INGRID JONACH

When the World Was Flat
(And We Were In Love)

STRANGE
CHEMISTRY

STRANGE CHEMISTRY
An Angry Robot imprint
and a member of the Osprey Group

Lace Ma
54-56 H
Nottingl
UK

www.str
Strange

A Stran
1

Copyrig

Ingrid J
identific

A catalogue record for this book is available
from the British Library.

ISBN: 978 1 90884 457 6
Ebook ISBN: 978 1 90884 459 0

Set in Meridien by EpubServices
rinted and bound by CPI Group (UK) Ltd, Croydon, CR0 4YY

For my husband Craig

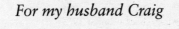

"Logic will take you from A to B. Imagination will take you everywhere."
Albert Einstein, 1879–1955

1

I remember when I first heard his name – Tom. I was sitting in the cafeteria with my best friends, Jo and Sylv, in the last week of our sophomore year at Green Grove Central High School, scraping Wite-Out off my nails and wondering whether I could stomach the burger on the tray in front of me, when the news broke about the "new guy".

It was a lifetime later – three months, twenty-four days, eight hours and three minutes – before I came face to face with him and before he literally turned my universe upside down and inside out.

His arrival in our small town was heralded by Melissa Hodge, who had heard the news from her father, who had heard it from his accountant, who in turn had heard it from the local gallery owners.

Green Grove, Nebraska, has a population of four thousand, six hundred and something, which results in about two degrees of separation between the butcher, the baker and the candlestick maker. But during his first summer in Green Grove, Tom was like the Loch Ness

9

monster or some sort of sasquatch. You know what I mean; seen only by a friend of a friend of a friend.

Melissa had a photo on her cell, but given our social standing we were the last to get a look. She snorted through her snobby nose about it whenever we saw her at the shops or the pool over summer, but it ended up being one of those grainy shots they put on the news when some hillbilly spots a UFO. It could have been Tom, or it could have been Mr Brady, the hermit who lives in the grasslands with the prairie dogs.

Then we heard that Tom had enrolled in our school and would start at the end of August.

Looking back, I wonder if I had an inkling that my life was about to go from ordinary to extraordinary. I like to think of it as BT and AT – *Before Tom* and *After Tom*. I must have guessed. I mean there were the dreams after all – nightmares, really. They started a couple of nights after I heard about Tom. You might think it a coincidence, like I did. But I can tell you now that the two were well and truly linked.

In the first nightmare, I was murdered in my bed. In my dream, I woke to see a figure standing beside me, silhouetted in the light from the open window. I screamed as he – she? – leaned towards me, coming so close that I could feel the scratch of what I thought was a beard on my cheek.

I was suddenly racked with cold, like I had been thrown into a bathtub of ice. I screamed again and the sound echoed in my ears as if it came from someone else.

I woke with a start and found Deb shaking me with both hands, like a child with a snow globe.

"Lillie! Lillie!"

I slumped against her, breathing in her scent of lavender as she rocked me. It had been a long time since I had allowed her to hold me like that, a long time since we had been in the role of mother and daughter. My tears left damp patches on her nightdress.

"Hush. Hush. Hush," she whispered to the rhythm of our rocking.

I continued to repeat the word in my mind after she had stopped. They say you can talk yourself into anything through repetition, which is why they replay TV commercials about a thousand times. They call it the "rule of repetition".

I managed to calm down after what seemed like a few hundred hushes and looked up at my mother through swollen eyes. "I dreamed I died," I told her between hiccups.

She rubbed my back. "Death symbolizes a new beginning, you know. It means the death of the past and the birth of the future."

My mother considered herself a dreamologist, amongst other things.

She cupped my face in her hands, considering me with crinkled eyes. Suddenly, she frowned and wiped my top lip with her thumb, showing me a smear of blood; a nosebleed.

My bottom lip quivered. A nosebleed? From a dream?

"Poor Lillie," Deb clucked, holding a tissue to my nose. "Let me make you a cup of chamomile tea. I could add valerian," she mused. "And I think I have marshmallow root."

My mother made herbal teas that were akin to dirty dishwater. Her herbologist credentials came from a couch surfer who had stayed with us last summer who had also read tea leaves. I used to tip my tea leaves into the trash before she could tell me there was someone tall, dark and handsome in the bottom of my mug. I was used to couch surfers and their sideshow talents. When I was about four years old a guy had me convinced he could pull a handkerchief out of his thumb. He stayed for so long that I started calling him Dad. He packed up and left the next day, leaving behind the handkerchief and its rubber thumb.

I drank the tea that night, but the dreams went on and on – a summer of nightmares. Deb continued to wake me with soothing noises and hot cups of tea, as if it were medicine.

In another dream, I was being chased. My sneakers thudded on an uneven flagstone path with dips and crevices that turned my ankles. My breath was short. My heart beat fast. A row of shrubs lined the path on either side and red birds flitted in and out of their branches, their wings waving like warning flags.

I looked over my shoulder at a figure dressed in black and realized the scratch of his beard had been the wool of a balaclava.

Like my other dreams, this dream ended with a chill that spread through my body, from my head to my toes. It brought my lungs to a standstill and stopped my heart dead. The sensation followed me into waking hours, blurring the line between my dreams and reality.

Cold. Cold. Cold, I thought, as I stood in the shower the next morning, my mind like a mouse on a wheel, turning, turning, turning. I shivered under the hot stream of water. The rule of repetition.

2

The day before Tom was due to start at Green Grove High, I was hanging out with the girls in my shoebox-sized bedroom, like we did every Sunday. We were supposed to be taking photos of Sylv, or at least I was, because she was going to be a famous model, but talk had turned to Tom.

"I bet he has a six pack," Sylv said.

Jo snorted. "I bet he has two heads," she said facetiously. She was kneeling in front of my bookshelf, alphabetizing my library, which consisted of a ton of photography books and a few novels from school.

Sylv shrugged. "I would take two heads in this town."

Sylv hated her mom for giving birth to her in Green Grove, instead of a city like New York or London. "How am I supposed to be scouted in Green Grove?" she complained, as she changed into a silver sequined top with a V-neck that ended at her navel.

"Kate Moss was scouted at an airport," I reminded her. I loved trivia. I spouted stuff I had heard on second-rate cable shows or read in trashy magazines, as if from an encyclopedia.

"Great," Sylv said. "I suppose I should go hang out at the airfield then, in case a model scout arrives on the weekly flight from Newark." She threw a cushion at me, a lime-green monstrosity my mother had crocheted when I was a baby. I ducked, letting it hit the wall instead.

We all hated Green Grove. For three quarters of the year it was flat and brown, for the other quarter it was waist deep in snow, which made its name as misleading as the sign that declared it the gateway to the renowned wine region, the Open Valley. We were more like a backdoor, or even a cat flap, to the rolling vineyards which grew, out of place, next to our desert-like town.

Even the flowers in Main Street had died two months after they were planted, despite the thousands of dollars the city council had spent on an irrigation system, against the advice of the community. "The community" being the Hodge family, principally Mr Hodge. He was king of Green Grove, owning about half of Main Street. I guess that made his daughter the princess.

Princess Melissa was in our grade at Green Grove High. She had shiny black hair to her waist and a spectacular smile without the embarrassment of having had braces for two years like me. Oh yeah, I had been called Brace Face, Metal Mouth, Train Tracks, you name it, not to mention the day Paul Gosling came at me with an industrial magnet, courtesy of Melissa.

I know your jaw will drop when I tell you that we used to be friends with Melissa, best friends in the case of Sylv. The two of them had even got their ears pierced together without telling their parents in third grade. They were competitive though. I remember the day Melissa arrived at school with a new haircut. Sylv immediately took a pair of scissors into the bathroom and hacked her own hair above her ears, at least three inches shorter than Melissa. Then Sylv hit puberty early, aged nine and a half, and Melissa started spreading rumors about Sylv, telling everyone she had gone to second base with Simon Caster.

I wound the film on and snapped a shot of Jo. She ducked her head as the flash bounced off the lemon-colored walls.

I had been bitten by the photography bug when I was nine. Deb had gone to a wedding where they had given the guests disposable cameras because they had been too cheap to hire a professional photographer. She had brought hers home unused. She hated photography, claiming it was a science, not an art. Deb liked to think of herself as an artist. I think it gave her an excuse to be half-baked.

She said she would paint the reception instead, but managed to put down about five brush strokes before she moved on to basket weaving, followed by woodcarving. Her list of unfinished projects was as long as her wavy hair, which flowed down to her backside. Not that she had a backside. She was straight up and down. We both were. But while it was good, enviable even, for a forty-one year-old to be as thin as an A-list celebrity, for me it was hell to be flat-chested at sixteen.

"I look like a boy," I complained, as I snapped a shot of myself in the mirror.

"At least you look like a hot boy," Jo told me. "I look like an ugly boy; an ugly, fat boy, like Jack O'Lantern."

Jackson Murphy was an overweight kid we had known in Elementary. He had lost his front teeth in second grade like the rest of us, but, by fifth grade, there had been no evidence of his adult set. He was given the nickname Jack O'Lantern, which he had put up with until he moved with his family to Kentucky or Texas or Hawaii, or wherever he went to escape the witch-hunt.

"Neither of you look like boys," Sylv said. "If you did, I would have hit on you by now." She pointed at me. "You look like a pixie." I put my hands up to my ears self-consciously, knowing they were kind of pointy, but Sylv moved her attention to Jo. "And you look like…"

"A boy," Jo finished. "Just say it. I know it. You know it. Lillie knows it. We all know it!"

It could be said that Jo was a bit masculine. Her mom had died of breast cancer when she was three and she had been raised by her dad – a truck driver. When Jo was eight, our teacher called Child Services because her dad had left her at home by herself for a week while he delivered a load of grain to New Jersey. She started spending so much time at my house after that it was like we were sisters. We shared a love of musicals and knew the words to all of the songs from films like *Oklahoma, Singing in the Rain, Meet Me in St Louis, Oliver*… and the list went on.

"I was actually going to say a bitch," Sylv joked.

Jo laughed, despite herself.

"Now," Sylv said. "Do you think we could stop talking about how you girls look and start talking about how I look? Last time I checked, this was my photo shoot." She shook her shoulder-length hair, which was currently blonde with two pink streaks, and struck a pose that looked pornographic.

While I snapped and Sylv posed, Jo continued to tidy my books, followed by my photos, stationery, shoes, clothes, etc. "You have so much… crap," she complained.

"Thanks," I said sarcastically.

"You know what I mean. You have a sweater from when you were like five years old on the floor of your wardrobe." She held it up against herself and peered into the full-length mirror on the back of my door. "Hey Sylv, I think this is your size."

"Hilarious," Sylv said, rolling her eyes.

"And when have you ever skated?" Jo asked, picking up a pair of ice skates that used to belong to Deb, proving she had been into materialism once upon a time in a land far, far away. The leather had split and one of the blades was bent. "I think you need to do some serious spring cleaning."

"I like my crap," I pouted. Each pen, each book, each photo represented a moment in time, a memory.

I had no need to hop from hobby to hobby like Deb. I knew who I was when I looked under my bed and saw the hundreds of empty film canisters from seven years of photography. Or opened my desk drawer and found pens out of ink from years of homework.

It was like having a ball of twine to guide me through a maze.

That was what I loved about photography. I could follow the ball of twine back to second grade by walking into the living room where Deb had hung my school photo next to her Feng Shui good fortune coin. Second grade was the year she had been into henna. I could tell, because there was a spray of stars tattooed across my right cheek. And within an instant I could revisit the first year Deb had baked a tofu turkey for Thanksgiving and had accidentally used silken tofu instead of firm. I had set the camera on a timer and the photo shows us sitting around a table eating a four-bean salad, Jo and her dad included.

"You used to be tidy," Jo complained, tossing worn-out sneakers into a tub labeled "shoes". "I think this summer has fried your brain."

The summer, or the nightmares? I wondered, watching her wrinkle her nose at a sock before throwing it into my laundry basket.

While I rewound the film in my camera, Sylv pointed out that if I used a digital camera we could see the shots now.

"If you wanted instant photos, you should have used the booth at the Ezy-Buy," I said. I liked to develop my own photos in the darkroom at school. I could spend hours in there. It was like being in another world.

"As long as you develop the roll before Thanksgiving," Sylv said. "I have to be discovered before my folks start nagging me about the SATs. As if I want to go to college!"

"As if you could get into college," Jo quipped.

Sylv stuck out her tongue, flashing the silver stud in its center. "I have contacts."

"A one night stand with a college guy is not a contact."

"What about a one night stand with a college professor?" Sylv asked.

Jo stuck her fingers in her ears and squealed. "Eew!"

We were constantly blocking our ears around Sylv. We had staged an intervention with her last year after she had pulled a packet of condoms out of her handbag during biology. We had been learning about the reproductive system and Sylv had decided to turn the lesson into a show and tell, which had not gone down well with our teacher, Ms French.

We had pointed out to Sylv that she was adding fuel to the fire that had been started by Melissa.

"When life gives you sour grapes, you make lemonade," she had said.

"You mean lemons," Jo had responded.

"I know you are, you said you are, so what am I?" Sylv had quipped and I have to admit that I laughed. Meanwhile, Jo had probably been wondering why we were even friends with Sylv.

Deb had a theory that we were friends because we were like the four elements – Water, Earth, Fire and Air. She said I was Water, because I was "as deep as Big Mac." It sounded like a burger, but it was the deepest lake in Nebraska. Jo was grounded, which made her Earth. Sylv was burning out of control as Fire. And Melissa had drifted to another group of friends because she was Air.

"An airhead," Jo had corrected.

••••

The girls stayed for dinner – veggie burgers and tabouleh. We were joined by the latest couch surfer, an artist-slash-hippie called Bill who talked non-stop about making candles.

Sylv kicked me under the table whenever he said, "Hot wax." That girl could make a sermon sound sexual.

When Bill invited Sylv to make candles with him, I choked on a mouthful of burger. It stuck in my windpipe and Jo had to give me a couple of thumps on the back.

As I sucked in a breath, a sudden shiver ran down my spine.

"Are you OK?" Jo asked.

"I think someone just walked over my grave," I said with a cough. Cough. Cough. Cough. Cold. Cold. Cold, I thought, as a now familiar chill settled in my stomach.

3

On the morning Tom started at Green Grove High – "T-Day" – the constant cold in my stomach was, at least temporarily, replaced by butterflies. I squashed them, telling myself I was being stupid.

I chanted the word "stupid" as I put on mascara and cherry lip gloss. At the last minute, I also put the gloss on my cheeks, for a healthy glow. Well, that was moronic. It shone like glitter. I smeared it with my hand and my chin shone too.

"Idiot!" I scolded, sticking a washcloth under the faucet. It squeaked as I turned on the water and the pipes banged inside the wall. Bang! Bang! Bang! "Idiot! Idiot! Idiot!" they seemed to shout.

This old house was falling down around our ears. I looked at the tiles, cracked and broken on the side of the bath, and then at the rusted drain hole, the chipped basin, the split and rotting windowsill. It was a dump, like half the houses in Green Grove. They had this temporary look about them, as if the builders thought no one would live here longer than a couple of years.

I continued to study myself in the mirror after I wiped my chin and decided I was wasting my time. Who was I kidding? As if the "new guy" was going to look twice at me: just look at my track record. Since my freshman year there had been three new additions to our grade at Green Grove High. Two had been male and neither had looked in my direction since they had set foot in this town. It was like I was invisible to the opposite sex. Maybe because girls like Melissa had breasts and I was as flat as an ironing board.

At least I had clear skin. Jo and Sylv both had spots, no matter how much they squeezed and scrubbed. They had more color in their complexions though. My skin was sallow and I had perpetual dark circles under my eyes, like smudged mascara.

I guess I could have blamed them on waking up at odd hours, gasping for breath like a fish in a bucket – the nightmares were like having sleep apnea – but I had basically been born with my dark circles. A guy who dated my mother when I was in Elementary used to call me "Panda Eyes". I tilted my head this way and that to see if they were highlighted by the fluorescent light that flickered above the mirror. My eyes glinted green, my one remarkable feature. But no one called me "Emerald Eyes".

"He probably has two heads anyway," I said, mimicking Jo, and then laughed, half at what I had said and half at the fact that I had said it out loud.

I was running about ten minutes late thanks to my primping and preening. Normally, I would have rolled out of bed and pulled on a few worn-out clothes. Today, I had spent at least fifteen minutes selecting a white cheesecloth top to pair with my customary light blue jeans and a pair of gold-colored ballet flats. A couple of large plastic bangles jangled on my wrist.

My wardrobe came from Tree of Life, one of those stores that sold gemstones and incense. Deb worked there part-time and I pulled a few shifts here and there, which meant we got their clothes discounted or for free when they overstocked. I went for the non-hippie-ish items, meaning no tie-dyed dresses or crocheted vests. I did have a pair of hemp shorts though, and the cheesecloth top I was wearing that day. That being said, made by hand, as in knitted, stitched or dyed, was non-negotiable when you were shopping free trade.

I checked the clock and realized Jo was running late too. We had walked to school together rain, hail or shine since kindergarten. When she did arrive, I saw she was wearing about a gallon of perfume and a skirt.

"You have a tear in your tights," I pointed out. The fact that she even owned a pair of tights or a skirt was kind of headline news, but I kept my mouth shut.

"Dammit," she cursed, looking at the ladder, which ran from her knee to mid-thigh. "My only pair too." She pulled at her hem, but she would have had to let it down about five inches to cover the hole. Jo was the opposite of a tart, but no one wore a skirt past their knee at Green Grove High, despite the efforts of Principal Turner – otherwise known as "Turnip" – and his tape measure.

Our school had a strict dress code which no one followed. Heavy make-up was banned, as were skirts above the knee. For boys it was rude T-shirts, sleeveless tops, torn jeans, jewelry and bandanas. Not that there were any gangs in Green Grove, unless you counted Melissa and her lapdogs, who we liked to call the Mutts.

I found Jo another pair of tights in my dresser.

"Thanks," she said.

I nodded and knew well enough to face the wall while she pulled them on. She was modest, unlike Sylv.

It took us fifteen minutes on a good day and twenty on a bad day to walk to school. I thought it was going to be a good day until a red bird flew across my path and my legs locked-up as I recalled my nightmares.

"Look," Jo said. "A red crossbill."

I had to laugh, even though my chest was constricted, as if by a large rubber band. "When did you become an ornithologist?" I teased.

We got to school a few minutes before the bell. I could tell that every girl at Green Grove High had added an hour or so to their routine that morning. The corridors smelled like tanning lotion and teachers were busy sending students to the bathroom to wipe off eye make-up and lipstick. It was the routine whenever a new guy came to our school.

"Is he here yet?" Sylv asked breathlessly when she met us at my locker.

She was wearing a white micro miniskirt and black ankle boots. Her sparkly red top had a plunging neckline which showed a black lace bra. She was beyond breaking the dress code – she was annihilating it. Turnip was going to have a stroke.

"No," Jo sighed, and I wondered if she was sighing about Tom or about Sylv and her choice of wardrobe. I guessed it was the latter when I saw her wince as she looked Sylv up and down. I heard a few giggles behind me and knew without looking who was the laughing stock.

"What I want to know is: what have you done to your hair?" I asked.

Hairdressing was Plan B for Sylv if modeling was a dead end. She had managed to flunk Hairdressing 101 overnight though, because she had dyed her hair as orange as a tangerine. She had also teased the roots and unloaded a can of hairspray into it, like they used to in the Eighties. She kind of looked like Cyndi Lauper.

"Why would you want to be a redhead?" Jo asked. Her own hair was strawberry blond, but she put a brown rinse through it once a month, turning it a mousey color with a hint of orange. It hung to her shoulders with a couple of kinks at the back, which gave it an unbrushed look. I wanted to smooth it constantly, like I was her mother, tucking in her shirt or dabbing at her face with a wet tissue. Jo would have slapped me silly though.

"The packet called it 'Tangerine,'" Sylv said.

Well, whaddayaknow? I was right.

"Anyway, I like red hair," Sylv continued, looking down the corridor at Taylor Blackwood. Sylv had been crushing on Taylor since he got suspended for riding his skateboard in the gymnasium last March. To her, he was a daredevil. To me and Jo, he was an oil slick, with greasy red hair that made a cheese pizza look fat-free.

"Ariel was a redhead," I said, "and Jessica Rabbit."

"They were cartoon characters," Jo pointed out.

The bell rang, but no one moved. The boys continued to lean against their lockers, looking around for their competition. The girls were gathered in groups, wondering if Tom was going to be a no show. We were cutting into class time, but no one gave a hoot about English, except for Jo, and the teachers, who were shooing students out of the corridors, like we were a herd of cows blocking the road.

"Gotta go," Jo said, leaving us in her wake.

"Give your lover a kiss for me," Sylv called after her. It was an ongoing joke that Jo had it bad for her English teacher, Mr Bailey. She spoke about him like he had invented the English language. I guess he was kind of good-looking, if you were in the market for a father figure. He was about fifty-something with gray hair. Eew. That being said, me and Sylv were in the lower classes and had Mrs Baker, who had a moustache. Double Eew.

At lunch we sat in the cafeteria at our regular table opposite the double doors. There was a window behind us, but our view would be obscured by a layer of dirt or snow, depending on the season. At the moment, it was the former.

For nine months of the year, dirt swirled through the air, as if God had shaken a picnic blanket over Green Grove. It got into our clothes, our shoes, our houses, our cars. I often wondered what the town would look like naked, without its brown or white coats. Maybe the cars would look newer or the paint on the houses fresher, but I knew it was more likely to look like an actress on one of those stars without make-up specials.

The janitor did stretch himself to clean our window now and then, but when he did all you could see on the other side was a brick wall.

There was a commotion across the cafeteria.

Sylv nodded and gave a low whistle.

"Would you take a look at that?" Jo said. "One head."

The butterflies filled my stomach again and I hesitated before turning in my chair, as if I could see the fork in the road. When I did turn, I saw Tom walking through the double doors of the cafeteria, looking like he belonged in an advertisement for Salvatore Ferragamo. Oh yes, I knew my labels. Thanks to Sylv.

He was wearing a gray T-shirt with roughed-up jeans. They looked brand new though, as did his white sneakers.

He ran a hand carelessly through his hair, which was brown and short, but not too short for that tousled, bed-head look. He was about thirty feet from me, but I could see his face as if it were inches away, his broad cheekbones, straight nose and strong jawline, as symmetrical as you like. There was a scar too, just under his chin. It was too small to see from where

I sat, but I knew it was there, even though we were strangers.

How? I wondered, but then he met my eyes and it was like my thoughts were sucked into a vacuum. I saw that his irises were a light blue, rimmed by a darker blue. It was like looking into glaciers, unlike the plain brown or gray varieties that were common in Green Grove. Of course, I had guessed his eyes would be as remarkable as my own, if not more so.

It would have been nice to say it was like worlds colliding for him as well, but the look Tom gave me was not even that between a brother and sister. It was a dead-behind-the-eyes look and in that split second we locked gazes he was as connected with me as Jo was with her femininity. I may as well have been a piece of bubblegum stuck to the concrete or a dust mote floating on the breeze.

Looking back now, I understand the look he gave me. I know what was going through his mind. But at the time it was like being spat on.

I suddenly realized I was out of my seat and sat back down with a nervous giggle. Jo was giving me a what-the-hell look. I blushed like it was going out of fashion, staring at the ground and wondering if the entire cafeteria was laughing at me or if all eyes had been on Tom.

Please. Please. Please, I thought, as I bit the bullet and looked up. It was the latter, of course. I could have juggled lunch trays while balancing on a stack of chairs and no one would have looked twice at me. Tom was magnetic, and girls were being pulled in left, right and center, me included.

Melissa was on his arm in an instant. They looked like a couple as she paraded him around the cafeteria, the Homecoming King and Queen. Tom looked bored as she introduced him to the Mutts. I smiled, even though I knew I should care less, given Melissa was basically royalty and I was one of a million dust motes.

"Was it as good for you as it was for him?" Sylv asked as we walked through the corridors to class.

"What?"

"The eye-sex."

"The what?" I asked in a high-pitched voice.

"The eye-sex," Sylv repeated. "You know, when your eyes meet across a crowded room." She surveyed our blank looks and sighed, as if we were stupid. "Like this." She held Jo by the shoulders and gazed into her eyes like they were in a soap opera.

"Get a room," I complained.

"Should I be pressing charges?" Jo asked.

"Come on, Lillie. I saw him looking at you. Spill."

"He looked at me for like a second," I protested.

"Premature ejaculation?" Sylv joked.

"Stop it!" I looked over my shoulder, worried that Tom was within earshot.

I spotted Melissa and her entourage a few yards back, *sans* Tom. They were having their own powwow about our new addition. I heard his name mentioned three times in the one breath, as Melissa fanned herself with a manicured hand.

Jo joined in on the innuendo. "Was he that bad?"

"No!"

"Which means he was good?" Sylv asked.

I gave up.

I sat behind Melissa in Economics, staring at her shiny black hair. Of course, Tom would go with her in a heartbeat. They were like two thoroughbreds in a stable of donkeys. She was known for her string of boyfriends, but unlike Sylv she had standards. One of those standards was that they had to be out of high school – the oldest had been a senior at Green Grove State College – but I could see her making an exception for Tom.

He was no Jack O'Lantern.

My heart played Double Dutch when I saw Tom at my locker that afternoon. For a moment, I thought he was waiting for me, but then he spun the dial of the locker next to mine and my heart stopped jumping rope.

Get a grip, I told myself, as I spun the dial on my own locker. This connection between me and Tom was one-sided. I took a deep breath and went about my business, but two seconds later my business became our business when a box of tampons fell out of my locker and bounced on the linoleum.

Tom bent down to pick them up, as if on autopilot. My cheeks burned and I closed my eyes, praying that when I opened them I would see the dream-catcher

Deb had made from an old coat hanger and a bunch of chicken feathers that hung above my bed, but then I heard Tom clear his throat and I knew that this was no nightmare. Oh well. At least I was safe from the man in the balaclava, if not from Tom.

I opened my eyes and saw him holding out the box of tampons, offering them as casually as you would a packet of mints. He stood about half a head taller than me, tall enough to look down on me, but not tall enough for me to crick my neck.

"Earplugs," I joked. "For Algebra." I laughed and took them from him, but when our fingers brushed, the hairs on my arms rose, as if charged with electricity. I laughed again. Magnetic? Electric? Tom was starting to sound like one of the X-Men.

He looked at me and his irises slid through a spectrum of blues like a kaleidoscope as they caught the fluorescent lights. It was mesmerizing, but I lowered my eyes to his chin. There I saw the scar, a thin white line, a flaw on an otherwise flawless face. I knew that scar. I knew Tom. Again, I asked myself how.

A memory knocked on the door of my mind, begging to be let in. It was like having the name of a song on the tip of my tongue. I flicked through my memories, like flicking through a photo album, but there were no snapshots of Tom.

Tom turned back to his own locker with no hint of a smile at my joke. In fact, his eyebrows were furrowed, as if he was bothered by my comment, or maybe by me.

••••

It was Monday, which meant the girls and I walked to the Duck-In Diner for an after school snack.

"How about I color your hair tonight?" Sylv suggested, as the waitress delivered our order. The Duck-In Diner had a menu to rival IHOP, with its waffles and buttermilk pancakes stacked to the ceiling. The uniform, however, rivaled Disneyland, with waiters and waitresses walking around wearing duck bill visors and white aprons with plastic feathers.

"This diner quacks me up," Jo said whenever we walked in.

I looked up from checking my waffle for hairs – the chef had the arms of a gorilla – and realized Sylv was talking to me. "You know what? I think I'll pass on getting suspended from school, but thanks."

Sylv had been suspended at least five times due to her hair color. She liked to change it a couple of times a quarter. You know, mix it up. Her current orange hair looked natural when compared to the purple and green streaks she had put in last winter.

My hair was brown. Thankfully not a mousey brown, but more of a chestnut color. I had let Sylv put highlights in it once. I know, what was I thinking? It ended up looking like caramel. Jo had smacked her lips and joked about having a sweet tooth for at least three weeks until it faded.

Of course, Deb would have done backflips if Sylv had dyed my hair all the colors of the rainbow. When I was twelve, she told me I was too conservative, saying it like it was a dirty word. She had made me sleep with a bundle of witch hazel under my pillow for six months to cultivate my creativity.

I wondered whether there was a delayed reaction. Maybe the witch hazel was the reason for my dreams. It could also have been the reason for my newfound messy streak. Between me and my mother the house had not been vacuumed since spring.

Sylv slumped in her seat. "You girls never support anything I do."

"What do you call the photo shoot yesterday?" I asked.

"Have you developed the film?"

"Of course not."

"I rest my case." I knew her case was not rested though when she sat up straight, ready for a rant. "I was looking forward to inviting you to Paris with me for Fashion Week, but you would probably miss the flight, knowing how you are with deadlines."

"There was no deadline," I protested.

"Actually, the deadline was Thanksgiving," Jo said, as she poured more blueberry syrup over her pancake stack. "Remember? You said you had to be discovered before the SATs."

"Which gives me three months," I said. "Please let me come to Paris with you."

We knew deep down that Sylv was as likely to go to Paris for Fashion Week as I was to be with Tom, but a girl had to dream when she lived in Green Grove.

Dream, I thought as I stabbed my fork into my waffle, once, twice, three times. Dream. Dream. Dream. The word chilled me to the bone. These dreams, or nightmares, were taking their toll. Last week, I woke up with my own hands around my throat. Yeah, I know. A psychiatrist would have a field day. Even Jo had commented that my dark circles were looking black, instead of their standard shade of gray. I wanted to tell her about my dreams, but she was no dreamologist, or psychiatrist come to that. I knew her answer would be to pop an Ambien.

"We should all go to Paris," I said brightly, shaking off my dreams. "We could sit and gasbag in a French Duck-In Diner. Do they have Duck-In Diners in France?" I paused, wondering if the franchise had made it out of Green Grove, let alone Nebraska or the country, before my mind drifted to the photos I could take in Europe. I wondered if Africa was nearby and then grimaced at these holes in my knowledge. To think, geography had been my favorite subject last year.

"Count me out," Jo said. "My dad. You know."

I did know. Jo had been looking after her dad for two and a half years. He had prostate cancer and had been through chemotherapy, radiation and a bunch of operations. He lived with a colostomy bag attached to his bowel, which he liked to tell us meant he could go to the bathroom in his La-Z-Boy, like it was a joke. It was no laughing matter, of course, especially when you considered what had happened to Mrs Green.

Deb sent bowls of tofu stir-fry to their house a few times a week.

"Are you trying to kill me with this vegetarian crap?" Mr Green always asked, but the containers came back empty every time.

"You know your dad wants you to have a life," I told Jo.

Jo gave a barking laugh. "In Green Grove?"

I shrugged. "Or Lincoln or New York–"

"Or Paris," Sylv said, flicking a spoonful of grits at Jo, who retaliated with a spoonful of syrup.

I put up my hands and stood up from the booth, deciding I would rather not wear my waffles, no matter what Sylv said about the latest fashion in Milan.

When we got to the end of the block, Sylv set off for West Green Grove, while Jo and I set off for North.

"Is everything OK?" I asked when it was just the two of us. "I mean, with your dad?"

Jo shrugged. "Yeah. Fine. I guess." Her chin trembled and I suddenly felt sick to the stomach.

Jo was not the kind of girl to burst into tears at the drop of a hat. In fifth grade she had split her shorts from the crotch to the waistband on the jungle gym. Melissa and the Mutts had been there to point and laugh and catcall. If it had been me, I would have run home in a flood of tears, but Jo had continued to swing upside-down from the monkey bars until I handed her my sweater to tie around her waist. If Sylv had been there I think she would have used my sweater to strangle Melissa instead.

"He seems... sicker." Her eyebrows furrowed under her mousey bangs. "He keeps forgetting stuff, like how to change his colostomy bag and that I have my license now."

"What about his doctor? What does he say?"

"She," Jo corrected and then shrugged. "He has a check-up next week."

I nodded and we continued to walk, in silence except for the scuffing of our shoes on the sidewalk.

When we got to my house I ran inside for a bowl of leftovers for Jo and her dad.

When Deb came out to see her "second daughter", Jo let her hold her for a moment, before taking a couple of steps backwards, out of our front yard and onto the sidewalk.

"You have a cracked aura, sweetheart," Deb said, following her through the gate. "Do you want me to fix it?"

Jo shook her head. She believed in that mumbo-jumbo as much as I did.

"Your dad will be OK," I said, as she turned to go. "Yeah?"

She smiled sadly and nodded. "Yeah."

OK, OK, OK, I thought as I watched her walk down the street, as if the rule of repetition could cure cancer.

Because Deb had it in her mind that she wanted to fix an aura, I gave in and let her practice on me. At least it saved me from the pan pipe for a few minutes. She was into her second week of music lessons, courtesy of a couch surfer called Fawn. It sounded like the wind through our broken back window.

I sat on a footstool that Deb liked to tell visitors had been carved by a witch doctor in Peru, but I knew her friend Jordie had bought it at Venice Beach.

"Focus on your energy vortex," she told me, placing her hands on my shoulders and closing her eyes.

"My what?" I asked.

"I can see a red light," she murmured.

I closed my eyes and was surprised to see a red light as well, until I realized it was the lamplight through my eyelids.

Deb clucked her tongue. "Your aura has died."

A sudden lump formed in my throat, as I thought of how many times I had died in my dreams and the chill filled my stomach for a moment, before I made myself tune back into her voice. She was telling me to visualize my aura spinning around, and moving up and down. It was starting to sound like an aerobics class.

I burst out laughing.

"You're ruining the vibe," Deb complained.

Just then, Fawn came in to announce the rye bread they were baking had risen. "What do I do now?"

"Take it out of the oven," I said, rolling my eyes and wondering how guys like Fawn made it out of Elementary.

"How about we continue this later?" Deb asked.

"Sure." I knew not to hold my breath for part two. I guessed that Reiki would be as short-lived as palm reading and basket weaving.

When I went to bed, I thought about setting my alarm ten minutes earlier to give myself time to get glammed up. Then I remembered my joke about the box of tampons and flopped back onto my pillow, thinking about Tom and how his eyebrows had furrowed at my comment.

Dumb, I thought, slapping my forehead with my palm.

I closed my eyes and recalled his profile – that chiseled brow, nose, cheeks and chin, and, of course, the scar.

Tom was on my mind as I drifted off and I wondered in that moment between wake and sleep if I could make myself dream about him, instead of about the man in the balaclava. But it turned out the man in the balaclava was ready and waiting.

In this dream, I was standing stock-still, my breath ragged from running. I was in a courtyard paved with the same uneven flagstones from my other dreams. A fountain was to my left, the man in the balaclava in front. He was moving towards me and I stumbled backwards, hemmed in by manicured hedges. My hands went to my stomach instinctively and I looked down, my eyes growing wide with wonderment. It was swollen, extended, as if I were pregnant.

"Tom!" I screamed. "Tom!"

4

It was two weeks before I processed the photos of Sylv. "I know, I know, tomorrow!" became my catchphrase.

You have to understand that Sylv wanted to be a model like Cinderella wanted to go to the ball. When we were in Elementary, Sylv and Melissa used to rope us into doing runway shows in my backyard. I had taken the photos and Jo had assembled the audience; family and friends, and whatever couch surfers had been staying with us at the time.

But while Sylv had been on my case about the photos, in the two weeks since school started there had been no close encounters of any kind between me and Tom. World History was the one class we had together, but he sat up front with Melissa. He had French with Sylv, but she said he sat on his own and had spoken once in his first week when the teacher called on him to answer a question.

"He got it wrong."

"He seems smart in physics," Jo offered.

His background had remained the subject of spec-ulation and walking down the corridors was like downloading a podcast that broadcast news about him 24/7. Names of English boarding schools were thrown around like confetti and rumors ran rampant of someone knowing someone, who knew someone else, who may or may not have bumped into him pre-Green Grove.

There was a lot of giggling and fluttering of eyelashes from the freshman and sophomore girls whenever he was within a mile radius. A few of the senior girls had plucked up the courage to ask him out, but were turned down. I heard a few college girls had as well. But we juniors knew that Melissa had dibs on Tom. She hung onto his arm like a leech with a fake tan.

He sat with her at lunch on her table near the noticeboard, but while others would have kissed the bottom of their this-season pumps to sit with Melissa and the Mutts, Tom continued to look bored by them, and by Green Grove in general. He seemed to spend a lot of time staring at his lunch tray or at the ground. I heard a rumor he had not spoken more than a few words to Melissa.

I tried not to look at him, because when I did I remembered my dream and my hand went to my stomach. But it was like trying not to look at a brilliantly cut diamond.

I know what it sounds like: like Sylv had been pushed down my to-do list because I was otherwise occupied with Tom. But you can blame the man in the balaclava. I was jumping at shadows, as if my killer was going to pop out from behind the vault horse in the gymnasium or climb out from under a table in the cafeteria. A few of my dreams had been set in the darkroom too, which had turned this former heaven into a kind of hell and made me avoid it.

Deb had come within an inch of a black eye when she had woken me at the crack of dawn on Sunday. I had decided not to apologize when I heard her reason.

"OK! OK!" she had yelped, rubbing her jaw where my swing had connected. "Fawn and I will watch the sunrise on our own then."

It made me wonder if my mother knew me at all. I mean, in what universe would I want to sit on the damp lawn in my pajamas and watch the sunrise with a guy who plays the pan pipe?

The next day I decided to bite the bullet and develop the film for Sylv. I walked down to the art block, which was buried at the back of the school, about a hundred yards from the main building.

"Like a fish in a barrel," I whispered, closing the door on the outside world.

I told myself I was being silly as I placed the film into the developer, but my heart continued to thud as I rocked the tray, letting the soup slosh across the negatives. I tried not to think about how much the liquid looked like blood under the red light.

My silliness increased tenfold when I came back at lunch to do the prints. As I focused on the negative, I thought I could hear breathing other than my own. I froze, as rigid as an ice sculpture, and the sound stopped.

My ears were like antennae searching for a signal. I could hear a faucet dripping in the basin behind me and the light above my head hummed like an old refrigerator. I let out my own breath with a sudden whoosh, before returning to my print. Of course, that was when the sound started again.

It was about five or six minutes later, after I had checked under the tables and in the cupboard, that I put two and two together and realized the noise was the sound of the bellows on the antique enlarger as I turned the focus knob.

I switched to the second enlarger, in case the first was leaking light.

By the end of lunch, Sylv was hanging from every peg in the room and I could see her cleavage from every angle. I came back before sixth period and took down a few that had dried to show the girls.

I was running about five minutes late to class thanks to Sylv and her goal to be the next Gisele Bündchen, so I took a shortcut across the quad, which backed onto the cafeteria. It was littered with the remnants of lunch: wrappers, soda cans and half-eaten apples. A potato-chip bag blew across the concrete like a tumbleweed.

I pulled out my camera and connected the macro lens, deciding Mrs Baker and her moustache could wait a few more minutes in the name of photography.

I was crouching down, snapping some shots of a carpenter ant carrying a crumb and whispering to him, "Go right. No. Right. Fine. Left," when a shadow made me jump out of my skin. The photos tucked under my arm dropped to the ground, fanning out on the concrete.

It was Tom.

I would have hit him over the head with my camera for giving me a cardiac arrest, but he was crouching down to pick up my photos.

"You should get your hand-eye coordination checked," he said, as he straightened up.

"Excuse me?"

His accent was British, no doubt about it, with a hint of South African or maybe Australian. It was like hearing my favorite song on the radio, but again there were no memories to explain when, where, why and how I knew Tom.

"You took these?" he asked, flicking through the photos as if they were part of a public portfolio instead of my personal property. He paused on a photo I had taken of the lime-green cushion in my bedroom and made a "huh" sound, as if he had spotted a long lost friend in the frame. Maybe I was reading too much into it, but I watched as he traced the cushion with his finger as if reminding himself of its pattern. He finally shook his head and then flicked to the next photo, which was of Sylv.

"There you are Tom!" a voice called out. Melissa. Great. "I thought you were going to make me sit alone in pre-calc," she huffed. I know. Like Melissa would sit on her own when she had ninety-nine point nine per cent of the student body at her beck and call.

I smiled smugly, as Tom looked at Melissa like she was bubblegum on the bottom of his shoe.

He handed back the photos and, maybe it was all in my head, but he seemed to linger when our fingers touched. "Good, but over-exposed."

"The photos or Sylv?" I joked automatically.

"Both."

My smile was ironed out by his response, but then I saw the corners of his lips curve upwards. The transformation to his features was like throwing gasoline onto a bonfire, and I stood and stared until he allowed Melissa to pull him across the quad and through the doors of the cafeteria, like a parent being pulled into a toy store. He threw me one last look over his shoulder as he went and it could not have been further from his dead-behind-the-eyes look. I suddenly wondered whether our connection was one-sided after all.

"He liked the photos though, right?" Jo asked later when I recounted his words at the Duck-In Diner. "He said they were good."

"Damn straight," Sylv said loudly. She was showing off, seeking the attention of a booth of college guys. They were ogling her thighs, which were bare under another micro miniskirt, which she continued to wear day in and day out, even though it was now fall.

"He also said they were over-exposed," I pointed out, still stinging about my over-the-top reaction to his smile and final look. I would not even rate a passing thought with Tom. Meanwhile, I was dreaming about having his baby. It was ridiculous. I was ridiculous. "I mean, who the hell does he think he is? Helmut Newton?" I continued.

"Helmut!" Sylv exclaimed, and slapped her thigh as she laughed. I heard the college guys guffaw, like it had been for their benefit. It had been, of course.

"I think you like him," Jo said with a smirk.

"Who?"

"Tom. Who else?"

I flushed. "No way."

"Yes way," Jo teased. "You love him."

"I hate him."

"How can you hate him? You've spoken to him once."

"Twice," I corrected. "But he was too rude to respond the first time."

"The lady doth protest too much, methinks," Sylv crowed.

We stared at her.

"What?"

"You just quoted Shakespeare," Jo said.

"So?"

"So, those flashcards we made you are working."

Jo and I had quizzed Sylv for two and a half hours at the weekend, because Mrs Baker was planning a pop quiz about Shakespearean lovers on Wednesday.

"Was Juliet the sun or the moon?"

"Who said, 'The course of true love never runs smooth?'"

"Does love look with the eyes or the mind?"

Yadda. Yadda. Yadda.

"If you paid attention to Mrs Baker like you do Paul Gosling and Simon Caster we could be at the movies," I had complained as we studied.

Instead, Sylv had spent the past two weeks flirting like a dime-store hooker with that pair of acne-covered sleazeballs. She played it up because Taylor "Greaseball" Blackwood sat next to them, not that he ever looked up from scribbling on his desk with a sharpie.

But Sylv was giving it away for free at the Duck-In Diner this afternoon, making rude gestures involving her tongue. The college guys returned the signals threefold.

Sylv withdrew her consent when the sexual sign language got too hot and heavy. "Home time," she declared, standing up from the booth.

"Hey! Where are you going?" the college guys called out.

Sylv ignored them.

"I said, 'Where are you going?'"

"You mean you 'asked' where are you going," Jo threw over her shoulder as we walked through the doors, leaving them scratching their heads. She was a stickler when it came to grammar. Sylv said it was because she was in love with Mr Bailey, not with the language, but I think it was because she had her head stuck in a book all the time. She literally corrected the text as she went with a red pen, even library books. She had been banned from Green Grove Public Library for editing *War and Peace*.

Jo and I split from Sylv at the end of the block as usual, but as we walked down the street I felt the hairs on the back of my neck rise, as if we were being watched. My mind went to the man in the balaclava.

I looked around and saw a man hosing his dead lawn a couple of houses back – nope, not him – and a woman pushing a pram towards Main Street – nuh-uh. A green car with a dent in its fender drove by, its engine groaning like a wounded beast. It was followed by a sleek black SUV that looked like it cost ten times the average wage in Green Grove.

"What a jerk," Jo commented. "That has to be Mr Hodges."

I wrinkled my nose as I watched the Mercedes-Benz disappear around the corner, taking with it the adrenaline that had coursed through my body at the thought of the man in the balaclava. "An out-of-towner, I would say."

"Speaking of out-of-towners. Tell me how you hate Tom again."

I snorted. "You mean speaking of jerks."

Jo guffawed. "Told you so."

"What?"

"You like him. You want to have his babies." She put her fingers in her ears and sang, "Lillie and Tom, sitting in a tree, K-I-S-S-I-N-G," childishly until we reached my front gate. "See you tomorrow," she called out, before walking down the street with her ears still blocked.

I shook my head. Of course I thought Tom was good-looking. To say otherwise would be like saying summer in Green Grove was cold or Sylv was frigid, but I also thought he was an ass.

And I would have to be an ass to like him, I thought, thinking of those intense blue irises. The blood began to throb in my ears, as I remembered my dream where I was pregnant with his baby. Thud. Thud. Thud. Ass. Ass. Ass.

5

I was on the path that led to the courtyard. My clothes were damp with sweat and I knew without looking that you-know-who was hot on my heels.

I sped up, navigating the uneven flagstones in the dimming daylight until I suddenly tripped and fell forward. I heard a crunch as my cheek struck a rock.

The cold was like a wall of water and I woke in my bed, gasping for breath. I sat up and put a hand to my cheek, expecting to find a broken cheekbone. I was relieved when I realized it had been another dream, but then my tongue touched a chipped tooth.

I rolled out of bed and turned on my bedroom light. I lifted up my lip and surveyed my molars in the mirror. It was a small chip, but it was a chip nonetheless.

I dropped my lip and stared at myself in the mirror, realizing I had finally crossed the line between dreams and reality.

I thought about my chipped tooth all morning, touching it with my finger or tongue and checking it in the bathroom mirror. It was at the forefront of my mind until I saw Tom at his locker after third period, and then my mind was filled with thoughts about him instead.

He was wearing another pair of torn designer jeans, which I guessed were worth upwards of a few hundred bucks.

"And I get sent home for having my skirt too short," Sylv complained, suddenly a cheerleader for the dress code and its clause on torn jeans.

"You could see your underwear," Jo pointed out.

"Turnip should have been thankful I was wearing underwear at all."

We laughed and Tom turned. I stopped laughing when he said my name.

"Lillie."

I was surprised he knew it, but at the same time it was as if the word had passed his lips a thousand times, his rounded accent rolling over the syllables with an ease that comes with familiarity. He was hardly at ease though, as he looked at the girls.

"See you at lunch," Jo said meaningfully, before dragging Sylv off stage left.

I turned to my locker, busying myself with the combination. I could feel his eyes on me and I let my hair fall forward like a curtain to hide my flushed face. It seemed like an hour before I found my textbook. Luckily, my tampons were safe and sound in their new hiding place on the top shelf. There would be no earplug jokes today, thank you. In fact, the comedy routine had also been shelved.

I held my textbook to my chest like a shield as I closed my locker door.

Tom was waiting for my full attention. "I believe I was rude to you yesterday," he said formally.

"You think?" I asked rudely. Ironic, I know.

His pinched expression made it as clear as a New York billboard that his apologies were as rare as his smile. He probably wanted to maintain his image of being a gentleman, given he was into picking up handkerchiefs for damsels in distress, or at least tampons and photos.

I sighed. "Forget it."

"No." He moved forward one small step, and the slight scent of his cologne made me heady. "I want to apologize," he said in a low voice. "It was unlike me." He held my gaze and his eyes seemed to be trying to tell me what he could not say aloud.

I looked down at my scuffed sneakers, breaking our connection. I was being ridiculous again. I felt like telling him that his rudeness had fit him like a glove from what I knew of him, but instead I changed the subject. "Do you like photography?"

"I hate photography."

It was his third and final insult, and it made me laugh.

He stared at me for a moment and then opened his mouth as if to speak, before closing it again without a word. I watched as he shut his locker with a clang and turned down the corridor.

A few steps into his exit, Melissa sidled up to him and hooked her arm into his. I gritted my teeth as I noted he neither encouraged nor discouraged her touchyfeeliness. I also noted she was wearing a scoop-neck top that showed off her cleavage and her skirt was hitched up, revealing long, toned legs that made mine look like a popsicle stick that had been snapped in two.

Melissa could have her pick of guys in Green Grove. The entire male population was wrapped around her little finger, but she was going for the one guy who liked no one but himself. I wondered whether to tell her to strap a mirror to her forehead.

I laughed again at the thought and Tom looked over his shoulder. I ducked my head before I could read too much into his look and when I looked up it was Melissa who met my eyes, watching me like a well-fed cat watching a mouse. There was no reason for her to pounce.

At lunch, the girls wanted the gossip on Tom.

"Did you two get it on?" Sylv asked with a smirk.

"Shut up," I begged. "I hate him. He hates me. End of story."

"Sounds like a love story to me."

"Jo," I warned.

"Or a porno."

"Sylv!"

But Sylv was on a roll. "Starring Lillie and Tom," she crowed.

I heard a titter behind me and turned to see Melissa passing our table, giggling like her sides would split out of their Spanx. Next to her was Tom. His expression was as somber as a funeral director's as usual, but his complexion was flushed, the color highlighting his cheekbones.

I think I would have welcomed the man in the balaclava with open arms in that moment, but the girls were in hysterics. Sylv had tears running down her cheeks, streaking her make-up.

I forced myself to smile, stretching my lips as wide as I could, even though I wanted to follow my ball of twine back to at least five minutes ago.

A double period of art studies that afternoon should have cheered me up, but when I showed Mr Hastings my photos of Sylv he said, "Good, but overexposed." Ugh. He sounded just like Tom.

"Listen up," he announced to the class as I slumped in my seat. His voice was like a whisper above the commotion of the classroom, but he continued to talk regardless, his care-factor below zero.

If anyone hated Green Grove more than me and the girls, it was Mr Hastings. From what I understood, he had been born here, but had moved to New York in his early twenties to become a professional photographer. His star had burned bright in that decade with his work exhibited in the Guggenheim and two books under his belt, which were now fifteen years out of print. Sylv had bought me a couple of copies online.

"The theme for your major work is 'Identity,'" Mr Hastings droned. "Make of it what you will. And you need to partner up. The school board wants you to learn about teamwork."

There was a collective groan and murmurs of "Really?" and "Is he on meds?" The class was made up of a mixture of social outcasts, who preferred their own company.

I looked around, putting together a blacklist of potential partners. There was Kate, the emo-slash-goth, who produced nothing but black canvases with a variety of dead insects glued to them: potentially a serial killer. Next on my not-to-do list was Darnell, the comic book nerd who liked to draw Manga. Hang on. Let me translate that for you – he liked to draw half-naked women with big breasts and short skirts. And then there was Jenna, who could make your ears bleed with her non-stop talk about fairies.

I should blacklist myself too, I thought, as my tongue touched my chipped tooth. Lillie, the girl who thought her dreams were reality.

I turned down two candidates, before we realized there was an odd number in the class.

Please. Please. Please, I silently willed Mr Hastings, as he tapped his pen on his desk. He paused and his mouth opened. I thought I was off the hook. I really did. In my mind, he said, "Lillie will have to do this one on her own." But what he actually said was, "Lillie will have to team up with Kate and Dirk." His pen fell to his desk like a guillotine, as he stood up to go have a cigarette.

I grabbed my bag and stalked across the classroom, pulling out the seat next to Dirk. A split second decision by my teacher was going to ruin this class for the rest of the year.

"Are you into Manga?" I asked curtly.

He shook his head. "*Dungeons and Dragons.*"

"Of course."

On the walk home, Jo seemed to know not to mention the T-word. Maybe it was because my face burned like a lighthouse beacon whenever I thought about the porno incident or maybe it was because I was kicking pebbles across the pavement with such force that they bounced at head height. I could have taken an eye out.

Of course, it could have also been because I was talking over the top of her whenever she spoke, just in case she said his name.

"Your dad has his check-up tomorrow, right?" I asked, having commented twice that it was too warm for September, asked if she was going to be working on the weekend and complained about art studies.

There was stutter in her step, before she continued on with a nod.

"And you have to go too." It was a statement, not a question.

Her dad complained she babied him, but Jo had to go to his appointments, even if it meant missing school and her beloved Mr Bailey. For a start, her dad needed someone to drive him. Jo was the only one in our group with a license for this reason. She also needed to hear it from the doctor first-hand, because Mr Green liked to keep his daughter in the dark. It had taken him four months to tell her he had cancer after the diagnosis.

"Last night I dreamed he died," Jo whispered.

It was like an ice cube had been dropped down the back of my shirt. I drew in a sharp breath and the words came automatically, "They say dying in a dream is good. It symbolizes a new beginning." And then I wondered why I had repeated this less than sage advice. Good? What was good about being woken up at all hours by the sound of your last breath? And who needed a new beginning three hundred and sixty-five times a year? I was like a slate being wiped clean every night.

Jo kind of nodded and shook her head at the same time, her lank hair heavy on her shoulders. I knew she was embarrassed that she had dropped her guard like that, even to me. Jo was like a draft horse, a Clydesdale. She could have saddled the weight of a thousand nightmares before her back broke.

"Call me after the appointment," I said when we reached my house.

"OK."

I watched her walk down the street again, wishing that I had a ball of twine for the future like I did for the past. Then we could stick to the highways, instead of these country roads with their potholes and dead-ends.

I told Deb about the appointment, which was a mistake. After dinner, she knelt before a candle with her hands together in prayer and invoked the Great God himself on behalf of Mr Green.

I covered my laughter with a yawn. "Night," I said, but she was deep in conversation with Asclepius and his daughters, the Six Sisters of Healing.

6

Sylv and I sat in the quad together at lunch the next day. Well, I sat. Sylv stretched out on a bench, using her bag as a pillow, her underwear on full display.

"How about you take a photo?" she called out to two sophomores, who were hovering like gnats around a bug zapper.

The sophomores burst into laughter and turned towards the cafeteria. I watched them shadow-box each other as they walked and suddenly it was like watching a rerun on TV, as in déjà vu. Majorly. "I think you flash your underwear too much," I told Sylv.

"You would too if you wore red lace panties from Victoria Secret instead of boy shorts from Wal-Mart," she said, taking a bite from her apple and turning her head to look at Mr Bailey, who was on yard duty. Her eyes narrowed. "Do you think Mr Bailey will man up and make a move or what?" she asked. "I mean, have you seen how he and Jo look at each other? Talk about sexual tension."

I rolled my eyes. "There is no sexual tension."

"Whatever. I bet Mr Bailey is releasing the sexual tension at least five times a day." She made a jerking movement with her hand, and the apple bobbed up and down.

"Sylv! Cut it out!" I yelped. My eyes went to Tom, who was sitting across the quad with Melissa and the Mutts. He was not looking at me though. He had barely looked at me since Sylv had told the world about the porno starring Lillie and Tom.

Melissa giggled and made a show of flicking her hair. She took the opportunity to touch him as often as she could, patting his knee, stroking his arm. My heart squeezed with each contact, even though I had called out his name again in my dreams last night and I was beginning to think he could be the man in the balaclava.

"Lillie," Sylv said, with a warning tone.

"What?"

"I know we tease you, but jokes aside..." She sat up and looked at me with a sober expression. "Tom likes Melissa."

I blushed. "What are you talking about?"

"Look." She tossed her apple towards the trash. It missed. "I know what it takes to get a guy. In this porno, Melissa will get the guy."

"Love story," I corrected automatically.

"Whatever."

Of course, I knew I had as much of a shot with Tom as Sylv had of meeting a model scout at Green Grove airport. There were the reasons that were on display to all and sundry, such as my lack of female endowment, lack of social standing, lack of fake tan, etc., but I also sensed a barricade between me and Tom. It was as if a battle line had been drawn and we were on opposite sides with guns raised and at the ready. The reason was hidden in my memories, I was sure of it, but as I trawled through them they tangled like cobwebs.

The silver lining was that Melissa had no chance with him either. Ha! I thought smugly when he added a few inches between them on the bench after she touched his arm again.

When the bell rang I watched Tom pick up his bag and sling it over his shoulder. My heart sank as he also picked up a yellow handbag and handed it to its owner – Melissa. Of course he liked Melissa. Take a look at her and then take a look at me.

Ha! I thought again as we walked to the main building, but this time I was laughing at myself.

I sat behind Tom in World History. It was by accident, I swear. Melissa sat next to him by design.

I found myself staring at the nape of his neck for the next forty minutes, noting how the muscles in his back moved whenever he lifted his head from his textbook to look at the teacher, who was giving us a lecture on Napoleon and his invasion of Russia.

As my eyes roamed over his smooth skin I noticed a small mark behind his ear – a tattoo. I squinted, straining to make out the shape. It looked like a mix of numbers and letters, like Algebra. It looked familiar, but I could have been thinking of a guy I had once seen with $E=mc2$

tattooed on his arm. Jo had asked if he was being ironic, given he was walking out of the unemployment office. He wanted to know what she meant by ironic. "I guess not," Jo had said.

Tom turned his head as Melissa leaned in to speak to him and the tattoo was concealed by his ear.

"I guess Napoleon thought he had a shot at Russia," she said, looking at me out of the corner of her eye and making a clucking sound with her tongue. "He should have realized it was out of his league."

My mood went from bad to worse during study hall. I had no text messages or missed calls from Jo, even though I had called her about five times and texted twice.

I decided to suck it up and go down to the darkroom, despite my nightmares. After all, I had processed the photos of Sylv on Monday and lived to tell the tale.

I had processed two rolls of film into negatives and hung them to dry before there was a knock at the door.

I started at the sound and then scooped up the photographic paper that was open on the bench. Maybe it was Jo.

"All clear," I called out.

The door opened and a tsunami of sunlight flooded the room filled with specks of dust. I groaned inwardly, knowing they would cling to my damp negatives. A figure was silhouetted in the doorway. I put my hand up in front of my eyes before I was blinded.

"Who is it?" I asked, as they stepped into the room and the door closed behind them with a click.

"Me."

"Tom?"

My eyes readjusted, like sponges sucking in their surroundings. Tom was standing there with eyes as black as midnight under the red light. I caught the scent of his cologne and a thrill went through my body. He stepped forward and said, "I have to tell you–" before he vanished, as if in a puff of smoke.

I blinked at the empty darkroom. "Hello?"

I looked down at the bench. It was covered in paper. The paper I had packed up two seconds earlier. I held up a piece to the red light. It shone pink. It was unexposed. Tom had been a hallucination. No. Not a hallucination. A hallucination made me sound like I was in line for shock therapy. He had been a daydream.

"A daydream," I whispered, but my heart was doing double-time.

As I walked through the crowd of students to my last class, the sun dimmed and we tilted our faces towards the sky. Rain was a biannual occurrence in Green Grove and the hum of voices around me swelled as, sure enough, fat drops of water began to fall from low-lying clouds. There were a few shrieks as the students scattered, scurrying to class like ants.

The rain was like a light mist by the last bell. I was going to have to walk home on my own, because Sylv was going to the movies with pizza-face Simon. She told me it was her reward for passing her pop quiz on Shakespeare by two marks.

About five steps in, the rain started coming down in buckets.

"Great."

A stream of traffic passed on my left. This time of afternoon, it was like all of Green Grove converged on the school, with parents picking up their kids and a mix of juniors and seniors showing off in their crappy cars.

"Hey, loser!" I looked over in time to see the window of a Ford Mustang roll back up. The windows were foggy and streaked with rain, but I could make out Melissa on the other side, laughing. I could guarantee Blake was driving. He gave her a ride home every afternoon, even though she had been given a brand new Lexus for her sixteenth birthday and he lived in the opposite direction.

The traffic was bumper to bumper and moved at a walking pace, which meant the Mustang stayed at my side. I was sure Melissa was laughing her ass off at me as I got soaked through. I wondered how many of them were in the car and whether Tom was in there too. I was starting to shiver from the sudden cold, but my face burned with enough embarrassment to keep me warm.

When I reached the road, the Mustang left me in its wake. Its horn blared as it sped down the street and I knew Melissa would be leaning on it for a laugh.

"Bitch," I muttered.

The water squished in my shoes as I walked. Squish. Squish. Squish. Bitch. Bitch. Bitch, I thought. Water coursed in rivulets down my face and neck, drenching my short-sleeved cardigan. My jeans were stuck to my legs, chafing my thighs with each step.

And then, when I thought there was no way the afternoon could get worse, it started to hail.

The stones were small at first, but within a minute or two it was like the gods were teeing off golf balls.

"Are you kidding me?" I shouted at the sky.

I heard a vehicle pull up beside me, water fanning out from its wheels. For a moment, I thought it was Melissa and the Mutts back to rub it in, but then I saw it was a black SUV. The passenger door swung open and the driver shouted, "Get in!"

It could have been Charles Manson for all I cared at that moment. Hell, it could have been the man in the balaclava. I splashed through the puddles and climbed into the passenger seat, pulling the door shut behind me. A new car smell filled my nostrils. It had a leather interior. Nice. I saw the Mercedes-Benz logo and realized it was the jerk I had seen while walking home with Jo. I also realized it was worth more than twenty Mustangs.

"Thanks," I breathed, looking at the driver.

It was Tom.

7

Einstein once said that God does not play dice. He believed the universe was ordered, the world predictable. But his contemporary, Nils Bohr, famously asked Einstein to "stop telling God what to do with his dice."

It was a few months before I took an intense interest in Einstein and read this in the Green Grove Public Library, but I would have agreed with Bohr. God was a gambler. How else had I ended up in this SUV with Tom?

I flung open the door and slid out, putting one foot in the gutter. The water went up to my ankle, spilling over the rim of my ballet flat.

"Hey!" Tom shouted above the roar of the hailstones on the roof. "Are you trying to get yourself killed?" He reached across, his hand touching my forearm. I looked at it, absorbing the smoothness of his palm on my skin, before he withdrew it like I was on fire, instead of soaked through to my double-A bra.

I climbed back into my seat and slowly closed the door.

We sat in silence, except for the continual pounding of ice on metal, like the rat-tat-tat-tat of a machine gun. I cringed about the damage it would do to the expensive bodywork. Tom was looking straight ahead and I finally settled on staring out of the passenger window. Talk about awkward. But these storms came and went in a flash. A few more minutes and Tom could kick me to the curb. My heart sank at the thought.

"This will stop in a second!" I shouted.

"What?"

I winced. "I said, 'The storm will be finished soon!'"

He looked at me with a frown and then shook his head.

I frowned as well. "The rain. It will…" I suddenly laughed, giving up.

Tom gave me an under-the-microscope look, as I turned back to the window with a half-smile on my face.

Sure enough, within a couple of minutes the hail had stopped and the rain had returned to a sprinkle.

"Your hood," I said, nodding at the dents that were visible through the windshield.

He shrugged. "It can be fixed." Of course, what were a few thousand dollars to a kid whose wardrobe looked like it cost the average wage in Green Grove? There was probably ten K and a bar of gold in the glove compartment.

I took a deep breath and was about to thank my host for his hospitality when he turned on the blinker.

"Where do you live?" he asked.

I thought about our weatherboard house with its peeling paint and yard overgrown with weeds. "I can walk."

"I can drive."

I sighed at his stubbornness. "Fine," I said, deciding he could drop me at the corner. The house there was a modern brick home that belonged to Humpback Harding. I crossed my fingers she was playing bingo this afternoon. She was about seventy years old and had broken her back lifting patients out of bed when she was a nurse, which meant she walked around doubled-up like a folding chair.

Green Grove was nowhere near a metropolis; its grid of intersecting streets covered about fifty square miles, book-ended by the Open Valley on one side and the sand hills on the other. You could drive to my house in five minutes, but it seemed like five hours with Tom. For the next couple of minutes neither of us spoke, except for me to say, "Right at the roundabout" or "Next left."

I occupied myself with taking off my wet cardigan. I was all elbows and thumbs, the wool clinging to my skin. It would have been a challenge for a contortionist. The shift in my weight made my jeans squelch on the seat. I shuffled my feet and my shoes squelched as well. My color rose from pink to red. It seemed that the more I tried not to make a sound, the more it happened. Squelch. Squelch. Squelch. Oh. My. God.

I burst out laughing.

Tom looked at me like I had started singing at the top of my lungs.

"I think my cardigan shrank in the rain," I explained.

There was no response; maybe a slight nod.

"When I was little I used to think sheep would shrink in the rain." Oh no. Did I say that out loud? My face grew hot until it burned like a bonfire. I closed my eyes until my cheeks cooled.

When we stopped at the one red light in town, I turned to study Tom, who was looking through the windshield broodingly. My shoe squelched again and I cringed as I slid down into the seat.

Suddenly, Tom laughed.

I looked at him with wide eyes. It was a reluctant moment of mirth, but in that moment he was transformed, more so than by his smile of the previous day. The hard lines of his features softened and his white-knuckle grip on the steering wheel relaxed.

I stared at him, as if seeing an old friend.

The light turned green and Tom squared his jaw again as we drove on. "Sorry," he muttered and it sounded like he was apologizing to himself for letting his guard down.

I studied him with a furrowed brow. "Do we know each other?" I asked, as he turned onto my street. "I mean, have we met before?" I stopped short of adding "besides in my dreams" in case he freaked.

His lips tightened and he turned the wheel with a sharp movement. "Here you are," he said, pulling into the curb. He sat in silence, staring through the windshield with dark eyes.

"Thanks," I said, picking up my bag and climbing out of the SUV. Tom continued to look ahead without so much as a nod in response.

I was standing on the sidewalk, watching him drive away, when I realized that I was in front of my house.

A coincidence, I thought, as I watched his taillights disappear around the corner.

I wondered where he lived. It should have been common knowledge in a small town like Green Grove. It should also have been the talk of the town that he drove a Benz, but he had somehow managed to maintain his privacy on both counts in a town where the word "privacy" had long been erased from the dictionary.

I walked up the concrete path, which had dried within five minutes of the downpour, sucking the water into its porous surface. I bent down to move a snail into the garden before it got itself trodden on and suddenly realized Tom had sidestepped my question.

Of course the answer was "No." A girl like me would remember meeting a guy like Tom, right? But then there was the scar on his chin. The cause of that scar was buried in my mind and I wondered if I could dig it out. I shook my head, knowing it sounded as strange as Deb and her talk about reincarnation. Or as strange as chipping your tooth in a dream.

I found my mother in the hallway, painting a mural on the wall. If I had to guess I would say it had a marine theme. Or maybe there had been a sale on blue paint.

"Your aura is glowing today," she said, as I navigated the drop sheet. "Must be the Reiki from the other night."

"Must be," I said with a smile.

I called Jo again, but it went to voicemail. I thought about going to her house, but she had my number and at least five voicemail messages.

I drew myself a bath and sat in there for about an hour and a half, flipping through a stack of photography magazines and reheating the water as needed. I loved soaking in the tub for hours on end, until my fingers and toes wrinkled. It was like being in the darkroom at school; another world.

I hung a satchel of dried lavender from the faucet and let the water run through it, its scent making me sleepy. I lit a candle and watched the flame dance on its wick through half-closed eyes.

I thought I could see two people in its heart, embracing, spinning, holding each other tightly. I thought about Tom and how it would feel to have his arms around me. I continued to watch the couple in the fire, telling their story in my mind. She was pregnant and they were celebrating the news. "A baby," the rhythm of the flame told me and tears pricked my eyes. A baby. A baby. A baby.

Deb knocked on the door, bringing me back down to Earth. "Lillie? Fawn needs to use the bathroom."

I climbed out of the tub, realizing the water was cold.

8

Another dream about the man in the balaclava. This time I saw his hands as he reached out to kill me. They were thin hands, bony and feminine with dark veins visible, like mine. The dream made me doubt he was Tom after all. And, for the first time, I began to seriously consider the possibility that the man in the balaclava was in fact a woman.

I woke with teeth chattering and stared up at my dream catcher, which I would have asked for a refund on had it not been homemade. I let my eyes roam the ceiling with its spider-web cracks and peeling paint hanging in strips as I thought about Tom. I thought about his laugh and it warmed me in the pre-dawn chill, but then I remembered the look on his face when the girls had joked about the love story-slash-porno. I groaned, burying myself under the covers. What an idiot. He probably thought I was running around telling my friends that I was in love with him and vice versa.

He did save me from being stoned to death by the heavens though, I reasoned, and my heart rose enough for me to uncover my head. I had to admit it was kind of chivalrous, like when he had picked up my photos. Or when he had picked up a certain bag for a certain bitch called Melissa, I thought reluctantly. I pulled the covers over my head again.

I stretched an arm out into the cool air to retrieve my cell from the bedside table, knocking over a photo frame and coming close to toppling a glass of water. The screen told me it was ten past five. No missed calls or voicemail messages from Jo. I hoped she was OK; her dad too. I was such a bad best friend. I should have gone to her house to check on them. Instead, I had been completely and utterly wrapped up in myself and Tom.

Because sleep was no longer an option, I threw back the covers and went to my desk where Jo had bundled my photos into categories.

I used to do that back when I was organized, I thought, furrowing my eyebrows, as if I could see into the past. Jo had not been kidding when she said I used to be tidy. I used to color-coordinate my wardrobe and scrub my locker with baking soda every quarter, but it was like the nightmares had messed with my ball of twine over the summer and my tidiness had been caught up in the tangled knots.

I chose the bundle with the sticky note that read, "Friends" and the subcategory "Elementary". I liked looking at photos from those years. If I could go back to them I would in a heartbeat. It was a time before boys, before exams, before I had to decide what I wanted to be when I grew up. Junior year was proving to be a bitch. They say senior year is a holiday in comparison.

I paused at a pic Deb had taken at a school nativity play when I was in fourth grade. Mr Green had asked for a photo, because he had been on the road and wanted to see Jo in her starring role as the back half of the donkey. I had been the front half. I smiled as I remembered how Jo had volunteered to take the rear end, even though the costume had been used every year since Christ was born and stank like dirty socks.

I suddenly had the strange sensation I was being watched. I looked up and caught a movement in the window. I stood up and drew back the sheer curtain. My bedroom was at the side of our house, overlooking a veggie patch, or rather a dirt patch – another project Deb had started, but not finished.

The yard was gray in the early morning sunlight. It was also empty.

It must have been a bird that caught my eye, or a cat. But the cold that settled in my stomach said otherwise.

Jo knocked on the front door at 8.15am as usual.

"I called you a thousand times yesterday," I said, following her onto the sidewalk.

"I know."

I waited for her to go on, but then I realized I would be waiting a while. "Is everything OK with your dad?" I asked, searching her face, which was bowed, as if we were walking against a strong headwind. Her freckles stood out against her pale skin, like flecks of brown paint on a white wall.

"They think he has a secondary cancer."

"What does that mean?"

"A second cancer," she said unhelpfully. There was another silence, before she changed the subject. "What did I miss yesterday?"

I thought of my ride home with Tom. "Nothing. Nothing at all."

The school corridors were buzzing when we got there. The queen bee herself was spreading gossip like it was pollen about a new student that had flown into Green Grove overnight. "Fresh meat," Melissa announced, as she walked past my locker where we had congregated. "Jackson Murphy."

"Jack O'Lantern?" Jo asked. "He came back to Green Grove after all these years? He must be a glutton for punishment." She smirked and looked at me to check that I had picked up her reference to him being overweight. I smiled, relieved she could joke after the news about her dad.

"I guess I am," a voice said.

We turned and let out a collective squawk.

Jackson, at least I guessed it was Jackson, was leaning against a locker a few feet away. He was solid, but from what I could tell under his red hoodie it was muscle, not fat, these days. His grin showed us his adult teeth had come in, perfectly straight and brilliantly white. I wondered if they were porcelain veneers.

Jo colored until her skin matched her freckles.

Jackson was nowhere near as handsome as Tom, with features that instead seemed off-kilter: shaggy blond hair, wide-set eyes and a slightly skewed nose that looked like it had been broken. It brought him down a couple of notches on the hot-or-not meter, but gave him character.

Melissa was not into character though. "Welcome back to Green Grove," she said without warmth, before returning to her hive.

"I see some things never change," Jackson said with a laugh, his hazel eyes sparkling.

"And some things do," Sylv observed, raising an eyebrow in appreciation.

The bell rang and everyone moved to their own lockers. As I turned to get my books Tom walked up to his locker, dropped his bag at his feet and busied himself with his combination.

Say something, I told myself, as I listened to him spin the dial. I opened my mouth and a small squeak slipped out. I bit my lip and then drew myself up to my full height. "Hey."

"Hi," Tom answered, without looking out from behind the metal door.

"Thanks again for the lift yesterday."

He shoved a stack of books into his bag and stood upright, slamming his locker closed. "Don't mention it," he said with a gruffness that made it sound literal.

As he stooped again to pick up his bag, I glimpsed a crumpled photo, half-hidden beneath his books. It looked like a photo of Tom with a girl.

She was a brunette like me, but with golden streaks through her hair like wheat, not caramel. His arm was around her, pulling her close in an embrace. And he was laughing, easily, freely, naturally, which was less like the

Tom I knew and more like the Tom I had seen for a split second in his SUV. It reminded me of his words when he had apologized for being rude. "It was unlike me."

My heart plummeted to my feet, continuing until it got to Antarctica. Of course. It explained it all. He had a girlfriend back in England or Australia, who he was hung up on, and for all intents and purposes she was hung up on him as well. They probably poked each other on Facebook and Skyped for hours on end. My heart gave a twist. Fool. And another. Fool.

"Tom, we have Legal Studies," Melissa declared, swooping in and grabbing him like a hawk would a field mouse. She looked over her shoulder as they walked down the corridor, giving me a look that said, "back off".

I gave her a you-too-because-he-has-a-girlfriend look, but I think it was lost in translation.

I had a double period of Art Studies, but it may as well have been Math. My feet dragged, the soles of my shoes scraping on the concrete as I walked, chanting the word "hate" in my mind. I hated Tom. I hated that he was messing with my mind. I hated his girlfriend too. And Melissa. I also hated Mr Hastings. And, of course, I hated Dirk, who had decided to attach himself to me at the hip during Art Studies.

"Lillie! I thought of a location to shoot our project. I mean, for you to shoot and me to sketch. I was thinking of the National Park. You know how there are those moss-covered trees? They kind of look like the homes of dryads. Dryads are tree-spirits, by the way. They protect forests and woodlands, but if they leave their tree they can die. Their name means 'oak' in Greek."

"Uh-huh," I said politely, as I took my seat, flanked by my new bestie, Dirk, and my new enemy, Kate. Kate glared at me from underneath eyelids blackened by a combination of eyeliner, eye shadow and mascara. Like Sylv, she was high on the dress code hit-list.

"We have a new student," Mr Hastings said, with none of the pomp and circumstance such an announcement should hold in Green Grove.

Twenty-three pairs of eyes flew to the front of the classroom and to Jackson. His dimples told me that unlike Tom, he was a glass-half-full kind of guy. I was about two hundred and fifty per cent certain that coming back to Green Grove was going to turn that on its head.

Mr Hastings gave Jackson an overview of our major work, adding, "You can pair up with Lillie – our third wheel."

Thanks for that last comment, I thought, as Jackson walked towards me, wearing a wide smile. The corners of my mouth moved upwards too, as I realized I had been rescued from the King of the Nerds and the Queen of the Emos.

"I think Kate would be into that – what did you call it? Death Knight? – you were telling me about last class," I said to Dirk. His crestfallen expression lifted as he turned to Kate, whose purple-lined lips twitched into a small smile.

"Thank you," I breathed to my knight in shining armor, as we sat down at another desk.

"For what?" Jackson asked.

I tilted my head towards my former partners, who were deep in conversation thanks to my matchmaking.

Jackson grinned again and then squinted at me, as if sizing me up. "Photographer?" he asked. "A stab in the dark," he added with a nod to my camera. "I have psychic powers, you know." He placed his fingertips on his temples and closed his eyes. "You also like the color blue. Pale blue. Like the color of an iceberg."

I startled as I thought of Tom and his glacial eyes. How did he know? But then I remembered I was wearing a pale blue sweater. I rolled my eyes. "OK. You got me on both counts." I spotted a scribble of ink on the back of his hand. It was a map of the school, as if you could get lost between here and the main building. "Let me guess," I said with a smile. "You like to draw."

His mouth fell open. "You cheated."

I shook my head. "I have psychic powers too," I teased.

He laughed and I pushed up the sleeves of my sweater as his thousand-watt smile gave me a hot flash.

He leaned down and pulled a tattered sketchbook from an equally tattered bag. "Trade?"

I hunted through my own bag, which was a bottomless pit of lunch wrappers, crumpled notes, film canisters, books and pens. Six months ago I would have had a heart attack that it had become such a landfill. These days I was more concerned about the man – or woman – in the balaclava than a few half-eaten muffins squashed at the bottom of my bag.

I pulled out a bundle of photos. "This will be a lucky dip," I said apologetically.

The first photo was of the ant carrying the crumb, which had been taken minutes before Tom had criticized my photos of Sylv. I touched a shadow in the corner of the image, which I knew belonged to Tom.

I flicked to the next pic.

"Wait," Jackson said, putting his hand on mine. I blushed and moved my hand in order to bring back the photo.

"Let me guess," he said, rubbing his chin comically as he studied the photo. "This is a statement on consumerism through the representation of mass consumption. The ant symbolizes the spread of the manmade world to the natural environment."

I stared at him. "Um. No. It's just a photo of an ant carrying a crumb."

"Thank God."

"For what?"

"I thought you were an art snob." He pointed at the photography books I had pulled from my bag and I drew them into my chest, like a mother gathering up her children.

When Jackson showed me his sketches I saw they were as detailed as my photos.

"I use carbon, instead of graphite," he told me and I nodded, as if I was up on my pencils.

I traced a finger over the fine lines, recognizing the streetscapes of Green Grove: Main Street, the Memorial Fountain, the Fur Museum, Wal-Mart. I laughed as I recognized a figure on the sidewalk. "Jo!"

Jackson frowned. "Really?" He studied the drawing and nodded. "Huh. It does look like Jo. Funny."

I continued to flip through the pages. "Green Grove. Green Grove. Green Grove," I said as I surveyed the sketches.

Jackson shrugged. "I like this town."

"You like this town?" I repeated incredulously.

"I was born here."

I was going to point out that he had also been bullied here, but instead I said, "Me too, but... You like Green Grove?"

Jackson laughed and then leaned towards me with an earnest expression. "If you want to talk about identity then talk about this town. Both of us are products of Green Grove."

I hesitated. I could hardly say I was a product of New York or LA, but to tell the truth I was a product without an ingredients list at the moment. It was kind of hard to hold onto your identity when you had died about forty times in the past four months, even if it was just in your dreams.

I narrowed my eyes as I realized he wanted our major work to be about Green Grove. "No."

He raised an eyebrow. "No?" He looked thoughtful for a moment and then brightened. "What about family? Are you a product of your family?"

I thought of Deb. "No."

"No again?" He pouted. "I thought Mr Hastings said this was about teamwork."

I laughed at myself. "Fine. I guess I will have to learn to love Green Grove." It seemed like the lesser of two evils.

He beamed again. "I can pick you up on Saturday. Yeah? Two?"

He had a location in mind, but his lips were sealed.

"A teeny tiny clue," I begged.

He shook his head.

"What happened to teamwork?"

His dimples flashed. "Badlands Street?" he checked.

I frowned. First Tom had known where I lived, now Jackson.

"I used to live two streets down on Wyoming Crescent," he reminded me.

"Oh." I searched my memory.

"I knew you had forgotten. You remembered my nickname though: Jack O'Lantern." He grimaced, but it turned into a grin as he asked, "Do you remember when Jo stole my school bag in fifth grade and you wrote Jack O'Lantern on it with a sharpie?"

"I think so… I mean, yes. I do," I said, my face flushing with embarrassment.

"And then I wrote on both of your bags as payback. Jo was Freckle Face and you were–"

"Buck Tooth Bandit," I finished, wondering why he would bring up such a memory. Thank God for braces, I thought, touching my front teeth self-consciously. My mind automatically went to my tooth again, which I had decided I had chipped while eating nuts or candy. Hey. It was either that or acknowledge it had happened in my dreams.

"We all got detention," Jackson continued with a smile.

"I must have blocked that from my memory," I said, giving him a half-smile in return.

"He sounds hung up on being called Jack O'Lantern," Jo said after I recounted our conversation.

"He probably came back to Green Grove for revenge," Sylv said. "Like in that horror movie where that pumpkin goes bad-ass and kills all those kids." She clicked her fingers as she tried to remember the name of what sounded like a forgettable film.

"You said you wanted to sleep with him two minutes ago," Jo said.

"I do." Sylv threw a grape and Jo batted it back. Her hand-eye coordination was second to none. Me, on the other hand, I could have missed a beach ball.

"Where are you going on your date?" Jo asked.

I shrugged, ignoring her use of the word "date." "He wants it to be a surprise," I explained, which of course made it sound even more like a date.

"If he takes you to an abandoned farmhouse, slaughterhouse, warehouse," Sylv ticked them off her fingers, "nuthouse, trainhouse–"

"Trainhouse?" Jo and I asked in sync.

Sylv grimaced. "I would have said train station, but I was going for a theme."

"Haunted house?" I offered.

"Bingo! Anyway, if he takes you anywhere that ends in 'house' you need to–" She frowned. "Dammit. How did they kill the bad-ass pumpkin?"

"They turned him into soup?" Jo suggested.

I guffawed.

Sylv shrugged. "You can thank me when he turns out to be a serial killer. Or worse."

"What could be worse than a serial killer?" Jo asked.

"A virgin?" Sylv suggested with a smirk.

But my mind went to the man in the balaclava. Woman, I corrected myself, remembering her hands. I shook my head, snapping myself out of my daydream. "This is non-negotiable," I told the girls. "We have an assignment. Do you want me to flunk art studies?"

"When will you girls understand that grades are not life and death?" Sylv asked.

"Tell us that when your dad cuts up your credit card," Jo said.

Jackson was walking across the quad. He waved and I waved back, but like a moth to a flame, my eyes moved to Tom, who was leaning against brickwork of the main building. I was surprised to find him looking at me with an intensity that made me blush. He straightened and for one heart-stopping moment I thought he was going to walk over and strike up a conversation, but then he turned and disappeared inside.

"I remember now," Jo said suddenly. "We played cards during detention. You, me and Jack O'Lantern. I mean, Jackson. I think it was Snap. Or Uno?"

I squinted as if my memory went hand-in-hand with my eyesight and then shook my head. "Not coming to me, sorry." It was like my brain had become a sieve and my memories had fallen through the holes, hanging on like strings of spaghetti. Like my inability to remember how I knew Tom; how I knew his scar.

I guess I was in good company. They say Einstein had a bad memory. He had once forgotten where he lived and had to phone Princeton University for his address. It was the one piece of trivia that I knew about him BT – Before Tom. Now I also know that they say he had schizophrenia, that his mother thought him deformed when he was born and that he had been expelled from high school. He must have had a principal like Turnip.

When I went to sleep that night I thought I would have another date with death, but instead I found myself with Tom.

We were surrounded by lilies; tiger lilies, oriental lilies, asiatic lilies. They sprouted from pots at our feet or hung in baskets above our heads and I realized we were in a greenhouse.

I followed Tom to the edge of a small pond. It was also filled with lilies – water lilies. The sunlight filtered through the glass walls and ceiling, making the surface of the pond sparkle.

I watched a goldfish swim between the lily pads, as Tom sat on the concrete wall that circled the pond. He dipped a hand into the water and splashed me, making me squeal. He laughed as I splashed him back and as he did I knew it was a dream. Tom laughing? As if.

I was scooping up another handful of water when he grabbed my arms and pulled me towards him. My heart fluttered as I leaned in for a kiss and, at that moment, I woke.

I squeezed my eyes shut, trying to return to the dream. Squeeze. Squeeze. Squeeze. Damn. Damn. Damn.

It had been so detailed that I could recall his scent and the scent of the lilies. I put my hand out in the dark, searching for the warmth of his body, but found only empty space instead.

9

I took my time preparing for my date with Jackson on Saturday. Yep. You heard me. I had turned into Jo and was calling it a date, even though I knew our outing was for business, not pleasure. The thought of being picked up by a boy had my butterflies in a flutter. If it had have been Tom instead of Jackson I think I would have been completely carried away.

My selection of "date" clothes was limited. I pulled on my good pair of jeans – dark blue denim with a skinny leg cut – and tried on the three tops I had laid out on my desk the night before.

One was a white linen top with embroidered yellow flowers around the collar.

"Too hippie-ish," I muttered, throwing it back on the desk.

Another was a pale pink t-shirt with a sketch of a donkey on the front. "Too casual."

The third was a crème-colored halter-neck top made from satin, which billowed around my waist.

"Hmmm…" I turned in front of the mirror. It looked good, but I pulled it off over my head. "Too formal."

I yanked open the window to check the outside temperature, holding out my hand and letting the sunlight warm my palm. I ended up pulling on the donkey T-shirt, deciding there was no need for a jacket.

I applied my mascara and cherry lip gloss, and brushed my hair at least a hundred times before putting it up into a ponytail and then letting it down again. The girls said wearing it up showed off my cheekbones, but I knew it also showed off my pointy ears, which was why I let my hair hang straight, a hand-length past my shoulders day after day. It must have been a decade since my ears had seen sunlight.

I checked my reflection again, tilting my head up and down, and pursing my lips as I applied another layer of gloss. I considered asking Deb for her concealer to cover my dark circles. Thanks to the nightmares, I was starting to look like a vampire.

I called Jo for a pep talk, but there was no answer either at home or on her cell. I guessed she was at work and left a voicemail message asking her to call the cops if I was missing in the morning.

Deb was sitting at the kitchen table, which was strewn with beads and gemstones and tangled heaps of fishing line. She barely batted an eyelash when I told her I was going out. I suppose I should have added "with a boy," but I wanted to save myself a talk on Venus, the Goddess of Love, or worse, the Three Virgin Goddesses.

Her eyebrows crumpled with concentration as she beaded. She had been commissioned to make fifteen necklaces for Tree of Life. I saw she was halfway through her first and was wrestling with a knot in the line, cursing under her breath.

I decided to give her a hand, considering I had about forty minutes before my so-called date. I made a necklace with a mixture of clear beads and pink gemstones.

"Rose quartz," Deb commented as I connected the clasp and held it up to the light. "The crystal of love."

I hesitated as she restarted her first necklace, wondering if she knew about Jackson. I held the necklace against my chest and turned to check out my reflection in a saucepan on the stove. Maybe I should wear it around Tom, I thought.

This thought was cut short by a knock at the door. I peered down the hallway and saw my "date" through the front window. He was twenty-five minutes early.

"I have my cell," I told Deb, as I dropped the necklace on the table. I raced down the hallway and barreled past Jackson. "Hi."

"Hi," he responded, surprised by my speedy getaway. "I thought your mom would want to meet me, check my license and registration, and all that. Maybe call the cops to check my record, which is clean, by the way."

I laughed. "If you knew my mother you would know how silly that sounds."

"Hmmm..." He made a show of racking his memory, putting a closed fist under his chin and squinting up at the sky. "Happy pants? Peace beads? Camper van?"

I laughed again. "OK. You remember Deb."

"I remember she came to school in third grade to teach us how to tie-dye T-shirts."

I cringed. "Really?"

"And she took you and Jo to one of those Rainbow Retreats at Elkhorn Crossing after fifth grade. You guys were gone for like half the summer," he said as he opened the passenger door.

"Wow. What a memory," I said, as I sank into the passenger seat. I wondered whether I should be worried and my mind went to my stalker, the man-slash-woman in the balaclava. A cold shiver ran down my spine and I closed my eyes, conjuring up the red light of my aura and doing aura aerobics until my body temperature rose a few degrees. I know. Just call me Deb.

Jackson drove an old hatchback which was off-white with pockets of rust on the hood and side panels. The tan seat covers sagged like granny panties under my body weight.

He was as tight-lipped about our destination as he had been at school.

"You realize I know these roads like the back of my hand," I told him, as he turned onto a road that led to the railroad crossing. "This road goes to the vineyards."

He frowned. "I should have blindfolded you."

"What can I say? Sixteen years in Green Grove versus…?"

"Eleven." He paused to check for trains, before driving across the tracks. The railroad crossing marked where the landscape went from sepia to color, as we went from the dustbowl that was Green Grove into a world without water restrictions.

The Open Valley had been a well-known wine region before prohibition in 1920. They had reopened it in the Eighties, dividing the private estate into seven wineries again. The valley was as refreshing as a cool glass of water on a stinking hot day. Yes, the vineyards themselves – row after row of grapevines – could get old, but there were also the formal gardens that belonged to a few of the wineries and the old brickworks, on which I had used up a ton of film over the years.

We passed a couple of vehicles as we drove down the narrow avenues, out-of-towners on a weekend getaway. Jackson hugged the side of the road as a red SUV flew by and a white sedan followed, throwing up pebbles. I flinched as they sprayed against the side of the hatchback like a hail of bullets.

Jackson laughed. "Are you worried about the paintwork?"

I smiled, but sudden sounds were not my friend at the moment. Last night Deb had dropped a spoon on the floor with a clatter and I almost had to breathe into a paper bag for half an hour afterwards, as if the man-or-woman in the balaclava was going to spoon me to death.

I shifted my attention to the window and saw that Jackson had put ten miles or so between us and Green Grove. Here the road merged into one lane with ponderosa pines crowding us on either side. I wondered what would happen if we came across an SUV now. Not that we would. If Green Grove was the middle of nowhere, then this was the middle of the middle of nowhere. All we needed now was an abandoned farmhouse.

My eyes moved to Jackson, who was humming off-key and nodding his head in time to the music that blared from the radio. The speakers crackled with the heavy bass as his fingers tapped the steering wheel. They were slender, like the hands of the man-slash-woman in the balaclava.

He caught me watching and grinned. "Got you now, Lillie."

My armpits prickled with sweat. Had I misheard him? "What?"

"You thought you knew Green Grove. What did you say? Oh yeah. Like the back of your hand." He laughed and then looked through the windshield with a smug smile. His tone was bright though as he added, "Jackson: One. Lillie: Zero." He was like a ray of sunshine compared to Tom. If one of them was my killer it would be the latter.

I allowed myself to sag into the seat again.

Jackson eased off the gas as the woods ended and we passed through open gates. My stomach stirred, as if with homesickness, as I looked at the ornate wrought iron. The stone pillars that supported the gates bore a well-polished plaque.

"Rose Hill," I read, my lips wrapping around the words as if embracing a long lost friend. I had this sudden sensation that I was coming home. The words stuck in my mind, like corn in my teeth. What did I mean by coming home?

I consulted the filing cabinet of my mind, looking for a reason for the familiarity, but found locked drawer after locked drawer, until a memory from when I was about five or six years old opened.

Deb had brought me here. We had dressed up as if we were going to a wedding or an expensive restaurant. I had worn a yellow sundress, and Deb had worn a red dress and white sandals, instead of her uniform of happy pants and peace beads. Her hair had ended at her shoulders back then and I remember her spending half an hour or so in the bathroom, blow-drying it into shape while I sat as stiff as a board on the couch.

As Jackson drove down the avenue of trees, I caught glimpses of freshly mown grass and a man-made lake, rectangular like the Reflecting Pool in DC, but deep and dark. I wound down the window to breathe in the fresh air and listen to the trill of birds as they flitted through the branches. Red birds. Like in my dream, I realized with a start.

The tires crunched on the white gravel, sounding like someone shushing us – or shushing Jackson, who was commenting on the size of the lake and wondering about catfish.

"I should have brought my rod."

Shhh. Shhh. Shhh.

The driveway curved and I drew in a deep breath as a white building came into view. I exhaled, as another drawer unlocked in my mind. I remembered Deb holding my hand as we had walked up the front steps. I had been complaining about a piece of gravel in my shoe.

"Ow. Ow. Oooow!"

Deb had crouched to pull off my shoe, giving it a shake. I must have been younger than five or six, maybe four, because she had also wiped my nose with a tissue and combed her fingers though my hair, before rocking back on her heels to study me, giving me a nod of approval.

"...a hotel," Jackson was saying as I tuned back in to his channel. "It has, like, fifty rooms. How much do you think it costs a night?"

I shook my head.

"Go on. Guess."

"A lot?"

He laughed, but before he could answer his own question, a man dressed in old-fashioned coat-tails met us in the circular drive. He looked at the hatchback like a cow had ambled into Rose Hill, but he told us we could view the gardens, provided we minded the out-of-bounds signage.

As we walked towards the front entrance I was overcome by my connection to the estate. "I am in love," I breathed.

Jackson grinned. "Good. Because I was thinking we could call our major work 'From Green Grove with Love.'"

I wrinkled my nose. "James Bond?"

"Bingo."

"From Green Grove with Love," I repeated dubiously. Boys.

I stopped a few feet from the steps that led to the front entrance and raised my camera to take a photo. The shutter clicked as a figure descended and my heart rate suddenly went through the roof. Tom.

I tried to remain cool, calm and collected, but I knew I was gawking. I have to say, he looked like he belonged at Rose

Hill. He was dressed in a light gray T-shirt which hugged his chiseled frame, and there were no tears in his designer jeans today. Jackson looked like a kid in comparison, with his loose shirt, baggy jeans and skate shoes.

Tom paused when he saw us and, in that moment, he looked like some kind of modern day Mr Darcy on the steps of Pemberley. I frowned. When had I read *Pride and Prejudice*? Jo was the bookworm. Maybe I had seen the movie. I think it starred Colin Firth. And maybe Keira Knightly? Or was that the BBC series?

"What are you doing here?" I asked, lowering my camera as he descended.

"I live here."

"You live here?" Of course. His family was loaded. Living in a hotel was probably as normal as having butter on bread. I guessed this was where he had been hiding out during his first few months in Green Grove.

"What about you?" Tom asked, his eyes moving between me and Jackson. I became acutely aware of my childish T-shirt and scuffed sneakers. I thought about the girl in the photo, who had looked as polished as the brass handrail on the front steps. "What are you doing at Rose Hill?" It sounded like an accusation, as if we were trespassing on private property.

"Assignment," Jackson said, rolling his eyes as if it blew.

The gravel driveway crunched behind us and I turned to see the valet pulling up the Benz. Tom must have forked out for a panel beater, because its hood was free from hail damage. Or maybe it was a brand new car.

"I have to go," Tom said.

"Where?" I asked compulsively.

He looked at me for a moment and then at Jackson. "Tell Lorraine at reception to let you into the ballroom." He turned towards his SUV and then hesitated. "And steer clear of the out-of-bounds signage if you go into the gardens."

His tone made my blood simmer and boil as I watched him climb into the SUV. "Who does he think he is? Lord of the manor?" I muttered, looking at his silhouette behind the tinted windows. The accelerator was pressed down and the vehicle moved off with the slightest spin of his tires, as if it were a message to me – "F-you."

It was like we were in the middle of an argument that had started before he came to Green Grove. I was ready to bury the hatchet, but he continued to hack at my heart with his mixed messages. I put a hand to my chest as I watched him drive through the gates and into the Open Valley.

I let my hand drop as I followed Jackson up the front steps and through the double doors.

"See?" he said, gesturing around the white marble foyer. "James Bond would love Green Grove."

"Technically this is the Open Valley," I grumbled, but I had to agree as I surveyed the sweeping staircase with its ornate banister that looked like it had been hand-carved from mahogany or some other expensive, well-oiled timber. I lifted my eyes to the ceiling, which featured a dome of ornamental plaster the size of a small continent.

Lorraine was an equally glamorous woman pushing sixty. She wore a caramel-colored skirt suit with an oversized gold brooch pinned to its lapel. Her bright red nails were as fake as her botoxed brow. She was about as Green Grove as the Statue of Liberty. She looked down her powdered nose at us like we were a couple of stray dogs, until Jackson mentioned Tom. Suddenly, she was all smiles and bleached teeth.

"Follow me, darlings," she said in a posh accent, which I could tell hid a Texan twang.

Jackson stopped about halfway down the passage to sketch an antique vase that occupied a recess lit by downlights. I walked ahead, as Lorraine doubled back to tell him its history. I passed a number of doors on both sides, but I knew I wanted the double doors at the end. You could call it intuition, I guess. Like how I knew about the scar on Tom's chin.

I placed both hands on the brass handles and pushed. The ballroom looked like it belonged in Versailles with its mirrored walls and chandeliers, and, as I stood on the polished parquet floor with my reflection multiplied a million times on either side, my stomach was filled with the same sensation I got when I looked at old photos. A longing.

"Who would use this in Green Grove?" I wondered aloud.

"No one in Green Grove," Lorraine said, coming into the room with Jackson in tow and smiling at me like I was a stupid child. "The owner used to throw lavish functions here, before it became a hotel." She must have seen the incredulous look on my face, because she added, "Long before you were born. A good forty years ago, I would say." She laughed softly, looking around the room, as if imagining a bygone party. "My, my, that shows my age."

Jackson wandered around the ballroom, holding up his hands like a photo frame and squinting at the view. I should have been taking photos, but I peppered Lorraine with questions instead, wanting, *needing* to know all about Rose Hill.

Luckily, Lorraine was keen for company. Apparently, she had worked at Rose Hill on and off since she was a teenager. "This place has a hold on me," she admitted. "I came back last year after a decade working at the Bellagio in Vegas."

"Has the owner come back too?" I asked, wondering who would own such a decadent estate.

Lorraine shook her head. "Her daughter and son-in-law used to pop in now and then. The last time I saw them was before I headed out west. They brought their son with them. I spoiled him rotten. I have to say, I was tickled pink when he returned this year."

"Son?"

"Tom," she said lightly, as if she were jogging my mind instead of blowing it.

I did a double-take as I thought back to him standing on the front steps, looking like he owned the estate. He did.

Lorraine bit her lip, accidentally smudging her front teeth with lipstick. "He skipped out on his grandmother in England," she said and then lowered her voice, as if his grandmother could hear across the Atlantic. "She thinks he is at boarding school in Kent. I agreed to keep mum about it." She sighed and patted her wavy auburn hair. "Can you imagine saying no to that boy?"

"No," I answered honestly. It was as clear as the crystal chandeliers that hung above our heads that Tom was used to hearing the word "yes."

Lorraine sighed. "It seems someone did say, 'No,'" she confided. "A girl." Her lips pursed. "She broke his heart and that was why he came to Green Grove."

My mind went to the photo of the girl again. I suddenly realized that they were in the middle of an argument, not me and Tom.

I lowered my eyes to the gilded columns that lined the room and homesickness settled in my stomach again. I thought back to when Deb had brought me to Rose Hill as a kid. We had walked around the gardens for what seemed like no more than ten minutes before Deb had asked the woman at reception – Lorraine? – about a man called William.

It was such a small detail that I wondered how it had made it through eleven years of schooling without being overwritten by fractions or verbs or the capital of Sri Lanka, not to mention my amnesia of the past few months.

"Do you know someone called William?" I asked Lorraine on a whim.

She smiled. "You must mean Tom's father."

I frowned. Why would Deb be asking about Tom's father? I was about to ask Lorraine if she remembered us coming to Rose Hill all of those years ago when we heard the phone ring at reception, tinkling like wind chimes.

"Enjoy the estate," Lorraine said, as she trotted towards the passage. "But please note the out-of-bounds signage in the garden."

I would have moved on when I saw the black lettering that dictated "Keep Out" if not for the triple-dipping on the warning. They may as well have led me here and unclipped the chain across the path. My mind was running through the reasons for the sign, which swung in the afternoon breeze. Maybe it was about public liability. The flagstone path looked uneven. I frowned and moved in for a closer look. I had seen that path before…

It hit me like a slap in the face. It was the path from my dreams, the path that led to the courtyard with the fountain. My chest constricted.

"Excuse me, Miss."

I yelped and spun around to see an old man crouched by the rose bushes. I took in his beige coveralls and the pair of gardening shears in his hands.

"Sorry," I said with a hand on my chest, as if holding in my heart.

"This section of the garden is out-of-bounds," he said apologetically.

"Why?"

He shrugged as he pruned a rose bush. "Ask the boy. He put up the sign." He chopped a branch with gusto, muttering under his breath. I caught a couple of words that made me blush.

I guessed "the boy" was Tom. I had to shake my head at him turning up and taking over. This old man had probably been pruning these rose bushes for fifty years.

"And he calls me George when my name is Fredrick," the old man continued to complain, dropping his shears and picking up a spray bottle.

I made a sympathetic sound as I looked at the path again. There was no way, no how that this was the path from my dreams. I was blurring the line between my sleeping and waking hours again. I turned towards the stables, telling the old man goodbye and myself to get a grip.

My grip lasted about three minutes, which was when I saw the greenhouse. It was hidden behind a row of small trees and I had to pinch myself when I saw its glass glinting in the sunlight.

I cut through the long grass and saw that unlike the greenhouse from my dreams its windows were smashed and coated in grime. I held my breath as I peered through a broken windowpane. It was empty. There were no pots or baskets, and no lilies.

I exhaled and lifted my camera to snap a shot of the interior of the greenhouse, focusing on a vine that was creeping up the metal frame, before turning the lens on a mound of rubble. I frowned, wondering if it could have been the concrete wall of the pond in my dream.

"Hey."

"Jesus!" I yelped.

"You can call me Jackson," Jackson said with a wink. He stuck his head through a broken window. "I think they should have a word with their gardener," he said with a laugh.

"Do you want to get decapitated?" I asked, pulling at the back of his T-shirt.

Jackson looked up at the shards of glass and withdrew his head with a shiver. "Should we check out the stables? I think I saw a horse."

I nodded, following him back through the long grass and onto the lawn. I looked over my shoulder, thinking I had to have rocks in my head to think I had seen both the path and the greenhouse from my dreams.

I squinted in the sunlight and for a moment the greenhouse took on a pinkish hue, as if it were filled to the ceiling with lilies.

It took two and a half rolls of film for me and one sketchbook for Jackson before the sun began to set over the Open Valley and the light was leeched from the sky.

"Goodbye Jackson," Lorraine said, as we walked through the hotel. "And…"

"Lillie," I said.

Her eyes seemed to bulge. "Lillie?"

"Yes," I said slowly.

"Sorry," she said. "Tom said you…" She hesitated and then bit her lip. She may as well have applied lipstick straight to her teeth. "It is just such a thrill to see Tom making friends," she finally said and then gave a slight shrug of her shoulder pads. "Although that boy has always been a people person."

I swallowed a guffaw, thinking how biased she was about the antisocial Tom. He was hardly a social butterfly. Maybe he had been outgoing as a child.

Or maybe I have a lot to learn about Tom, I thought, wondering what he had told Lorraine. I was about to ask when she suddenly remembered that she had to speak to the kitchen about a room service order. "Lovely to meet you, Jackson and... Lillie."

There were no bouncers, but it felt like we were being kicked out of Rose Hill. I followed Jackson down the steps and into the dying light, wondering whether I would be allowed back again or whether I would just have to continue to visit in my dreams.

10

Jackson talked non-stop as we drove from Rose Hill. It was starting to drive me nuts.

"Have you noticed that people have stopped using their blinkers?" he asked and then continued to talk without waiting for a response. "A truck came close to cleaning me up this morning before I picked you up. I was like one second from being killed, all because of a stupid blinker." He shook his head and whistled under his breath. "And what about the road rage in this town? I mean the truck driver flipped me the bird. Me!"

I wondered when he breathed.

I stared out the window as he went on about being honked at for stopping at a stop sign, my eyes flicking from tree to tree. As they thinned, I saw rows of vines, their leaves turning red and falling from their branches. In another few weeks they would be bare, like stick figures hung out to dry on the trellises.

I wanted to see Rose Hill again, but it was over the rise. I closed my eyes and saw myself walking through its corridors with rooms on either side. I wondered which room belonged to Tom, or should I say which rooms plural? He probably had a butler too. He may as well have been King of the World for how much of a shot I had with him. I closed my eyes and leaned against the headrest, wondering whether I even wanted a shot with Tom. My attraction to him was making my head hurt, not to mention my heart.

"What the–?" Jackson exclaimed, slowing down.

I looked through the windshield at the railroad crossing ahead. Through the twilight, I could see a few cars parked and teens milling about on the side of the road. I recognized Blake, slouching against his Mustang. Melissa was sitting in the passenger seat with the door open, her silver pumps on the asphalt.

"They play chicken with the trains," I explained. It was how teens in Green Grove got their kicks. Yep. It seemed that racing a speeding locomotive was as good as it got in this town.

Jackson slowed and wound down his window as we approached the crossing.

"Go. Go. Go," I begged, as Melissa slunk out of the car and approached, like a lioness stalking its prey.

"OK. Stop," I said, as I spotted a certain SUV through the dusk.

Tom was leaning against his SUV. His face was in shadow, but it was turned in our direction. I suddenly realized it was me who was wrong, not Lorraine. He was a social butterfly after all.

"Hi Jackson," Melissa said, bending down at the window. She was wearing a sequined top that looked like it belonged to Sylv and her fake-tanned arms were covered with goosebumps in the chill of the evening. "Oh," she said, seeing me. "Hi…"

"Lillie," I said, as if she could forget my name when we had hung out for half of our lives.

A train horn sounded in the distance and a few of the teens straightened up, like prairie dogs.

"The 6.18," Melissa crowed. "Who's up?"

"Me," Jackson volunteered.

"What?" I looked at him as if horns had sprouted from his head.

"Come on, Lillie. Live a little." He grinned and revved the engine, looking at the railroad crossing a couple of hundred feet ahead.

"Yeah, and maybe die a little too," I said. "Forget it."

The train came around the bend, its headlight lighting up the track.

"Get out of the car, Lillie."

"So you can kill yourself? No way."

Melissa snatched a sweater from one of her lapdogs and waved it in the air. "On your marks!" she called out.

"Get out," Jackson ordered.

I knew he was going to do it. He had a look of determination on his face and his forehead was damp with sweat. I reached for the door handle, but the door was locked. "Jackson." I began to panic as the engine revved louder and louder. "Let me out!"

"Get set!" Melissa shouted.

Tom was no longer reclining against his SUV, but standing upright, poised as if he were also going to race the train.

"Sorry, Lillie," Jackson whispered.

"I said, 'Let me out!'" I shouted, my fingers slipping and scrambling to pull up the lock.

"Go!"

The back tires spun in the gravel and we were off.

"Stop!" I screamed, staring wide-eyed at the train, which was seconds from the railroad crossing. I took in its size; it must have been at least twenty cars long. It would take about a mile of braking before a train like that slowed, let alone stopped. The driver blew the horn as our white hatchback approached, its piercing sound mixing with my screams.

I looked at Jackson as we reached the tracks. His eyes were wide with horror. He knew he had killed us both. All those months of waiting for the man-or-woman in the balaclava had been wasted. I was going to be murdered by a boy in baggy jeans instead.

The tires barely made a sound on the tracks. I guessed we were airborne. I closed my eyes, hoping it would be instantaneous. I thought about Deb, who would probably lay the rose quartz necklace on my grave and pray to the Goddess of Reincarnation. I thought of Jo, of her dead mother and dying father. I thought of Tom.

The thought was followed by an earth-shattering smash and suddenly I was being thrown in all directions, as the car spun around and around and around.

And then the world stopped.

The train horn continued though, and I wondered if it had followed me into the afterlife. I could hear Jackson breathing heavily beside me. Maybe I was a ghost, looking down on my death. I opened my eyes and saw him beside me, his hands gripping the steering wheel, knuckles as white as his face. I felt a throbbing pain in my elbow. I lifted my arm and saw that my elbow was cut, bleeding.

I reached for the lock again, pulling it up with ease unlike my earlier attempts, before I opened the door and threw up on the road.

"Lillie! Are you OK?" It was Tom. His voice was hoarse, like someone had their hands around his throat.

I nodded, thankful my hair provided a curtain on either side of my face.

Suddenly, I heard Jackson being pulled from his seat. "What the fuck were you thinking?" Tom shouted. "You could have killed her!" I turned to see Tom pushing Jackson to the ground and following through with his fist. Once. Twice. The swings cut through the air and connected with well-practiced precision.

"Tom," I climbed to my feet, leaning on the open door for support.

"Sorry! Sorry!" Jackson shouted, his voice cracking. He waved his hands in surrender, as blood poured from his nose, staining his top lip and mouth.

Tom grabbed him by the front of his shirt and slammed him against the side of the hatchback.

"Tom! Please!" I screamed.

Tom looked up at me, a clenched fist in the air, ready to strike. His eyes cleared for a moment and I thought he was going to listen to me. I thought he was going to lower his hand and let his opponent lick his wounds, but his mouth tightened and his fist torpedoed towards Jackson, who screwed up his face, waiting for the blow. It landed inches from his face, as Tom smashed his knuckles into the car instead. I heard the metal buckle. It would have hurt his hand like hell.

He dropped Jackson, who slid to the ground like a sack of potatoes.

"Come on, Lillie," Tom ordered, stalking past me, towards the SUV.

I followed, stepping over the debris of the rear bumper, which had been ripped off by the 6.18. I thought I was going to be sick again as Tom reached for my arm and helped me into the passenger seat. Not on his leather seats, I thought, as my stomach lurched.

Tom shut the door and I leaned my forehead against the window until my stomach settled. When I lifted my eyes I saw Melissa through the dusk with her arms crossed and an expression icy enough to halt global warming.

"Are you OK? Are you sure?" Tom asked again, as he climbed into the driver seat and started the engine. His eyes searched mine as if looking for the answer. I nodded and then looked down at my hands, not wanting to be sucked into their depths.

A low hiss escaped his lips when he spotted my elbow. He reached under his seat and pulled out a first aid kit, before taking my arm. I had to remind myself to breathe as he swabbed the cut with antiseptic and applied the plaster gently to my elbow, running his fingers up and down until it adhered.

"Your hands are shaking," he said, turning up the heat. "You might be in shock." He leaned into the back seat and produced a black jacket. "Here. Put this on."

"Thank you," I whispered.

He acknowledged my thank you with a nod. "I think you should go to hospital," he said, releasing the handbrake.

"No. Please."

He studied me suspiciously. "You might need stitches."

I shook my head. As silly as it sounded, I was thinking of Jackson. He had just committed a misdemeanor, if not a felony. He could go to jail.

"Lillie! You could have been killed," Tom argued.

"Please, Tom."

He considered me for a moment, before turning his attention to the road. "Fine." He flicked on the blinker and pulled out, carefully crossing the railroad tracks and maneuvering around the hatchback, where Jackson was sitting in the dirt, holding his nose.

It was at least a minute before I broke the silence. "When you said you lived at Rose Hill, I thought you meant as a guest."

"I did. It belongs to my grandmother," Tom said curtly.

The silence settled again.

"I liked the ballroom," I finally said. "And the gardens." I hesitated, glancing at him sideways. "The greenhouse–"

"The greenhouse is out-of-bounds," Tom interrupted. "There should be a sign. I told George–"

"His name is Fredrick," I snapped.

Tom looked at me and his guard seemed to slip for a second. "Really?" He turned his attention to the road again as we pulled onto my street.

"Why were you at the railroad crossing?" I asked quickly before the opportunity passed by like the houses through my window.

He hesitated for a moment or two before he spoke and I thought he was going to sidestep the question. "I was off track," he finally said and then added, "Mind the pun."

I looked at him with a small smile. "Did you just make a joke?"

His lips twitched. "I guess I did."

I laughed.

He pulled up in front of my house and then turned in his seat. "Are you sure about your arm?"

I nodded.

"Positive?"

"Promise," I said with another laugh.

"You like to laugh, don't you?"

"And you don't." It was supposed to be a question, but it sounded like a statement.

"I used to," he said, looking at me sideways. For a moment I thought he was going to spill his secrets, but then he took off his seatbelt and leaned across to open my door.

As his hand rested on the door handle, I saw the knuckles on his right hand were grazed and swollen. I reached out and touched them tenderly.

He looked up at me and my lips tingled with anticipation, but then he flicked open the door and sunk back into his seat.

"Night," he said.

"Night," I echoed, climbing reluctantly from the vehicle.

Tom stayed at the curb with the engine purring until I reached the front door. I realized as I pushed it open that I was still wearing his coat. I pulled the collar up around my neck and breathed in his scent, laughing as I wondered what the girls would say. Sylv would probably tell me I was one step away from sniffing his underwear. I laughed again.

Tom was still watching and, in the glow of the dashboard, I thought I saw him smile.

11

I had hoped to see Tom in my dreams that night, but instead I found myself back in the car with Jackson. I guess I should have been grateful that the man-or-woman in the balaclava was nowhere to be seen, but I could hear the train coming – the 6.18 – its horn blowing like the wail of an ambulance. I screamed in sync.

We were milliseconds from the railroad crossing, but time was passing in hours. It was relative, as Einstein would say. But I knew what was about to happen. I knew we were going to hit the tracks and sail through the air. I knew the train would clip the rear bumper, making the hatchback spin out of control. Of course, then came the throwing up and Tom punching Jackson.

But before we reached the railroad crossing, Jackson decided to slam on the brakes.

The car skidded towards the tracks, its tires screeching on the asphalt. My eyes grew wide as I realized it was too little, too late. There was no way, no how that the hatchback was coming to a standstill before the railroad crossing. We were on a collision course with the train and the split second delay meant this time it would take off more than the rear bumper.

The headlight shone through my window, burning into my retina, and then the world went white and the cold spread through my body.

The next morning I tried to call Jo on her cell twice, before phoning her landline. We had become ships passing in the night and it was about time we dropped anchor.

"Hello?" a male voice answered.

"Mr Green?"

"Pipsqueak!" he exclaimed – his pet name for me. "Now who the heck is Mr Green? For the hundredth time, call me Dave."

"How are you?" I asked, unable to call him by his first name. I was one of those old-fashioned girls who said Mr or Mrs, unlike Sylv who called adults by their first name whether she had their permission or not. They say your manners reflect your upbringing, but I think mine reflected my personality instead. If Deb had given birth to Sylv she would be barefoot and pregnant by now.

"Brilliant, thanks to hearing your voice, sweetie," Mr Green said.

He told me Jo was working at Wal-Mart, so I pulled on a pair of jeans and a plain yellow T-shirt, deciding I was unlikely to run into Tom in Main Street, let alone in Wal-Mart.

●●●●

Wal-Mart was packed. Well, packed for Green Grove, with about thirty people browsing the aisles.

I had worked there with Jo for three weeks over the summer before they let me go. I thought I would be a model employee. I had aced the interview, but that was before the nightmares kicked in and I began to daydream. Of course, I had daydreamed before, but not as much as I did these days. It seemed my mind wanted to wander all the time. Exhibit A: my hallucination – I mean, daydream – of Tom in the darkroom. And then you can add my amnesia.

Jo was working checkout. Dammit. If she had been on customer service we could have talked. I stood in line behind an elderly woman buying hosiery, and two women with prams who were buying baby clothes and toys. I say women, but one was about two years older than me. Stephanie Crossly. She had popped out her first kid when she was fifteen and named it Beyonce. Yep. After the singer. Her second kid was named Jay-Z. I kid you not.

"Hey," I said when I reached the counter.

"Hi," Jo said, glancing up from restocking the plastic bags.

"How are you?"

"Fine."

Her tone told me otherwise. It was neither warm nor cold. It was monotone, as flat as the Great Plains. "Really?" I asked.

"Really."

"Cross your heart?"

She was supposed to answer, "And kiss my elbow." It was our favorite line from *Breakfast at Tiffany's*. But instead she looked at the line behind me. "I have customers."

"My house then? This afternoon?"

"I have to work."

"Your dad said you finished at two," I said, calling her bluff.

Her lips tightened, but she nodded. "Fine. See you then." She smiled at the next customer, a little girl holding a deck of cards and a ten-dollar bill.

I went next door to grab an energy drink at the Ezy-Buy. Humpback Harding was at the counter buying Advil and a lottery ticket.

"Hoodlums," I overheard her saying to Mr Kershaw, the owner-operator. "I hope the police catch them and teach them a lesson."

"You would think the kids in this town had a death wish," Mr Kershaw agreed, shaking his head. "A dollar thirty-nine," he said when he saw me with the drink.

I handed over the money.

"I say, 'Lock them up,'" Humpback Harding grumbled, looking at me like I summed up the youth of Green Grove. "That should stop them from racing trains."

My stomach churned. The train driver must have reported the accident. The cops were bound to find out who it had been in a town like Green Grove. Forget two degrees of separation. It was more like one.

I tossed my drink into a trashcan on the street. I needed caffeine like I needed a hole in the head.

••••

"Poor Jackson," I said to the girls when we congregated in my bedroom that afternoon. I imagined the cops putting him in the slammer, making him share a cell with a few of the local drunks and the Peck brothers who had a history of breaking and entering.

"Poor Jackson?" Sylv asked. "He could have killed you, Lillie. Good on Tom for smashing him." She sighed and looked dreamy. "Talk about loaded with testosterone. He would be great in bed."

"I thought you had the hots for Jackson," I said.

Sylv shrugged. "Do they both have Y chromosomes?"

I raised my eyebrows. It seemed the biology flashcards were also working.

"Just what you want," Jo suddenly said. She had been sitting at my desk in silence for the past twenty minutes, flicking through a magazine, as lukewarm as she had been in Wal-Mart. "A violent boyfriend." Her voice was soaked in sarcasm. "I guess his money makes up for it though."

I furrowed my eyebrows at the venom in her voice, but she continued to flick through the pages, stopping now and then to underline a mistake with a pen. I knew she would email the editor later to point out the errors.

"Who wants to hear my good news?" Sylv asked, changing the subject. Without waiting for an answer, she announced she had been scouted.

I clapped my hands and gave a hooray, but it was short-lived. It turned out Sylv had been tarting around Main Street in her white micro miniskirt and knee-high boots when a middle-aged out-of-towner had given her his card and asked her to call him, claiming to be a photographer for some posh magazine.

"He said it was based in Europe," Sylv bragged.

"I knew those hours you put into slathering on the make-up would pay off," Jo sneered.

I frowned at Jo, but then bit my lip. "Are you sure about this guy, Sylv?"

"What do you mean?"

"Well…" I spoke slowly, knowing I was treading on thin ice. "Why would a fashion photographer come to Green Grove?"

"Kate Moss was discovered at an airport," she reminded me.

Jo snorted. "He sounds like some sleazy guy who wants you to take your clothes off."

Sylv stood up. "I knew it! I knew you would bring me down."

"She has a point," I ventured, even though Jo was being a bit of a bitch.

Sylv went as red as a beet. "What are you saying, Lillie?" she demanded. "Am I not model material? Am I not pretty enough? Jo?"

Jo held up her hands, backing down. "I never said that."

"You say it all the time," Sylv spat. "I slather on the make-up, do I? Well, I would rather slather it on than look like a man. Would a lick of mascara kill you? Huh?"

Jo looked like Sylv had punched her in the gut. She looked down at her magazine, blinking a few times before circling a headline.

"Sylv!"

Sylv whirled on me, her gray eyes flashing like lightning in storm clouds. "And you! You think you have it all, because guys like Jackson and Tom like you. Well, guys like me too. This guy thinks I can be a model, unlike my so-called friends." She grabbed her shoulder bag from my bed. "Excuse me. I have to go call some sleazy guy who wants me to take my clothes off."

I thought the bedroom door would come off its hinges when she slammed it.

The room seemed to shudder in the wake of what had happened and we sat in silence until Deb poked her head in. She was carrying a bowl of orange chips. "Pumpkin chips?"

We both shook our heads.

"This room has a lot of negative energy," Deb observed. "I think it needs to be cleansed."

Jo went home a few minutes later, as Deb sat in the lotus position on my bed chanting to Hestia, the Goddess of Home and Hearth. I sat down at my desk and tried to do my homework, as my mother performed three concentric circles of the room in both clockwise and anti-clockwise directions.

Needless to say, Algebra was making about as much sense as a guy like Tom moving to a town like Green Grove. I stared at the string of formulas on the page, thinking of the tattoo behind his ear. What did it mean? It was as if the meaning was buried in my memories, like everything else about Tom.

When Deb left me in peace, I took his coat from the

back of my chair and put it around my shoulders. I lifted the collar and breathed in his scent again. If I closed my eyes I could feel him pulling me close, like the girl in the photo. My heart seemed to shrink, but then it then swelled again when I remember he had mentioned me to Lorraine. Yeah. He had probably said, I have this stalker called Lillie, I thought, letting my heart shrivel up like a prune.

I took off the coat and folded it carefully, before placing it in my bag. I would return it to Tom on Tuesday, tomorrow being Labor Day. I sighed, thinking of how the girls and I used to get excited about long weekends, planning slumber parties and late nights with bottomless coffee at the Duck-In Diner.

The dream returned that night; the one where I was calling out to Tom, screaming his name. I was in the courtyard. The speckled sunlight had dimmed and my killer was there in front of me, his or her hands reaching out. I stumbled against the edge of the fountain, but before I fell backwards into the water I reached out and pulled off the balaclava, my fingernails catching in the scratchy wool.

Long brown hair tumbled down around narrow shoulders and a fine-featured face looked back at me, flushed with anger. I gasped before I was pushed under the surface of the pond and the cold enveloped me.

It was confirmed. The man in the balaclava was a woman. But what was more, she was… me.

When I woke in a cold sweat, I wondered what Deb

would make of my dream. It seemed symbolic. Maybe I was having an identity crisis. That was typical for a teenager. Right?

My heart pounded in my ears as I lay in the gray light of dawn, wondering whether or not to go back to sleep. I finally rolled out of bed, deciding I was not ready to face myself again.

12

Tom skipped school on Tuesday. I looked for him all morning, scanning the faces that passed me in the corridors and hurrying to my locker between classes. My heart rose whenever I caught a glimpse of short brown hair or the blue of his favorite sweater in the crowd, and then sank like a stone when I saw it was just one of the jocks or the blue of a backpack.

Melissa cornered me before third period, demanding to know what had happened between me and Tom on Saturday.

"None of your business," I said, as I opened my locker.

She flicked her mane and stamped her foot, like a bad-tempered pony. "He was supposed to meet me for lunch on Sunday, but he stood me up." These last three words were said with a what-the-fuck tone.

"I think you should talk to him, not to me," I said, loading my books into my bag. "Call him." Maybe she could let me know what had happened between us too once she had talked to Tom.

She adjusted the yellow handbag on her shoulder. "I would if he had a cell." She trailed off, as if hearing his lie in her own voice. Of course it was a lie. Tom was rich enough to have every piece of technology ever invented, five weeks before it came on the market. He probably owned half of Apple.

"Is that his jacket?" she suddenly asked.

I slammed my locker shut, concealing the evidence.

Her eyes became tiny slits of mascara and pink eye-shadow as she stepped forward, getting up in my personal space. "Listen to me, you skank."

Her grape bubblegum perfume gave me a headache. Or maybe it was the chemicals in her fake tan.

"You think you have a shot with Tom? Talk about pathetic." She laughed nastily. "As if he would be into a freakshow like you, whose mom thinks she is Cleopatra reincarnated or some stupid shit like that."

I blushed, wishing Deb had passed on the interview with the *Green Grove Post* when she was invited to become a member of the American Society of Psychics and Mediums last year.

"Let me keep that in mind next time I go to his house," I said coldly. Her eyebrows shot up. Of course, she had no clue that his house was Rose Hill.

I picked up my bag and turned on my heel, well aware that I was at the top of her hit list now. I knew what they said about friends in high places, which meant I could guess what they said about enemies.

Like Tom, Sylv had skipped school, leaving me to spend lunch with a girl who told me she was Jo, but who bore no resemblance to my best friend of sixteen years.

Her mousey hair had been dyed jet black overnight and hacked into a ragged bob with blunt bangs. It looked alternative and I guess you could say sophisticated. It was kind of 1920s flapper. I half-expected her to pull out a cigarette and smoke it in one of those long holders while using words like "sugar" and "toots".

"Who are you supposed to be? Liza Minnelli?" I asked, but there was no smile, even though we both loved her character Sally Bowles in *Cabaret*. There was no answer either. She sat through lunch in silence, not touching her tray of nachos.

She was reading *The Catcher in the Rye*, which I knew she had read a thousand times before. I rolled my eyes whenever I saw her circle a word, wondering what mistakes she could find in a book that had been in print for over fifty years.

But when the bell rang I realized I would rather sit there for another forty minutes watching Jo edit than go to fifth period – Art Studies.

I knew Jackson would be there with his puppy-dog eyes – or one puppy-dog eye, because the other was bruised and swollen. I had seen it at lunch, before I had turned my head and pretended to be deep in conversation with Jo. Yeah, right. As if. She had already shut down my attempts to ask her about her new look and whether her dad was OK. "I will let you know when he dies," she had said snippily, leaving me as stunned as a mounted deer head.

When I walked into the Art Block I was, for all intents and purposes, going to sit on my own or even with Dirk and Mary Sunshine, otherwise known as Kate. But then I saw Jackson, sitting there with an empty seat beside him and those aforementioned eyes. His left eye was the bruised one, a mottle of blue-black tinged with red and yellow that ran down the side of his nose, courtesy of Tom.

I slumped in the seat next to him, realizing I was going to have to talk to him sooner or later if I wanted to pass Art Studies.

Mr Hastings was talking about the Renaissance. I noticed his voice was animated and above twenty decibels. I looked around the classroom, checking if Turnip was sitting up the back assessing him or something. Nope. Maybe the school board had a camera installed. I decided to work on my acting skills too, by impersonating a model student. I opened up my folder and began taking notes on a fresh, lined page.

"Lillie," Jackson whispered.

I chewed on the end of my pen, looking at the front of the classroom, as if spellbound by Mr Hastings and his talk on linear perspective in painting.

"Lillie," Jackson whispered again.

I wrote, "The Renaissance began in the Fourteenth Century", taking my time with my cursive, like those monks who wrote in old-fashioned calligraphy. They say a lot of them died of poisoning from the mercury in their ink.

"I want to apologize." He drew in a deep breath. "Sorry."

Sorry. Sorry. Sorry, I thought with each stroke of my pen.

"I was an idiot," Jackson continued. "Why did I do it?" He groaned dramatically. "Why?"

"I think they call it peer pressure," I hissed.

Mr Hastings gave us a look.

Jackson sighed. "I know. I have a problem."

"Maybe you should see someone about that," I said snidely.

"Lillie," Mr Hastings warned. OK, there must have been a camera, because normally you could talk on your cell in his class without complaint.

A moment or two passed before Jackson muttered, "I would have thought three years of therapy after I left Green Grove had done the trick."

My eyebrows shot up.

"Spare me your surprise, Lillie. You know how it was for me in Elementary."

"Then why did you come back to Green Grove?"

Mr Hastings raised his voice another twenty decibels. "The first Renaissance artists emerged in Florence in the 15th century during a competition to sculpt a set of bronze doors for a cathedral."

Jackson bent down to scribble a few notes and I thought that was the end of our discussion, until he slid his notebook across the desk.

I looked at the words, "At the end of a fear of flying course you have to take a flight."

I looked at him with furrowed eyebrows. "And?"

"Green Grove is my flight," he whispered.

"And your parents agreed with your therapist?" I pictured them uprooting their new life to return to their old one.

"My mom is my therapist. My parents are both shrinks."

Mr Hastings cut into our conversation. "Jackson, please move to the other side of the classroom."

My mouth fell open. Mr Hastings was doling out discipline? It was as if both he and Jo had gone through extreme makeovers overnight.

Jackson swept his books and pens into his bag. I touched his hand, as he stood up.

"Sorry."

He looked at my hand and then at me, his lips twitching into a small smile. "Me too."

"Jackson," Mr Hastings warned.

"I hope no one turns you in," I added.

"Me too."

That afternoon I waited for Jo in the quad as usual, scanning the sea of bobbing heads for her new haircut.

I checked the time on my cell at the four minute mark. And again at the six. And then at the seven.

"Two more minutes, Betty Boop," I muttered, as if she were telepathic. "OK. Three." It was about five minutes later that I spotted her across the quad, at the entrance to the cafeteria. She was talking to Mr Bailey. I groaned and slouched against a brick wall, realizing we could be here for hours.

Jo turned into Jell-O around Mr Bailey, stuttering and stammering to the point where it took her about ten minutes to say hello. It made me wonder how she had managed to top his class, considering he had been her teacher for two years and counting.

Today she seemed to have developed a nervous tick too, punctuating each sentence with a flick of her jet-black hair. Hold on. I squinted across the quad. Was that her hand on his arm? Seriously? I straightened up, as Jo threw back her head and let out a laugh that echoed around the quad. Oh my God. She was flirting with Mr Bailey. Flirting!

My mouth hung open as Jo waved goodbye with a flutter of her fingers.

"Are you... OK?" I asked, as we walked down the driveway.

"Fine."

I bit my lip. "Cross your heart?"

"And hope to die."

Wrong answer. I frowned. "But–"

"What are you? My mother? I said I was fine." She quickened her pace and I had to skip a few steps to keep up.

The lady doth protest too much, methinks.

There was a stack of books next to my bedside table which Deb had given me after I had asked about the meaning of dreams. I shook my head at myself as I opened one of them – a dream dictionary – and flipped through the pages until I got to "death".

"To dream you are dying indicates a transitional phase. You are about to reach enlightenment."

I closed the book and leaned against the pillows. Good news, I guess. I was about to become enlightened.

I picked up another book. This one was a dream guide. My eyes scanned the chapter headings, "Premonition".

"Dreams can be a message from the universe," I read, skipping the boring bits. "You may be visited by a loved one, or even by yourself. Blah, blah, blah. Bad news or a warning. OK. Prophetic." And then this: "Abraham Lincoln dreamed about his death two weeks before his assassination."

"Oh my God," I whispered. Maybe the dreams had been warning me about the railroad crossing. But that had come and gone, and the dreams had continued. I bit my lip as I considered this conundrum. When had the dreams started? The beginning of summer? I sat in bed with the book open for a long while, not reading.

How much longer do I have? I wondered.

13

My breath caught in my throat when I saw Tom at his locker the next morning. It was like my body temperature increased to a thousand degrees whenever he was around. I noticed his hair was less tousled. He must have had a haircut.

"Hi," I said.

"Hi," he responded, his attention on the contents of his locker.

I dropped my bag at my feet and looked at him sideways. His lips were slightly parted, as he busied himself with his books, and I realized he was drawing in deep breaths, as if calming himself. I was the one who needed to be calmed though, as I watched his chiseled chest rise and fall under his T-shirt.

I spun the dial on my own locker. "I missed you yesterday," I said quietly and then blushed. Of course, I meant he had cut school yesterday, not that I had missed him, even though I had. I needed to change the subject ASAP. "You got a haircut." And now I sounded like a stalker. Brilliant. Just brilliant.

"Lillie."

"Yes?" I asked breathlessly.

"What do you want?"

You, I thought, looking at him like a junkie at a crack pipe. What had Melissa called me? Pathetic? Yeah, no kidding. I turned my head from side to side and whispered, "Nothing. Nothing at all."

I returned to my locker, but in my peripheral vision I could see him looking at me, one hand fiddling with his locker door. I kept my eyes on my Algebra book, thinking how stupid it was that I had spelled "Mathematics" in full on the front. Not once had I said, "I have Mathematics homework tonight," or "I have a Mathematics quiz next period." It was always Math, short and simple. It would be like calling Tom, Thomas. I wondered if his full name was Thomas. Thomas Windsor-Smith.

Thomas William Windsor-Smith, a voice whispered in my mind. "Is your middle name William?" I suddenly asked.

Tom looked alarmed, but then composed himself. "I made a mistake last weekend," he said.

I closed my eyes, telling myself he was talking about being at the railroad crossing with Melissa and the Mutts, not about driving me home. But I was kidding myself. If Melissa was a pony then Tom was a stallion. And me? Well, I was a donkey. Yep. Like the T-shirt I happened to be wearing at that exact-same second. A complete and utter ass.

I pulled his coat from my locker. "Here," I said, pushing it at him.

He caught it in the stomach, like a medicine ball. "Lillie," he said in a pleading voice. "Please understand. I came to Green Grove to be on my own – not to get involved with anyone, especially you."

His last words were like a slap across the face. Especially me? I glared at him. "If you want to be on your own then maybe you should stop hanging out with Melissa." I slammed my locker shut and hauled my bag over my shoulder.

Loser. Loser. Loser, I chanted in my mind as I walked through the corridors, not sure if I meant him or me. The sound of my shoes on the linoleum seemed to echo the rhythm. Click. Clack. Click. Clack. "Lo-ser. Lo-ser," until it became, "Lil-lie. Lil- lie."

I took a break from the world at lunchtime and went down to the darkroom to develop the film from the weekend.

As I watched the negatives develop in the tray I realized there would be no break from Tom, because there he was in the first frame, walking down the front steps of Rose Hill.

His association with Rose Hill meant I saw him in all of the negatives after that. He was there in the ballroom, leaning against a pillar. He was standing on the grand staircase in the foyer. He was walking towards me, out of the frame and although the image was in black and white I could see the pale blue of his eyes, burning through me like the center of a Bunsen burner.

I cringed as I thought about wearing his jacket, about smelling the collar. I really was pathetic.

I was relieved when the bell rang and I was able to leave the negatives behind on the line to dry. I took my time with walking to my locker, knowing I had World History with Tom.

I spotted Jo in the quad and called out her name.

"Want to cut class?" I asked when I had caught up. "I think we both need a break."

She shook her head. She was wearing a bucket load of gray eye shadow and heavy black eyeliner today, which had smudged under her left eye, giving her a look that was half-goth, half-hooker. "I have English last period."

I rolled my eyes. "Mr Bailey will be here tomorrow and the next day. He probably comes in on weekends too."

"I have to hand in an assignment."

"But we can get rocky road milkshakes from the Duck-In Diner," I angled. "My shout."

She glowered. "What? Do you think you can bribe the fat girl with food?"

"Jo. No. You know I–"

She raised her hand like a traffic cop. "I said 'no' and I mean 'no,' Lillie. Maybe next time you should throw in a couple of Twinkies."

My blood boiled as I watched her walk to class. Who was this girl and what had she done with my best friend? I wanted to bombard her with photos of us swimming in the river at the Rainbow Retreat. I wanted to tape her eyes open and make her watch a twenty-four hour musical marathon. I wanted her to be Jo again.

"Have fun with your boyfriend Mr Bailey!" I yelled, my voice bouncing off the brick buildings and turning a few heads.

Jo spun around with a face like fury.

I stood my ground as she stalked towards me, her black boots clomping on the concrete.

"And you have fun with Tom and Jackson," she spat, stabbing a finger into my chest. "Maybe you could spare a few for the rest of us."

I raised my eyebrows. Was she calling me a slut? "Maybe I would if you dressed like yourself, instead of like a freakshow." It was what Melissa had called me and I was sorry as soon as I said it.

Jo stared at me for a moment and I saw her chin wobble, before she turned and clomped across the quad to class.

Shit. Shit. Shit, I thought as she went.

I decided to cut class on my own. I went via the playing fields, instead of the driveway, where Turnip would have swooped on me in a second.

Jo and I had agreed to disagree a thousand times during our friendship, but I could count our fights on two fingers.

Once was when we were ten years old. Jo had accused me of cheating while playing Casino, a card game made up by Sylv, where we had dressed up like hookers and smoked twigs like they were cigarettes. Sylv had decided to start a fire with a lighter and our twigs, and I had thrown a couple of cards onto the flames. Jo had hit the roof because one of the cards happened to be from her hand and she had been about to win for the eighth time in a row. It was three years before I admitted that I had known it was the ace of hearts, which trumped all other cards in Casino.

The second was when Deb had bought me a training bra. Jo had thrown a tantrum because her dad was as likely to buy his little girl a bra as he was to turn vegetarian.

Jo had snarked that I was as flat as a tack and I had told her she sounded like Melissa. "Are you going to spread rumors about me and Simon Caster?" I had asked.

We had stopped talking for three days and fourteen hours and twenty-five minutes, which was when she admitted that she had been taping her breasts for three months.

We ended up asking her dad about the training bra together. You know what they say about safety in numbers.

"What are you in training for?" he had asked.

"Big boobs," I had responded.

Deb ended up buying the bra for Jo, which she had to hide from her dad, washing it in the bathroom sink and drying it in her cupboard.

As I walked around the corner of the art block, I collided with the defensive tackle on our football team. At least, I thought it was the defensive tackle, because it was like being hit by a wrecking ball, but then a hand closed around my arm, holding me up, and I realized that if it were a jock he would have let me fall.

"Sorry," I muttered, glancing up.

"Lillie?" It was Tom. His forehead was creased with concern. "Are you OK?"

I pushed past him and broke into a half-run, suddenly needing to get away from school – from Jo, Tom and Green Grove altogether.

From Green Grove with Love. Yeah, right.

Deb was working at the Tree of Life, so I went home and drew a bath, dissolving three bags of lavender in the water before pulling down the blind and lighting a candle. I looked for my dancers in the flame, but instead I saw two figures pushing and pulling each other, wrestling, fighting, until they merged into one. Then the figure was gone and all I could see was a flame.

For the first time in my life I wished I had learned meditation from Deb. I thought of how relaxed she looked as she performed yoga in the morning, chanting "Om." She had told me the sound of om represents the four states of the Supreme Being.

The four states of Tom, I thought miserably.

I sank down into the water until it reached my chin, letting the warmth wash over me.

"Ommmmmmmmmm," I said, and then spluttered and choked as water entered my mouth.

Once I had recovered from my near drowning, I let myself slide into the bath until I was floating with my face above water, but my ears below. My knees were tucked up tight given the small dimensions of our tub.

"Ommmmmmmmmm," I said. I could hear the sound loud and clear in my head, like it was echoing within my skull. I repeated it over and over.

Suddenly I felt a hand grip my throat and I was pushed under the water. I screamed, bubbles coming from my mouth and nose as I thrashed in the tub, sloshing water over the sides. The water went cold, as if a bag of ice had been poured into the bath and then as suddenly as it had happened my neck was released. I sat upright in alarm, water coursing from my hair and ears. The bathroom was empty. It had been another hallucination.

The door flew open. It was Deb.

"Lillie! Thank the Great Goddess. The school called and said you had cut class. I checked the Duck-In Diner..." She trailed off and put a hand on her chest. "I was calling you and calling you."

"I was under the water," I said in a daze.

"Are you OK?" She sat down on the toilet lid. "Why did you ditch school?"

I have to say that was one of the perks of having a hippie as a mother. Most parents would be yelling at their kids, grounding them for a century, etc., but Deb was a firm believer in sick days. She called them Mental Health Days and took them regularly herself from the Tree of Life.

"I had a fight with Jo," I said and then burst into tears.

"Oh, Lillie. Let me make you a hot drink. It will calm you down."

And that was the downside. I ended up spending the evening having homeopathic remedies shoved down my throat until I smelled of mugwort and peppermint.

14

The next morning I got to school an hour and a half before the bell. It was either that or lay in bed staring at the ceiling like a corpse in an open casket, thinking about my life going to hell. At least I could finish developing my photos from the weekend, tick that off my to-do list. And I mean that literally. I was a to-do list kind of girl. Told you I used to be organized.

When the first bell rang I made a beeline for my locker, where I was relieved to see Jackson waiting for me instead of Tom. The two were like apples and oranges. Jackson was an open book, easy to read, his thoughts were there on the page in black and white. Tom, on the other hand, was like a locked diary.

"Load me up," Jackson said, as I pulled a stack of photography books from my locker. He pushed up the sleeves of his sweater and stuck out his arms. "Five hours of weights a week," he said with a wink, as if I had commented on his bulging biceps.

"Thanks," I said, piling the books on one by one.

He gave a melodramatic grunt as I loaded the last book. "No. Thank you."

"For what?"

"For letting me throw out these books. Finally." He turned towards the trashcan.

I laughed and made a grab for them, rescuing a book about my favorite photographers, the Geldings, which the girls had bought for my eleventh birthday.

"What?" Jackson asked, lifting the rest of them above his head. "Did you think I was carrying them to class?"

I thumped him with the book.

"Ow. OK. OK. Kidding!"

"Hilarious."

As we walked to class Jackson asked if I was going to the Masquerade Ball next week. Flyers advertising the ball were wrapped around every pole and trashcan in school. The Dance Committee had stopped short of stapling them to our foreheads. Just.

"Yep."

"And Jo and Sylv?"

"Yep."

For a moment I thought he was going to ask me to the ball, but then we rounded a corner and passed Blake and Melissa, who took a few steps to her left to sideswipe me with her oversized handbag.

"Hey!" Jackson said.

"Yes?" Blake asked, muscling up to him.

Jackson stood his ground.

"Go on," Melissa said with a curled lip. "Stick up for your loser girlfriend."

"Forget it, Jackson," I said, tugging on the back of his T-shirt. This was not about him. This was about Tom. I felt like telling Melissa that Tom was no longer an option for me. That no one in Green Grove was an option for him. He wanted to be on his own.

Jackson and Blake continued to square-off until Melissa called off the dogs. "A word of advice," she said, as if she was about to give me a tip on blow-drying. "Watch your step," she warned, before click-clacking down the corridor in a swirl of fuchsia, Blake at her heels.

"Sorry," Jackson said, as we continued to class.

"For Blake being a meathead, or Melissa being a bitch?"

He laughed and then looked at me sideways. "She called you my girlfriend."

"Loser girlfriend," I corrected and we both laughed.

When I showed Jackson my photos of Rose Hill, he flicked through them with a puckered mouth.

When he got to the photo of Tom he tossed it to the side, letting it slide across the desk until it balanced on the lip, like a seesaw. "What about the sand hills instead of Rose Hill? Or the National Park?"

I snatched the photo before it toppled to the ground. "I thought you said James Bond would love Rose Hill."

"I said James Bond would love Green Grove," Jackson corrected. "And I have it on good authority that Rose Hill is technically in the Open Valley."

I laughed and then flipped through the pages of his sketchbook. "Are you sure? These sketches could have got us an A." I held up a drawing of the banister, which detailed the carvings along its side. I noticed a family crest among them. I had to smile to myself that Tom had a family crest. What a jerk.

"You mean an A plus," Jackson said with a wink. It seemed his ego had been successfully stroked. "Fine. How about we line up a second date to Rose Hill?"

I should have said no, given he had come close to killing me on our first "date", but my heart fluttered at the thought of returning to Rose Hill. I also had a soft spot for Jackson. His constant chatter, which had grated on me in the car, was a good pick-me-up. And he made me laugh. A good belly laugh, not the schoolgirl giggles I had around Tom.

"This weekend? Saturday?"

"Saturday," I confirmed. I should have at least hesitated or consulted my schedule before I answered. I looked like I had no life. But this was Green Grove.

I was walking to the driveway to meet Sylv – Jo had track – when I heard my name. I turned and saw Tom.

"You made up with him?" he asked.

"With who?"

"Jackson." He spat out his name and took a step forward, closing the gap between us. "Lillie, he could have killed you!"

I shook my head. "He made a mistake."

"We all make mistakes," Tom said through clenched teeth.

I lifted my chin. "And we can all be forgiven."

"What about a murderer?" he asked, his eyes flashing like lightning. "Would you forgive a murderer?"

I hesitated. "A murderer?"

Tom stared at me for a moment, as if waking up from a dream.

I stepped towards him, causing him to take one step backwards and then another and another. "If you can be friends with Melissa then I can be friends with Jackson," I said. "If you recall it was you who wanted to be by yourself, not me."

"I have to be by myself," he said. "It has nothing to do with what I want."

"I suppose it has something to do with the girl in the photo then?" I asked. She had been playing on my mind since I had heard about his broken heart. He had probably moved halfway across the world to teach her a lesson. He was rich enough to do whatever he wanted. "Is she your girlfriend?"

"What?" His eyes flared up again, but this time it was with alarm.

"Your bag was open. The photo was sticking out," I explained. "I saw it for like a second." I sounded like such a snoop.

The color was sucked from his eyes until they became like glass. "The girl in the photo…" he said in a controlled voice "…is dead."

This final word hung in the small space between us, like a curtain. I suddenly realized that I was the ass for bringing up his dead girlfriend.

"Tom," I started, but he jammed his hands in his pockets and turned to stalk across the quad.

Meanwhile, Melissa stood at the entrance to the cafeteria, giving me a look that could have killed a thousand girls in a thousand photos.

15

Tom skipped school the next day and the next and the next. Each morning I went to my locker with bated breath, ready to say sorry.

Maybe next week, I consoled myself.

On Saturday the time for my second "date" with Jackson came and went. I watched the clock, telling myself he would turn up before the second hand reached the twelve and then before it reached the eight.

I texted him and then called him twelve minutes later. I got his voicemail. "Jackson? Lillie here. Where are you? Call me."

Maybe I had the wrong day. Did he say Saturday or Sunday? I thought back to the conversation, but it was tangled up in my ball of twine, like so many of my other memories. I seemed to have one memory of him saying Saturday and another of him saying Sunday.

My cell rang. It was Sylv.

"Are you OK?" she asked.

"Yes. Why?"

"The cops arrested Jackson."

"What? When?"

"Like two hours ago."

There was a knock at the door. I poked my head into the hallway and saw two police officers through the window.

"Crap," I said.

"What?"

I hung up and walked up the hallway with small steps as if I were walking to the gas chamber.

"Lillie Hart?" the shorter cop asked when I opened the door.

I nodded.

"We need you to come down to the station. We have to ask you a few questions." He held up his notebook, as if we were playing charades.

"Is your mom home?" the taller one asked. His nametag read "Officer Davidson".

"Am I being arrested?"

Officer Davidson smiled. "No."

"Not yet," the smaller one corrected.

Good cop. Bad cop. I swallowed a laugh.

They let me call Deb. She must have sprinted from Tree of Life, because she was breathless when she arrived at the station. She grabbed my shoulders and scanned me from head to toe as if I had been in a car accident that afternoon, instead of last weekend.

"Relax," I muttered.

"Relax? You could have been killed!" She sounded like Tom.

Tom. I suddenly realized he had turned in Jackson, which made him the ass again.

The interview took about twenty minutes. I played it down, telling the cops there had been miles between us and the train, passing it off as a near collision.

The smaller officer called me out. "We saw the damage to the vehicle. It was inches from being a write-off."

"And a fatality," Officer Davidson added, making me think of my dream with the alternate ending.

I hid my shiver with a shrug. What was this, the Spanish Inquisition?

Officer Davidson closed his notebook. "Jackson has explained that you were an innocent party. We just needed your account of the incident. Thank you."

"What will happen to Jackson?" I asked as we all stood.

"It will be decided by the court," the smaller officer said, pushing in his chair with a screech.

Jackson was sitting on a bench near the front entrance, waiting for his parents, who were signing paperwork. I bet his mother thought her therapy was as nuts as I did now.

"Jackson, are you OK?"

His eyes were red, but he nodded. "Fine," he lied. "I have a court date in a couple of weeks." He shuffled his feet on the linoleum. "I guess I still have a few enemies in Green Grove."

Just one, I thought. Tom.

Deb was like a witch doctor on steroids that afternoon. She put together a bag of protection stones – amethyst, serpentine, citrine and whatever else she could find in the house, including a jade ornament that she scooped out of the fish tank – and told me to hang it around my neck with a worn piece of leather.

"I need to add agate," she said, pouring boiling water into a teapot and pulling on the cozy. "I can pick up a few stones from the store on Monday." She let the tea-leaves steep, before pouring me a cup. "Are you going to put on the necklace?"

"No." I was suddenly overcome with PMS, as in pain-in-the-ass mother syndrome. "I am not putting on the necklace," I told her. "I am not drinking the tea. And I am not praying to the goddess of complete and utter stupidity!" I stood up from the kitchen table and my chair toppled against the wall. "How about being a mother instead of a nutcase for two seconds? Ground me! Lecture me! Make me wash the dishes for a week!"

"But we have a dishwasher," Deb said stupidly.

I grabbed my camera from the breakfast counter, before racing down the hallway, my hair flying out behind me and my face as hot as a road in the middle of summer.

I marched down the street, my hands clenching and releasing as I thought about Tom. His face came to mind, but I blurred it immediately. This was not the time to think about how his cheekbones looked like they had been chiseled by Michelangelo. Instead I thought about the apology that had been on the tip of my tongue these past couple of days. Now he was the one who needed to apologize, both to me and to Jackson.

I walked until the soles of my feet ached as much as my head. I had covered at least fifteen blocks, walking up and down the intersecting streets. The sun was setting, spreading its golden rays over Green Grove. It was blinding and I put a hand in front of my eyes to shield them, squinting through my fingers.

I was at the railroad crossing. I could see tire marks on the road where the hatchback had spun out of control. I crouched and raised my camera, but as I took the first shot I heard the thud-thud of a vehicle crossing the tracks and stood up in alarm, not wanting to be run down. The vehicle slowed and I realized I was looking at a sleek black SUV. Tom.

I turned and half-walked, half-ran into the woods beside the road. I heard him pull up, his tires crunching the loose gravel. A door opened and then slammed shut.

"Lillie."

The sound of his voice, smooth but husky, made my heart speed up, but it slowed down when I remembered Jackson, who was going to have to go to court because of Tom. I picked up the pace, heading down an old cattle trail.

Tom continued to call out to me, but I pushed through branches, the trail becoming thinner and the woods thicker. I was alarmed to hear him following me and my mind went to my nightmares, but I could not remember having been killed on a cattle trail. I suddenly hit a dead end. I slapped at the branches like a toddler throwing a tantrum, before growing up and turning to face Tom.

The dust had been kicked up and floated in the air around me, looking like glitter in the last rays of daylight.

I squared my shoulders, as he walked through the golden haze.

"You were in the middle of the road," he said breathlessly.

I looked at my sneakers, my hair falling in front of my face.

"Lillie." He drew back my curtain and I looked up into his flawless face. No. Not flawless. There was the scar. My scar.

I reached up as if in a trance and then withdrew my hand when he trembled beneath my touch. "Sorry."

He closed his eyes. "No," he whispered as he shook his head. "I am sorry."

I frowned, having expected at least another three weeks of him being hot and cold before I got my apology.

"I should have told you the truth when I arrived in Green Grove," he continued.

I cocked my head as I realized his apology was not related to Jackson. I watched as he took a deep breath, as if preparing to plunge into deep water.

"You asked if we knew each other," he said.

"Yes?" I whispered, suddenly realizing he meant the truth about the last six months, about the last sixteen years. How I knew him. How I knew Rose Hill. I wondered if this was a hallucination, if he was going to vanish, like he had in the darkroom.

He bit his lip. "What if I told you we had met?"

I knew it! I frowned as I searched my memory, wondering whether we had met in Green Grove. Maybe it had been in Lincoln. "When?"

His face scrunched for a moment, as if preparing me for his next words. "In another life," he said. "Another world."

I frowned and rocked back on my heels. "You mean like reincarnation?" I asked, wondering if he was as loopy as Deb.

"Have you heard of the theory of everything? Albert Einstein?"

I laughed, but the sound stuck in my windpipe. "Einstein?"

He smiled. "It sounds like a science lesson. I know."

I suddenly remembered Jo saying he was smart in physics.

Tom walked around in a circle, the dust billowing around his feet. He looked at me a couple of times, as if deciding whether or not to dive deeper into the water. "Einstein wanted to read the mind of God," he finally said. "But he died before he could finish his unified field theory, which is also called the theory of everything. Physicists have been picking up the pieces for decades." He looked me in the eye. "You might have heard of string theory?"

I was thoroughly confused by the conversation. When did the theory of everything become the theory of Tom and Lillie? "What was the point of the theory of everything?" I asked. "World peace? Everlasting life? More red M&Ms per packet?"

Tom gave me a quizzical look.

"I like red M&Ms." I knew I was babbling, but I felt like I was taking a test without having studied.

Tom took another deep breath, his carved chest rising under his sweater. "The theory of everything led to the discovery of… parallel dimensions."

"Parallel dimensions?" It sounded as absurd as reincarnation, but then a slideshow of memories of other lives – of other me's – started flicking through my head. I tried to focus and the pictures paused at a birthday party with a clown cake and a man who had the same color hair as me and ears that were kind of pointy. "Dad!" I called out to him in my memory, before the slideshow flicked on.

I frowned, knowing there had been no birthday party and no father.

"You see, where I come from," Tom continued. "Einstein accepted a life-saving operation and lived long enough to finish the theory of everything."

"England?"

He shook his head, his forehead creasing slightly at my stupidity. "Another dimension."

I gave a barking laugh.

Tom walked towards me. "You know it, Lillie. Deep down. You know what we are."

"Soulmates," I whispered, before coming around from my swoon. "No," I said, taking a small step backwards and shaking my head back and forth. "You and me. Out of the question. Not in this lifetime. Not in any lifetime." I frowned at him. "This is crazy. Totally and utterly insane."

"Let me show you," he begged, reaching out to me. His hand on my neck made my pulse shoot up, but I stepped back again, pressing my back against a tree trunk. I suddenly realized how completely and utterly alone we were here in the clearing. If I were to scream...

He drew back as I opened my mouth. "Forget it," he said, shaking his head. I closed my mouth as I realized he was not going to hurt me, at least not physically. "Like you said this is crazy. Totally and utterly insane."

"Tom," I started. I was unable to deny our connection, parallel dimensions or no parallel dimensions.

He took another couple of steps backwards. "I have to stop saving you, Lillie."

I swallowed a barking laugh. "Is that what you call what you did to Jackson?" I asked incredulously.

His face hardened into stone. "Jackson. I see. You do like him." He sounded like a jealous boyfriend.

"Of course I like him." I had a heart, unlike him. "And I hate you for what you did to him."

Tom flushed angrily. "I did it for you. Though I wonder why I bothered."

I clenched my teeth, wondering why he would think I wanted him to turn in Jackson. "You and me both."

We stood there like a pair of pigheaded children, until Tom set his jaw and turned on his heel. There was a moment when he looked over his shoulder and I thought he was worried about leaving me alone in the woods. It seemed there were limits to his chivalry though, because he pushed through the branches with barely a break in his step. He seemed to suck the last of light from the sky as he went, leaving me in the twilight. I heard the branches snapping until he reached the road and then a car door slammed and its engine roared to life before disappearing in the direction of Rose Hill.

I sat down miserably on a fallen tree, listening to the chirp of crickets from the darkness as I collected my thoughts. Einstein? The theory of everything? Parallel dimensions? Huh? Huh? Huh?

Now and then I jumped at the crack of a twig, imagining they were footfalls. "Hello?" I called. "Is someone there? Tom? Hello?"

When I got home I was greeted by a sage smudge stick, which my mother used to cleanse the house whenever we had an argument. I rolled my eyes as she told me to inhale the smoke, as if it were a toll to enter the house. I breathed it in, too tired for another argument. I also let her rub herbal cream into my blisters. It smelled of dusty earth, the smell reminding me of being in the clearing with Tom.

When I went to bed I dreamed I was there again. I called out to the darkness and the killer responded.

"Hi," she said, in what sounded like my voice.

16

The next day my conversation with Tom was like a book with missing pages. I remembered talking about Einstein and the theory of everything. Did I bring up red M&Ms? And what did he say about string? It made me think of my ball of twine.

I did remember the word that had come to me automatically – soulmates.

I shook my head, as if I could shake out the memory. Deb believed in that mumbo-jumbo, not me. It had to be a joke, or a hallucination. Maybe I had drunk the tea Deb had made for me and had fallen asleep with the bag of stones around my neck.

Yes. That sounded logical, more logical than parallel dimensions anyway. It had been another dream.

The rumor mill was working hard when I got to school on Monday. The first rumor I heard was that Jackson and I had been locked up. Another was that he had fled the country and I was going to meet him in Cuba as soon as I could. I saw a few faces fall when they realized it was hogwash.

Jackson was allowed to stay in school until his court date the following week. He was innocent until proven guilty, as they say, although he was banned from the Masquerade Ball.

"Lucky you," Jo said coldly when he told us. She was in a mood as dark as her eyeliner. Her head had been buried in another book all morning and she was generally responding to questions with a one-syllable yes or no.

I was surprised she was talking to me at all after our fight in the quad. What is her deal? I wondered, but I decided not to ask again in case she bit off my head and wore it as a hat. I watched her draw a thick red line under a sentence and realized it was her physics textbook.

"What do you know about Einstein?" I suddenly asked.

Jo continued to read as if my voice were the distant sound of a dog barking or a car alarm.

"Jo?"

She looked up, but her eyes were glazed beneath her bangs.

"Have you heard about the theory of everything?"

"No."

"String theory?"

"No."

I sighed as she circled another word. "Can I borrow your cell?" I asked. "I need to use Google." Jo had a smartphone with internet connection. Her dad had given it to her for her fifteenth birthday, as a sorry-I-screwed-up-your-childhood present, given he had been on the road for seventy percent of her life. Deb must have missed that memo.

"No," she said again.

Sylv raised her eyebrows at me and mouthed the word "bitch". But I had too much on my mind with Tom to think about Jo. If he had turned up to school today I could have asked him about Saturday. I was not completely convinced it had been a dream.

I ran into Melissa as we walked to Biology. Literally. I turned the corner and bam!

I readied myself for a tongue-lashing, but instead she smiled. Her straight white teeth were shark-like. "I heard you and Jackson got arrested on Saturday."

I pushed past and continued down the corridor.

"I warned you to watch your step," she called out meaningfully.

It was like she had dropped a piano on my head. Melissa had turned in Jackson, not Tom. "You bitch!" I shouted, whirling around and throwing myself at her like a rabid dog. My open palm connected with her cheek, making a sound like the crack of a whip.

She took a step backwards, clutching her cheek. Her blue eyes were wide as she looked around for her guard dogs, but Blake and Ethan had retreated as well, looking at me like I needed an exorcism.

Sylv grabbed me before I could slap Melissa again. "Let the tramp lick her wounds," she said.

Melissa bucked up when she saw me restrained. "Who are you calling a tramp, you slut?" she asked Sylv.

Sylv released me and gave Melissa a slap on her other cheek.

There was a smattering of laughter from a few of the bystanders, especially those who knew the history between Sylv and Melissa. I think everyone else was in a state of shock. If you laid a finger on Melissa you were finished in this town.

Even so, we had a spring in our step as we walked to class.

"I think karma just bit Melissa on the ass," Sylv crowed.

I rolled my eyes. Deb carried on about karma too. If I sprayed a wasp she told me I would get stung one of these days, leaving me to point out that a wasp was more likely to sting me without the spray. "I think we should get the kudos, not karma," I told Sylv.

"For biting Melissa on the ass?" Jo asked. Her voice was monotone, but I think it was a joke.

"I should have slapped that girl years ago," Sylv continued, looking at her hand like she had discovered a super power.

"Girls Gone Wild, here we come," Jo said.

Turnip called me and Sylv to his office half an hour later.

"Hairdressing, here I come," Sylv moaned.

Turnip was an elderly man with white hair and watery eyes, who looked like he could use a feed, but he could stare you down until you thought you would spontaneously combust.

We took a seat in front of his desk, which was covered with manila folders crammed with reams of paperwork.

Turnip pre-dated computers. I think he pre-dated cologne too, because his office smelled like old man. He studied us without a word for what seemed like an age, before he said, "I understand you slapped a fellow student."

Sylv nodded. I bit my lip.

"And that student was Melissa Hodge?"

Sylv nodded again. I thought I could taste blood.

"Are you sorry?"

I laughed, a sudden burst of nerves.

Sylv looked at me in shock.

I took a deep breath, swallowing the sound. "She–"

Turnip raised his hand. "I will not tolerate violence in this school," he said. "You should consider yourselves lucky that Miss Hodge decided not to press charges. Her father wanted to take it to court, but after a twenty-five minute phone call I have managed to convince him otherwise."

I scowled. I hated the Hodges.

"After school detention for both of you. Level two. Classroom Four."

As we were leaving, Turnip said, "Miss Dartmouth you can also consider yourself lucky you have not been expelled. You are on thin ice. Very thin ice."

"You would think we had tried to assassinate the queen," I grumbled in Algebra.

"Well, she is Green Grove royalty," Sylv said.

"Yeah," I agreed. "A royal pain in my ass."

Sylv spent the hour in detention staring at the clock, willing the hands to move. She had a second date lined up with Simon.

I had checked out a few tomes on Einstein from the school library, but there had been no books on the theory of everything or string theory. I read how Einstein had died in the early hours of April 18, 1955, in Princeton Hospital. The internal bleeding could have been stemmed by surgery, but he insisted he had done his share and it was his time. Very Hallmark, I thought, moving on to a book on the theory of relativity, but it was like it was written in another language. I finally slammed the dusty cover shut, giving up. I was going to have to learn about it from the primary source – Tom.

Mr Hastings looked like he wanted to be there as much as we did. He alternated between looking at the window and looking at the clock. I wondered if he was dying for a cigarette.

When he released us with six minutes to go, Sylv grabbed her handbag and booked it.

"Wait," I said, as I packed up my bag.

"See you tomorrow, Lillie," she called over her shoulder.

I walked to my locker alone, my footsteps echoing through the empty corridors. When I spun the dial and opened the door the box of tampons fell out, bouncing on the concrete. I thought of Tom again and how he had not turned in Jackson after all.

I thought back to the clearing on Saturday. He had said... I racked my brains. He had said, "I did it for you." My color rose as I realized he had been talking about punching Jackson, not about turning him in to the cops. Of course. I should have known that Tom was out of the loop on Green Grove gossip. The rest of the town would have known about our run-in with the police two seconds after the fact, but he would have been in the dark, both then and now.

As I walked out of the main building a clatter of footsteps across the quad made me spin around. I recognized the worn-out shoulder bag, the short, ragged bob. Jo. She should have been home by now. I guess she thought so too, because she was running like she was at a meet.

"Jo!"

I could have sworn she sped up.

"Jo!"

"Leave me alone, Lillie!" she screeched without turning her head.

"Wait," I begged, but track had given her more stamina in her little finger than I could muster from head to toe. I stopped, bending over to catch my breath, before trying to call her cell. No answer.

"Dammit!" I threw my phone on the ground, where it broke into two. I scooped it up and thundered down the remainder of the driveway, watching Jo disappear into the distance.

"Jo. Jo. Jo," I chanted to the beat of my bag, as it bounced against my back, as if the rule of repetition could bring her back.

17

The next morning I walked to school without Jo. In my mind, I saw her running as if from the Grim Reaper, or from the woman in the balaclava.

By the time I got to the quad, my stomach was like a front loader on a spin cycle. Jo was the kind of girl who packed extra underwear and socks for camp. She was the girl who did her homework on a Friday night instead of waiting until Monday morning like the rest of us. She was Old Faithful. But lately…

I was halfway to my locker when I heard the rumors – not about me and Jackson, but about Jo.

"Oh my God. Did you hear what happened?"

"That girl Joanne–"

"Josephine."

"Whatever. She shagged that teacher."

"Which teacher?"

"Mr Bailey."

"Eww."

"I heard it was a threesome with that skank Sylvia."

"I heard that too. Gross."

"Double gross."

"Triple gross."

I met Sylv at my locker. "This is BS," I said.

"You can say the word bullshit, Lillie. We are not two year-olds," Sylv said, snapping her gum.

"Fine. This is bullshit," I said, but then I remembered how Jo had been running yesterday. "Right?" I asked, clutching my stomach as its contents started to spin again.

"Of course," Sylv said. "As if you would catch me dead in a threesome with Jo and Mr Bailey." She laughed at her own joke, but stopped when she saw me put a hand to my head and close my eyes. "Wake up, Lillie. You know they talk shit in this stupid town."

I leaned against my locker. "Should we call Jo?" I asked and then answered my own question by reaching into my bag. "Damn," I said, as I remembered my cell was broken.

But Sylv was dialing her own cell with fingernails coated in liquid paper and red hearts, drawn on with a marker. "Voicemail," she told me. "Hey biatch. Rumor is you got lucky yesterday. Hit me back." She hung up. "We have to pay her a visit. Stat."

I was used to flying under the radar in Green Grove, but these last few weeks it was like a flashing neon sign had been strapped to my head. My nerves tickled my insides and gave me the giggles, as we walked down corridors lined with spectators.

Jackson fell into step long enough to ask, "Is Jo OK?"

I shook my head, unable to speak in case I burst out laughing from sheer adrenaline.

Melissa crowed like a rooster as we passed her locker. I was about to speed up, but then I saw Tom. He was leaning against the next locker with his arms folded across his chest.

My giggles dissolved like sugar in coffee. I wanted to grab him by the shoulders and shake him until he explained the theory of everything. I wanted to ask him if it was related to my nightmares or my mixed up memories. But he was as disconnected as an unplugged TV. It was the dead-behind-the-eyes look from his first day and it made me think that I had hallucinated last Saturday after all.

Sylv grabbed my hand and pulled me towards the driveway. By the time we reached the road she had made up her mind that the rumors were complete crap. "Jo is too frigid," she said.

"Shut up!" I said, suddenly erupting like a volcano. "This is your mess!"

Sylv looked at me with wide eyes. "How?"

"You called her a man."

"I said she looked like a man," Sylv corrected, like it was a compliment by comparison.

"Well, you might have noticed that Jo cut and colored her hair after that and started reading about twenty books a day instead of her standard ten." I sighed at my own realization. "She was doing it for Mr Bailey."

"She was doing it for Mr Bailey alright," Sylv said with a grin, but she stopped smiling when I turned and stalked down the street.

"Grow up, Sylv."

••••

Mr Green nearly slammed the door in our faces when we got to his house.

"You!" he said, looking thinner than I remembered. The dark circles under his eyes were worse than my own. I wondered if it was because of the cancer or his daughter, or a bit of both. "I should string the pair of you up. I know you have something to do with this!"

"Good to see you too, Dave," Sylv said brazenly.

"Can we talk to Jo?" I asked. "Please?"

Mr Green sighed heavily and shook his head. "Sorry, Pipsqueak. She locked herself in her room last night. No dinner, no breakfast and I would reckon no lunch too. The school called…" he trailed off and then sighed again. "Yeah. OK. Give it a shot."

We stayed for about an hour, talking to her bedroom door. I even got on my hands and knees and pleaded through the gap between the wood and the carpet. I could hear the sound of a nose being blown. It was muffled, like she was buried underneath three duvets and a pile of pillows.

Mr Green made us coffee afterwards, unable to hold a grudge. I wanted to ask about his health, but thought it would be out of line in front of Sylv. Plus, I could see the answer for myself from the state of the house, which looked like a bomb had hit it, followed by an asteroid.

"You girls have gotta watch out for each other," he said as we sat around the kitchen table, which was covered in magazines, bills and old coffee mugs. "Keep your eye on the ball."

He looked at me when he said this and I flushed. My ball had been bouncing between Tom, Melissa and Jackson these last couple of months and Jo had kind of been dropped. Well, Deb did like to remind me that my first word had been "Lillie". It was all about me. Me. Me. Me.

Me and Tom, I corrected myself, swirling my mug between my two hands and watching the grains of instant coffee float up.

When I got home I curled up on the lounge under a hemp blanket and put on a musical. Deb had driven to the state park to meet up with a group of fire dancers, which meant I had the house to myself.

I chose *Chicago*. Jo had been in love with Richard Gere since we had watched a rerun of *Pretty Woman* in sixth grade. It was like her prayers had been answered when he signed up to do a musical.

As he belted out *"Give 'em the old Razzle-Dazzle"* I looked at him with a nagging thought in the back of my mind. He looked like someone I knew. By the time he finished his tap dance I had worked out who. Mr Bailey. Yep. The same eyes. The same gray wavy hair. They could have been twins.

I hunted through the cushions for the remote and turned off the TV. As the house sank into silence, I thought I heard a sound on the porch. I sat up straight and waited for a knock, but instead I heard the front door creak open.

"Deb?" I jumped to my feet and looked down the hallway, but the front door was closed, deadbolted.

••••

I was murdered in the lounge room in my dreams that night. The killer pushed open the front door with a creak and came down the hallway towards me. Richard Gere-slash-Mr Bailey had finished his tap dance and was befuddling Amos on the stand when the woman in the balaclava walked through the doorway.

I ran into the kitchen and heard her laugh as she followed, as if we were kids playing hide and seek.

I grabbed a knife from the counter. For the first time I had a weapon, even if it was a bread knife.

The woman in the balaclava laughed again and I recognized it as my own laughter.

"Is this a dream?" I asked.

She smiled, her emerald eyes crinkling behind her balaclava. "All that we see or seem, is but a dream within a dream," she said cryptically before she grabbed me by the throat.

I dropped the knife as I fell against the counter, the cold washing over me.

18

The rumors continued the following day.

The three top picks were: 1. Jo was pregnant; 2. Mr Bailey was in jail; and 3. Jo had been given top marks in return for lap dances, as if Jo were the lap dancing type.

Jo was absent, of course. Mr Bailey too, which sparked another rumor that they had hit the road, moving from state to state, from motel to motel like Humbert Humbert and Lolita.

Tom was at school, but continued to treat me like the Invisible Girl. I was a social pariah anyway. Sylv too. We would have given out a few slaps if not for Turnip, who patrolled the corridors like a prison warden with a clipboard instead of a gun. We had to be on our best behavior after his word of warning, especially Sylv, who was going to be pulled out of school by her parents if she ended up on the wrong side of Turnip's law again.

We decided to go to the Masquerade Ball that night. We both needed a pick-me-up.

"Plus, I told Brandon he would be getting lucky tonight," Sylv said.

"I thought it was Simon," I said.

Sylv shrugged. "I got bored of Simon."

We got ready for the ball at my house, but the mood was like getting ready for a funeral.

Sylv was wearing a long red sparkling dress, but she made up for the modest hemline with a plunging V-neck that required double-sided tape to hold in her girls and a pair of red stilettos, which promised a sprained ankle by the end of the night.

My dress was kind of like a smock or a tunic, or even a caftan. It was made from a dusty pink fabric with three-quarter length sleeves and a square neckline. It was from another era. Or another dimension, I thought with a shiver.

I knew my feet would freeze in my sandals, so I pulled on a pair of worn-out cowboy boots. They were the color of toffee, reminding me of Jo joking about eating my hair after Sylv had made it look like caramel. Poor Jo.

Sylv curled our hair and then begged to do my make-up. "Come on, Lillie."

I shook my head. "My mask will be on in any case." My mask was pink and I had glued a tiny white bow to the top right-hand corner. Sylv had added horns to her mask, which she had coated in red glitter.

"Please?" Sylv pleaded, taking a swipe at me with her mascara and then with her eyeliner, until I gave in. It was either that or lose an eye.

I studied my reflection afterwards to make sure I was more model-esque than stripper-esque. I definitely looked different. Thanks to her concealer there were no dark circles underneath my eyes, which had been rimmed with brown eyeliner and pink eye shadow. Sylv had smudged the eye shadow along the top and bottom lids before sweeping white eye shadow along my brow bone.

My emerald eyes came and went as I fluttered eyelashes as long as falsies above painted cheeks. It seemed a shame to put on my mask.

"Enjoy," Deb called out as we climbed out of the beat-up sedan she had been driving since our camper van broke down. It had belonged to a couch surfer who had stayed with us for a week last January, but I guess it belonged to us now.

"Holy Mary," Sylv said as we stepped into the gymnasium.

"Mother of God," I concurred, once my eyes had adjusted to the thousands of fairy lights that had been strung around the gymnasium and the ton of balloons that were floating above us. I heard a few popping over the drumming of the music, probably pulled down and stomped on by the skaters.

Our eyes were not on the decorations though. Jo was walking across the basketball court towards the bathroom. At least, I thought it was Jo, but the Jo I knew wore flats, not killer heels decorated with metal studs. She was dressed completely in black as expected, but her LBD was drawing dirty looks from other girls and a few wolf whistles from the boys.

We followed her into the bathroom, which was filled with girls standing at the sinks, fixing their make-up and bitching about each other. The cubicles were empty though and we spotted her walking into one at the far end.

"Hey," a senior complained, as I pushed past. I put my hand out as Jo closed the door, pushing against the painted wood.

"Please, Jo," I begged.

There was a short stand-off before she relented.

As I closed the door behind me, I heard one of the girls at the sink mutter, "Lesbians," before Sylv threatened to take them to the showers and show them a real-life lesbian. Yep. She liked to play up the rumor that she had kissed at least one girl in her sixteen years. She had started a rumor last year specifically about her and Melissa.

I was face to face with Jo, both of us wearing masks. I pushed mine up, but she continued to look at me through her eyeholes. Her lips formed a tight line below her mask which had been decorated with black satin and lace, but then I saw them wobble as she burst into tears. She dropped her shoulder bag on the floor and flung her arms around me, burying her face into my neck.

"Sorry," she choked. "I screwed up."

I gave her a tight squeeze, wringing her like a dishrag before putting at least two feet between us again. Jo was hardly a touchy-feely girl and I also liked my personal space.

"I should be the one apologizing," I said.

An argument followed about who was sorrier, and so on and so forth. Jo pushed up her mask, revealing cheeks that were streaked with mascara. They were also as red as two tomatoes, as was her nose.

"Are you drunk?"

"No," she said incredulously, but her eyes flitted to her shoulder bag. My eyes followed and we both dived for it at the same time. There was a tussle, the zipper cutting into my hand as the shoulder bag was pulled back and forth.

I spotted the neck of a whiskey bottle. "Jo," I moaned.

She suddenly let go and my back hit the door with a thud, the shoulder bag landing like a wrecking ball against my stomach.

"Like you can talk," she said. "Miss Irresponsible. You slapped Melissa, remember?"

I raised my eyebrows. "You went Goth," I threw back.

Jo frowned. "You got detention."

"You started wearing more make-up than Sylv."

"You got arrested."

My blood boiled. "And you got it on with a teacher." As soon as the words fell out of my mouth I wanted to catch them and cram them back in. Jo looked like she was choking on them too, her eyes bulging before she burst into tears again.

I followed suit. "Sorry," I blubbered.

Jo shook her head and sagged against the wall of the cubicle. "I was such a dunce, Lillie. I asked him for help with my homework and then I threw myself at him."

I bit my lip, thinking about the pregnancy rumors. "And?"

"And he has a wife and two kids who he loves, thank you very much!" She shook her head, tears streaming down her face. "Oh my God. Talk about humiliation." She grabbed her bag from me and fumbled through it, pulling out the bottle of Johnny Walker. "Want a drink?"

I hesitated for a second and then took a swig. I coughed as it scalded my throat. They say alcohol messes up your memories and I had a couple of memories I wanted messed up, like the one about parallel dimensions and the one where I died in my dreams every night. I took another burning mouthful and gagged.

Suddenly, a head appeared at our feet. It was Sylv, on her hands and knees, looking under the door. "I can see up your dresses. Nice panties, Jo." Her expression hardened when she saw the bottle. Sylv may have been a wild child, but she was a teetotaler because of her mom, who drank like a fish – and when I say like a fish I mean like an alcoholic fish. She had been sloshed on the eight or so occasions I had seen her in the past year, including once when Sylv had faked a migraine and was picked up from school.

Sylv finished crawling under the door and the three of us were crammed into the cubicle like sardines.

"Ow. Watch it," Sylv complained.

"How about you get off my foot?"

I took the bottle from Jo and sat on the toilet cistern, taking another swig and another and another. I had a sudden sensation of déjà vu and I searched my memory bank to see if the three of us had shared a cubicle before. Nope.

Sylv grabbed Jo around the waist.

"Damn girl. Have you been eating?"

Jo shrugged and shuffled backwards until Sylv let go. I noticed for the first time how much weight she had dropped over the past couple of weeks. Her legs were like candy rope under her skirt and her wrists looked like they would snap like twigs as she took the half gallon bottle from me with both hands. I also noticed her strawberry roots were showing, and her nose was bright red and flaky from being sandpapered with tissues.

"Spill," Sylv said.

"There was no kiss. And definitely no sex," Jo said. She shuddered at the memory, before taking another swig from the bottle. "What the hell was I thinking?"

"You weren't yourself," I soothed.

"No. I was. I am," Jo bawled. "I loved him. I still love him!"

Sylv rolled her eyes and opened her mouth to make a comment, but I gave her a shut-up-and-listen look.

"And now he has to leave Green Grove," Jo continued. "He said he had to report it. Turnip called my dad. He said I would have been expelled, but Mr Bailey decided to leave school instead." She choked for a moment on her words. "He got a transfer to Lincoln."

"Did you at least get suspended?" Sylv asked.

Jo shook her head. "Turnip thought it would put a stop to the rumors if I continued on as normal."

Normal? I suppressed a giggle at the thought. What the hell was normal about this? It was like being in another dream.

Jo sighed. "But the rumors will never stop."

"Of course they will," I lied.

"How stupid do you think I am?" Jo asked. "They feed off it, like vultures." She nodded her head towards the gaggle of girls outside the cubicle. "And this is juicy meat."

"Not as stupid as me," I answered, thinking of Tom.

"Or me," Sylv said. "Remember my modeling shoot? It turned out the guy was a sleazebag after all. He wanted me to go topless."

"What did you do?" I asked.

"I took my top off."

"What?"

"Just kidding! I told him to shove it and threatened to call the cops if he breathed a word to anyone. I lied and told him I was fifteen." She clapped her hands gleefully. "He almost shat himself."

Suddenly, Jo burst into laughter. And I am talking about proper belly laughter. It was a moment or two before we joined in, all laughing like our sides would split.

I was wiping the tears from my eyes when I heard Sylv say, "Cool tatt."

"What?" I climbed down from the cistern and rotated Jo, so I could see behind her ear. She struggled as I pushed back her hair and there, hidden behind the cartilage of her ear was a string of numbers and letters. A formula, like the tattoo I had seen on Tom. "What the hell?"

"Come on. Give me a break," Jo said, shaking me off. "You can poke fun at me tomorrow."

My face crumpled with confusion. Did Jo like Tom? I guess it would have explained her makeover. It would also have explained her coldness towards me. And why she had thrown herself at Mr Bailey. To draw attention to herself. To make Tom jealous. I could understand all of that, but a matching tattoo? No. Not my Jo. But was she my Jo? I frowned at those skinny legs sticking out from under her miniskirt.

"How about we get out of here?" I asked, suddenly claustrophobic.

The gymnasium was claustrophobic too. The crowd pressed in on us from all sides and the music vibrated through the floorboards, like we were in the middle of an earthquake.

"Bleachers?" I asked over the music.

The girls nodded and we moved across the basketball court, giving a group of seniors who were dancing up an alcohol-fuelled storm a wide berth. A girl wearing a yellow maxi dress and a feathery mask collided with me, knocking the air out of my lungs.

I let Jo take my hand and pull me towards the bleachers, even though her feet were as wobbly as mine thanks to a combination of alcohol and stilettos.

Suddenly, a guy in a balaclava and a black suit that was a size too large jumped out at us from the shadows. I opened my mouth to scream, but the sound stuck in my throat. The moment had arrived. At least the alcohol would soften the blow.

"This is a stick-up," he said.

"Jackson!"

I had been holding my breath and it whooshed out when I heard this exclamation from Jo. He put a finger to his lips and I remembered he had been banned from the ball.

As I scanned the crowd for Turnip, I spotted Melissa trotting across the dance floor with a silver mask in her hand. She was wearing a blue satin dress with a split up the side and sparkly stilettos. The crowd parted in front of her, as if she were Moses and they were the Red Sea, and suddenly there was Tom.

He was standing in the doorway, wearing a light gray lounge suit with a crisp white shirt underneath. He surveyed the gymnasium with an air of disdain.

Melissa pulled the silver mask over his head and moved in front of him to check it was on. She fiddled with it, tugging it to the left and then to the right, like a wife straightening a bow tie. My blood boiled. I imagined walking up behind her and grabbing her long black ponytail. I could hear her shriek in my mind.

Tom suddenly looked up, as if he could hear it too. I blushed and turned back towards my friends, following them to the bleachers. I am a good girl, I reminded myself.

Be. Nice. Be. Nice. Be. Nice, I willed myself with each step. Maybe I had finally hit puberty. That would explain my mood-swings. I looked down at my chest and giggled at myself. Yeah right. As if I would suddenly grow breasts four years after getting my period.

I was pulled onto the basketball court by the girls and Jackson. Sylv teased Jo, dancing sexily around her like a stripper around a pole. And I danced with Jackson, who had rolled up his balaclava until it looked like a stocking cap.

The alcohol had given me a buzz. I put my hands up in the air and shouted made-up lyrics to the song that was booming through the sound system. The ground swayed to the music and I swayed too, hitting the polished floorboards with a thud.

"Ouch," I said, before breaking into peels of laughter.

Jo grabbed my hands, but she also fell and we both rolled around on the floor of the gymnasium, laughing hysterically.

Jackson finally pulled us to our feet. First Jo, who fell a second and third time before he propped her up against the bleachers, and then he turned his attention to my sorry self. "Come on, Lillie," he shouted above the music, his hands around my wrists. "Up you get."

I laughed again as he lifted me. "Upsidaisy!"

I threw my arms around his shoulders as I found my feet, and as I did, my eyes fell on a face in the background. Tom. He was leaning against the wall with his arms folded. His lips formed a hard line below his mask.

I smiled and turned towards Jackson. I was about to close my eyes for our first kiss when he stepped backwards. He was shaking his head and motioning with his hands.

"What?" I shouted above the music.

It could have been the red lights, but his cheeks looked like they were flushed with embarrassment. His eyes shifted to Jo and Sylv.

"What?" I asked again.

"You. Me. Friends," he shouted over the music, as if I was a child and he had to spell it out. I guess he did.

My own cheeks began to burn like hotplates. It was hot. Too hot. I pushed through the throng, using my elbows as battering rams.

"Watch it!"

"Hey!"

"Ow."

"Lillie!" Jackson called after me.

I walked past Tom. Melissa was tugging on his hands, begging him to dance. It took me a while to find our pile of belongings in the shadows and I kicked the shins of a few canoodling couples before I found my new best friend, Johnny Walker.

The fresh air swirled around me as I found my way into the quad and booked it to the Art Block, dodging a couple of teachers who were standing guard to make sure girls like Sylv were in the gymnasium and not in the bushes.

I sat down on the stairs. Stupid, I thought as I unscrewed the lid on the bottle of whiskey and took a swig. Cough. Cough. Cough. Stupid. Stupid. Stupid. I had screwed up my friendship with Jackson and my... whatever it was... with Tom.

I heard a footfall in the darkness and my mind automatically went to my killer. "Is someone there?" I asked.

My answer was the distant sound of Michael Jackson singing "Thriller".

"Answer me!" I stood up, adrenaline rushing through my body like a flash flood in a storm water drain. "This. Is. It," my blood shouted as it pulsed through my veins. The dreams had become reality. I was about to come face-to-face with the woman in the balaclava.

My muscles twitched in anticipation. It could have been the alcohol, but I decided I was going to kick her ass. Of course, my self-defense training consisted of a kick to the groin, but in my imagination I had martial arts moves to rival Jackie Chan.

I reached up to remove my mask, as a figure stepped forward into the circle of light.

"Oh," I whispered and my knees went weak.

Tom caught me before I could hit the concrete and I rested my head against his chest before realizing that his body was as stiff as a board. "Are you drunk?" he asked.

I gave him a small shove as I stepped backwards. "Who are you? Turnip?"

"Lillie. This is not you."

I gave a short laugh. "You think you know me?"

"Yes. I do."

"Right. From another dimension."

He nodded. "Right."

I squinted at him, suddenly sober. "I thought it was a hallucination." I said. "The theory of everything. Parallel dimensions."

Tom shook his head. His fingers brushed my cheek, feather-light. I reached up to stroke his face in return.

"How did you get the scar on your chin?" I suddenly asked.

He chuckled, the sound making me smile, even though I had missed the joke. "An ice skating accident," he said, his cool eyes warm for a change. "A friend of mine thought it would be fun to go ice skating on the lake."

"At Rose Hill?" I asked, feeling like I had heard this story.

He nodded and rubbed his chin, his smile now sad. "We ended up having a fall."

"I have a pair of ice skates," I said slowly. "They used to belong to Deb."

"I know."

A memory suddenly burst into my mind, like sunlight flooding into a house that had been boarded up for a decade. I could feel the ice skates under my feet, wobbly and ten sizes too big, but hands held me tight, leading me onto the ice with small steps.

"Chicken," a voice goaded good-naturedly. "You were the one who wanted to go ice skating." The voice sounded young – a child – but the accent, a mix of British and something else, sounded like Tom.

I looked up and saw a boy about eight or nine years old. He seemed to radiate in the light that bounced off the ice, giving him an angelic appearance. A red scarf was wrapped around his neck and above it, his smile beamed, showing off his perfect teeth.

There was an innocence in his blue eyes, which sparkled like the lightest colored sapphires. An innocence that has long been lost, I thought as my mind returned to this dimension and the now grown-up Tom.

"Who am I?" I whispered, wanting answers for the past six months, the past sixteen years. "Please, Tom. I want to know."

Tom reached into the inside pocket of his coat and pulled out a crumpled photo. "They say a picture tells a thousand words."

I took it from him, a lump forming in my throat. "The girl in the photo is dead," he had said.

I looked at the couple in the photo – first at Tom and then at his girlfriend – and as soon as I did, my chest tightened and my breath became short and sharp, like I had been kicked in the gut.

My head swam, as memories bubbled to the surface, rising from the depths of my mind. The girl in the photo is alive, I thought, as I blinked at her high cheekbones, her pointy ears and her dark circles. She looked back at me with emerald eyes.

I lifted my own emerald eyes to Tom. "The girl in the photo," I whispered, "is me."

We startled as we heard voices at the top of the stairs. It was Jo and Jackson.

"We thought you had been kidnapped," Jackson said, looking at Tom pointedly.

Tom grabbed the photo and crammed it into his pocket again, before storming up the stairs. He watched Jo warily as he passed, like she was a wild animal about to attack.

"What is his deal?" Jo asked with a laugh.

I ran to the grass, where I fell to my knees and threw up.

●●●●

That night I had a new dream.

I was sitting on the steps outside the Art Block. "Is someone there?" I called out and, instead of Tom, I saw the woman in the balaclava.

I dropped the bottle of whiskey and it smashed on the concrete as I stumbled down the stairs and into the stairwell. I was trapped. I whirled around and tried to pull off her balaclava again, but she turned her head. It was then that I saw the tattoo.

"Jo?" I asked, but the laugh she gave was my own.

The cold went through me and I heard someone who sounded like Tom shout, "No!" It was like the wail of a wild dog and I woke with the sound echoing in my ears.

19

The fallout from the Masquerade Ball was like a nuclear bomb had missed its target and hit our no-name school. The word on the street was that a few girls had turned up high and one of them had thrown up on Turnip.

"Stupid stoners," Sylv said, because we were in the firing line as a result. A teacher had found the empty bottle of whiskey near the Art Block and Turnip was on our scent like a bloodhound, despite the bunch of seniors who had arrived drunk.

I could care less about Turnip. My mind was on the photo I had seen last night. Maybe it had been Photoshopped. It would take two seconds to cut and paste my face onto–

"Lillie." Jo broke into my thoughts as she grabbed my arm and shook it like a shake 'n' bake. "Turnip said if I ended up in his office again it would mean instant suspension."

"I think this will be instant expulsion," Sylv said.

Jo went as white as a sheet.

"Should I give her a slap?" Sylv asked.

I gave her a look.

"What? Just trying to help."

Jo was barely breathing by the time Turnip decided to have a junior-senior sit-in in the gymnasium. The Dance Committee must have been at school since the crack of dawn cleaning it from top to bottom, but I could see gold glitter caught between the wooden floorboards, which I could guarantee would be there for the next decade.

"We can sit here all day and all night if you want," Turnip said, his voice booming over the PA system.

"Bye-bye pop quiz," Sylv whispered.

Jo looked at her wide-eyed, as if speaking was akin to a confession.

I frowned. A few weeks ago Jo would have been laughing at Turnip, asking if he was going to take our fingerprints. That being said, a few weeks ago she would not have brought a bottle of whiskey to school.

As Turnip droned on, he stared through each and every student with those watery eyes. He seemed to stare at me for an hour and I stared back, like a deer caught in headlights.

"I am warning you," he continued as I shifted my gaze to the doorway, where a stray streamer hung like a forgotten cobweb. "I take underage drinking very seriously."

Jo let out a squeak that sounded like someone had stepped on a canary, and Melissa, who was sitting two rows in front, turned to look at her with narrowed eyes.

I elbowed Sylv, who elbowed Jo.

"Keep your trap shut, Jo," Sylv hissed, but we knew Jo was as capable of keeping her trap shut as Melissa was of buying her clothes from Costco.

I grimaced, as I thought about the pay-off. Jo would be expelled after using up her first and second strikes with Mr Bailey and Sylv would be pulled out of school by her parents. Jackson would probably be expelled too and his family would leave town, heading back to Minnesota or wherever they had been the past five years or so.

The pay-off for me, though would be a cup of chamomile tea.

"I will find out," Turnip promised, holding up the empty bottle, like a warlord with a severed head. "And when I do…"

Jo had gone green around the gills, reminding me of Lindsey Manning two seconds before she threw up in front of the class in fourth grade.

I took a deep breath, but before I could confess I heard a male voice say, "Fine. You got me."

There was a murmur as Tom climbed to his feet. Melissa was tugging on his jacket and hissing at him to sit down.

"What the hell is he doing?" I whispered.

"Who cares?" Jo said gleefully. "He got us off the hook."

"That boy is either getting laid by one of us or he wants to lay one of us," Sylv said, looking at me.

I flushed, both with embarrassment and anger. This was not about being chivalrous, about picking up photos or tampons or bags. This was about continuing to mess with my mind and my emotions. First with his talk about parallel dimensions, and then with the photo. I clenched and unclenched my fists. "It was actually me," I said, standing up.

A ripple of laughter went through the gymnasium, but Turnip silenced it with a piercing look. Tom gave me a piercing look of his own that asked, "What the fuck?"

I squared my jaw.

We were both suspended for a week.

Deb picked me up in the beat-up sedan. I could see her through the windshield, eyes closed, like she was harnessing her chi. Her cheeks were red, burning with emotion like mine did when I was put on the spot.

"Did you bring a cup of chamomile tea?" I joked as I opened the door. "Or maybe a thermos?" I slumped into the passenger seat, the wooden beads of the seat-cover rattling like a den of snakes.

Her eyes flew open and then homed in on me like a laser beam on a sniper rifle. They were emerald like mine and I wondered if mine flashed in the afternoon sunlight too. "This is not a joke, young lady," she said, in a voice unlike my mother.

I raised my eyebrows and laughed.

She flinched, as if I had slapped her across the face. "You think this is funny?"

I shook my head, pressing my lips together, but a giggle slipped out.

Deb pumped the gas pedal as she turned the key in the ignition. The engine spluttered and roared. "You used to be such a good girl," she said, as she pulled the rust-bucket into the turning circle. A couple of sophomores who were sneaking a cigarette at the side of the Main Building laughed at us as we passed.

I used to be such a good girl. The words hung between us, spelling out what I had known for six months. I had changed and not like a caterpillar changing into a butterfly. I was like an ice cube melting in a glass. I had become less, instead of more.

"Is that him?" Deb asked, slowing down. "The boy who got you drunk?"

I lifted my head and saw Tom walking towards his SUV, which was parked out of sight around the block, as usual. For one heart-stopping moment I thought Deb was going to pull over and give him an ear-bashing, but she flicked on the blinker and turned in the opposite direction towards our street, giving me an earful instead.

"You are not only suspended," she said, warming up to her role as judge, jury and executioner, "but grounded as well. That means no friends and especially no boys."

"Mom!" I was surprised when the word came out of my mouth.

I could tell she was surprised too, I had been calling her Deb since third grade, but she tightened her lips. "Yes. I am your mother," she said resolutely. "I am not your friend and I am not – what was it you called me the other day – a nutcase?"

I looked out of the window, my cheeks flushed.

"This is what you wanted, Lillie," she continued. "You wanted me to ground you, lecture you, make you do the dishes."

"And, as they say, 'Be careful what you wish for,'" I said dryly.

We sat in silence until we reached our street. "Deb?" I said, unable to contain my curiosity.

"What?"

I hesitated. "How do you know William Windsor-Smith?"

There was a sharp intake of air from my mother and the car slowed. "Where did you hear that name?" Her eyes were on the road, but she swallowed hard and blinked a few times, as if a bug had flown into her eye.

"I know his son," I said. I stopped short of saying he was the boy who supposedly got me drunk.

"His son?" She turned to stare at me and drove past our house. "Shit," she cursed, slamming on the brakes and shifting the car into reverse. The engine whined and the tire hit the curb, launching us onto the sidewalk.

"Deb!"

"I know! I know!" she shouted.

We managed to get the car into the drive without a fatality, although Humpback Harding came out onto the street to supervise and gave us both a heart attack when she tapped on my window with her cane.

"I thought you were that hooligan," she complained when I opened the car door. "What was his name? The Murphy boy. You know, the one they arrested for the accident down at the train tracks."

"Jackson," my mother said, frowning at me like her friends were Harvard Alumni, instead of a bunch of pot-smoking dropouts. "Jackson Murphy."

The girls came to see me after school, but my prison guard told them no visitors. I could hear a hint of a smile when Sylv gave her sass, but Deb was like an oak. A little lip from Sylv wasn't going to make her bend the rules – rules that included no TV and no cell, though my cell was broken anyway.

I waved to the girls through my bedroom window as they went. Jo walked backwards for half of the street, waving back at me. I knew she would be feeling torn up that I had taken the rap, but I had less to lose.

20

I slept in the next morning. Partly because I had spent a sleepless night thinking about Tom, but mostly because I had no reason to get up early. I could have gotten used to being suspended.

Deb slept in too. I could hear her cursing and banging around in the bathroom, getting ready for her shift at Tree of Life.

A few minutes later she pushed open my bedroom door. Apparently there was no such thing as knocking when you were in home detention.

"I finish at three and until then you're housebound," she said, pointing her finger at me, like a schoolmarm.

"What if the house catches fire?" I asked lazily.

She rolled her eyes and spun on her heel. A minute later I saw her coming back up the hallway, slinging a beaded handbag over her shoulder.

"But I need vitamin D," I called out to her. "They say rickets is a real risk." "They" were two couch surfers who used to sunbathe in the nude in our backyard despite the complaints from our neighbors.

"Fine," Deb said, her keys rattling. "You can go into the backyard."

I smiled, even though there was no reason to smile about going into our backyard. I guessed I could take a few photos of the dead veggie patch or the mildew on the north side of house. At least it would keep my mind off Tom. Maybe.

It was about an hour later that I rolled out of bed. I pulled on my knock-around jeans, which had a tear under the knee, and a white knitted hoodie with a stain on the front pocket. I scraped my hair back into a high ponytail, reminding myself that no one was going to see me today, tomorrow, or the day after that.

"You have to love being housebound," I said, looking at myself in the mirror.

I poured a bowl of muesli and, like the delinquent I was, went into the lounge room and switched on the contraband TV. I flicked through the channels, pausing on a program about urban legends and then stopping on another about cloning.

The presenter was talking about a bunch of scientists in Scotland who had cloned a sheep from a mammary gland and named it after Dolly Parton. I wondered how they could tell she was a clone as I scanned the flock of identical sheep on the screen. I guess if she had been human it would have been like having an identical twin – like the girl in the photo.

My daydream was interrupted by a rumbling out front, followed by the explosion of a car backfiring. I walked up the hallway, peering through the window beside the front door. A man with dreadlocks was pulling a duffel bag out of the trunk of a station wagon and behind him stood a woman in a long skirt, who was plaiting her hair and looking up at the sky as if searching for signs of rain. There were none, of course.

"Visitors," I sighed and we were not talking cup-of-tea-and-a-biscuit kind of visitors. No. I could tell from the size of the duffel bag and the junk piled up on the back seat of their wagon that these were the sleeping-on-the-couch-for-a-month kind. Deb!

I grabbed my camera and macro lens and opened the front door as the pair stepped onto the porch. The man had a set of bongo drums under one arm, along with the duffel bag.

"Lillie," the woman said in a breathy voice and when she saw my eyes widen she added, "We dropped in on your mother at the shop. She told us you would be home." She gestured towards herself. "I'm Dawn. And this is Blaze."

Blaze gave me an awkward wave as he balanced his belongings.

I nodded an acknowledgment before stepping out of the doorway and onto the porch. "I have to pop out, but make yourselves at home," I said, as if they needed an invitation.

I guessed Deb had told them about my incarceration when Dawn shifted her weight, skirt swaying, and started with, "You see…" and "I think…" before Blaze put a hand on her arm and shook his head.

"Thanks," he said to me as he moved through the doorway.

"You too," I responded with a begrudging smile.

The sun was shining, but my breath fogged as I walked to the park. I decided to photograph the fall leaves scattered under the trees before they rotted and turned brown, which meant I was lying flat on my stomach on the sidewalk next to the bleachers, snapping shots of the colored tapestry when I heard a vehicle coming down the street.

It was the Benz. My heart suddenly thudded against my ribs, like a prisoner rattling a cup against the bars of a cell. Clang. Clang. Clang. Tom. Tom. Tom.

I watched as the sleek black SUV slowed to a stop. Then I sat up on my haunches, brushing at my stomach, sweeping away dirt and fragments of crushed leaves. You have to love being housebound, I thought sarcastically, as I heard the engine cut out and the vehicle door open and close. I looked up and my breath formed a cloud in front of my face, blocking my view.

When it cleared, I saw Tom walking towards me, looking like he had stepped off a runway in Milan, as usual. He was wearing a light charcoal sweater today with a darker charcoal scarf swaddling his neck. I brushed at my top again, but it was going to need a three-hour soak in Tide Stain Release. I suddenly remembered my hair was in a ponytail and I yanked the band out, letting it fall around my shoulders, covering my pointy ears.

"Why?" Tom asked from thirty feet, his expression like a thunderstorm.

"Why what?" I asked, wrapping my camera strap around my hand nervously.

"Why did you confess?" He was a few feet in front of me now, pacing back and forth like a caged animal. "There was no need. I took the fall." He shook his head as if wondering why he had bothered.

I wondered why he had bothered as well, but instead of asking the question I shrugged, pulling the strap tighter, like a noose. My fingers throbbed as the circulation was cut off. I released the cord and watched them turn from purple to white and finally to a pale pink. "I wanted to ditch school for a few days?" I joked and was reminded of Deb asking if I thought this was funny. When I saw his face contained the same question, I added, "I did the crime. I should do the time, as they say."

"What about Jackson?" Tom scowled. "He did the crime and you let him off the hook."

"Off the hook?" I flared up. "He goes to court on Monday." I could feel hot patches rising like the midday sun on my neck and cheeks. "Is this about Jackson? Because if it is you should have stayed in your car. It would have been warmer."

I know it sounded like Tom was jealous of Jackson, but this was looking like a pride parade, as if he were a silverback beating his chest. Tom had stuck his neck out at the railroad crossing and then I had made up with Jackson. Now, he had taken the rap about the Masquerade Ball and it had been thrown back in his face again. Maybe I can mess with his mind too, I thought smugly.

"Are you cold?" Tom suddenly asked, unwrapping the scarf from around his neck in a fluid motion.

He held it out to me and we stood there motionless, like statues in the park – he, a marble god carved by one of the masters, and me, a lump of plasticine molded by a toddler – until I took it, slinging it around my neck awkwardly. The wool was soft against my skin, with a hint of his familiar cologne.

"Why did you take the fall?" I asked quietly.

The clouds cleared from his expression. "Because I cannot stop saving you, Lillie."

He reached out and put his hand on mine. When I looked down, I realized I had been twisting my camera cord around my fingers again. The cord loosened and the blood pumped into my purple fingers. Throb. Throb. Throb. Why? Why? Why?

"I wanted to give you a second chance," Tom whispered, answering my unspoken question. "I wanted to give us both a second chance."

I frowned. "Is this about the girl in the photo? Is she… Is she really me?" His lips were inches from mine. I could lean forward on my tiptoes and–

"Do you want to go for a drive?" he asked and then, as if his question had been ambiguous, he added, "I think we should go for a drive."

I rocked back on my heels, considering his proposal. Deb would probably make me take up yoga or drink a ton of green tea while chanting to the Goddess of Self-Control, but I nodded and followed him to his SUV as if attached by an invisible thread. The Goddess of Self-Control can go screw herself, I decided.

My feet rustled through the leaves, which seemed to

whisper, "This. Is. It." It was like reaching the last chapter of a good book. I wanted to skip ahead to the last page. I had all the questions and I knew Tom had all the answers.

He opened the passenger door and I looked down at him as I climbed up into the heated leather seat. The clouds had closed in again on his expression, as if he were battening down the hatches in preparation for our drive.

We were on the road from nowhere to nowhere, headed out towards the sandhills, when Tom finally spoke. "I heard you slapped Melissa."

I blushed. "She turned in Jackson."

"Loyal," he observed. "Loyal Lillie."

My eyes flew to him. Loyal Lillie had been my nickname in Elementary. Deb had started the trend when I was in first grade and came home wearing one shoe. "I gave one to Jo. Hers had a hole," my seven year-old self had explained. I liked it when Deb told me that story. It reminded me that I used to be a good girl.

"Who are you?" I asked Tom, fed up and flicking to the last page.

His expression darkened and in that moment he looked older than his seventeen years. "How long have we known each other?" he asked, looking at me sideways.

"A couple of months?" Six weeks, seven days, three hours, I thought.

Tom shook his head. "Longer," he said, like we were playing the game Hot and Cold. I imagined myself throwing numbers at him for hours and receiving the responses "warmer... warmer... colder."

I frowned, thinking of the woman in the balaclava standing in my bedroom six months ago. The hairs on the back of my neck stood on end, like soldiers standing to attention. Maybe it had been Tom after all. "How much longer?" I asked, my eyes scanning the pastures, looking for a farmhouse or an emergency telephone, but finding cow after cow instead.

"I stopped counting at four hundred and thirty-two," Tom answered.

"Days?" I asked. My mind somersaulted with the calculations and my fingers flew in my lap – one year and...

Tom shook his head. "Years."

There was no hint of a smile, as his jaw clenched and unclenched.

Years? my mind echoed. Years? And I thought parallel dimensions were a stretch. My eyes flickered to the door handle and I wondered if it was locked.

I could jump out, I thought, leaning towards the window and watching the road whooshing beneath us like water. I guessed we were going about fifty miles per hour. In my mind I saw myself opening up the door and launching myself out. I heard the sickening crunch of my skull against the asphalt and felt my skin being scraped from my flesh as I rolled towards the ditch at the side of the road.

I decided to stay in the vehicle, but two seconds later we slowed to a stop anyway. We had reached a crossroads and although my chest was straining against the seatbelt I decided to continue my journey with Tom.

21

We took the road that led to a rock formation called The Ox.

We climbed up its stone hide, sitting between its horns with our legs hanging over the ledge. It was afternoon and long shadows stretched between the undulations of the land like deep pools, but there was no water in the sandhills at the moment, even though their rainfall was twice that of Green Grove.

I was holding the photo of Tom and my identical twin. I squinted at the couple, as if I could dredge up the memories from the depths of my mind. "Is this photo from another dimension?"

"Yes."

"Is that you?"

He nodded.

My stomach somersaulted as I pointed at the girl. "And is that really me?"

"That photo was taken more than three hundred years ago," Tom said, looking out over the sandhills. He closed his eyes for a moment and then sighed. "Let me start from the beginning," he said. "Let me explain parallel dimensions."

Another science lesson, I thought, but this time I was taking notes.

"In your dimension, parallel dimensions are considered science fiction," Tom said, "but I studied them at school. I learned they are created whenever a person makes a decision, like choosing whether or not to have butter on their toast, or whether or not to push a button that ends the world. The dimension splits."

"Like being cloned?" I asked, recalling the program I had seen that morning on cloning. I looked at the girl in the photo again.

He nodded. "But in one dimension the person would have butter on their toast and in the other they might have peanut butter instead."

I wondered what the girl in the photo had for breakfast. "What if they decide to have coffee instead?" I asked.

"Then the dimension splits again. Three times. Four times. Five times."

I pictured the lifeline on my hand, which Deb had read when she was going through her palm-reading phase.

"You have a life-changing decision ahead," she had told me, tracing the line on my palm and pausing at a fork. "If you choose correctly you will have a long life." Her finger had indicated the deep line that ended at my wrist. "But if not..." She had brushed the short line, which trailed off into smooth skin.

Tom held his hands behind his back. "Pick a hand."

"Right. No! Left!"

His left hand emerged empty, but then he revealed his right, which was holding a small wildflower. I reached out, but he lifted it above his head and shook his head. "In this dimension you picked my left hand."

"Does that mean I chose your right hand in another dimension?"

He nodded. "You probably also chose not to pick a hand at all, knowing your pig-headedness." He twirled the purple flower between his fingers. "Do you feel like God?"

"Like God?"

He shrugged. "You just created at least two worlds."

The weight of his words fell on me for a moment, but then I had a thought that made me smile. "What if this is the dimension where I get to choose both hands?"

He laughed and handed me the flower. It was as small as a button and I held its stem between my thumb and index finger, its petals resting on my finger like a butterfly.

"I think I created another dimension earlier," I said, thinking of how I had opened the passenger door in my mind and... I shuddered.

"Lillie, dimensions are being created left, right and center. They are as infinite as the universe." He saw the look on my face, as I felt my skin being ripped off by the asphalt. "Are you OK?" he asked, touching my arm. The contact gave me a hot flash in the chill of the late afternoon. "I should have known not to dump it on you like this." His voice lowered, like he was talking to himself. "And they say practice makes perfect."

I hugged my knees to my chest, as I took deep breaths in and out. "Do you think this is what it was like when they found out the world was round?" I asked.

Tom shrugged helplessly. "Like I said, I was taught about parallel dimensions when I was a kid. For me it was like knowing the sky was blue or that summer followed spring." I heard a hint of a smile in his voice as he added, "I was also taught that the world was hexagonal."

My eyes widened for a moment, before he chuckled. "Hilarious," I said with a strained smile, as I pushed the thoughts of myself lying in a ditch by the side of the road out of my mind. "Sorry," I said, stretching my legs out over the ledge again. "I need to put my imagination on a leash."

Tom grimaced and I knew he was about to hit me with another bombshell. "Lillie, there is no such thing as imagination."

"Huh?"

"The human brain can record information, but it cannot make it up. What you call imagination is in fact your memories from other dimensions."

I frowned. "What about dreams then?" I asked stubbornly. "I used to have a reoccurring dream I was flying."

"Levitation. In a number of dimensions they have worked out how to harness the power of the mind." He shrugged apologetically. "There are also dimensions that break the laws of physics. Flying elephants. Upside-down buildings."

My voice dropped to a whisper. "And what if you die in a dream?"

Tom looked out over the sandhills. "It means you have died in another dimension."

I thought about Deb and her claptrap about new beginnings and a squeak of a laugh slipped out.

Tom gave me a curious look, but went on to explain, "A cold shiver down your spine also means you have died in another dimension."

"What if...?" I asked Tom with a catch in my voice. "What if someone kills you in a dream?"

His lips tightened and he picked up a couple of pebbles beside him, rattling them in his hand like dice, before letting them drop and scooping them up again.

"And what if that someone is me?" I pressed. "What if I killed myself?"

The pebbles fell, bouncing and scattering. Tom stood up. "We should go," he said. "Your mother will be wondering where–"

I climbed to my feet. "Tell me who I am, Tom. Am I...?" The words stuck in my throat like a jawbreaker. I finally managed to spit them out. "Am I a murderer?"

I thought of the number of times I had run down that path at Rose Hill and felt the cold spread through my body. I thought of how I had been killed in my bedroom, the darkroom, the kitchen, the bathtub and countless other locales. I thought of the dream where I had pulled off the balaclava and had seen my own face. Memories. My head throbbed. Memories. Memories. Memories.

Tom looked at me, his eyes as cold as the shadow cast by the rock. "Yes," he said dully.

My legs went like Jell-O and I fell forward, waiting to hear the crack of my knees on the stone. But then I realized I was being held up by strong arms in this dimension. Tom was holding me, pulling me into his embrace. I put my head against his chest, feeling the hard muscle under his sweater, and sobbed as I thought of another dimension, where Tom had decided not to catch me and I was lying on the ground with bruised knees.

He stroked my hair and I buried my face in the crook of his arm. "They say…" I started, my voice muffled until I drew back my head. "They say you should take the road less traveled. You know, when two roads diverge in a wood? They say it makes all the difference. But how can you make a difference when you take all roads?" I shook my head, trying to comprehend infinite roads and myself walking down each of them.

"I used to ask myself the same thing," Tom answered. "How do you make the toss count if you choose both sides of a coin, right?"

I nodded, looking at him through blurred eyes.

He cupped my face in his hands, his fingers caressing my tear-stained cheeks. "By falling in love," he whispered, as he leaned forward and kissed me. His lips were soft and warm against mine and filled with memories of the two of us, of our other lives together. I kissed him back, desperately, like a swimmer holding onto a life preserver in an endless ocean.

●●●●

"What did you mean when you said we had known each other for hundreds of years?" I asked Tom, one of a thousand questions I had been throwing at him as he drove me home. I now believed we had other lives in other dimensions, because the memories were floating through my mind like wisps of smoke, but I was sixteen, not five hundred and sixteen.

"I have traveled through thirty-four dimensions," Tom explained. "Thirty-five if you count this dimension. I have spent five minutes in some dimensions. And forty years in others."

"You look good for your age," I said with a small smile.

He returned my smile, but I think he had heard the joke before. "When I slide I go back to being seventeen," he explained. "That was my age when I started sliding between dimensions during the Evacuation."

I suddenly realized that with all this talk about infinite dimensions, not once had I asked about his dimension.

"What was the Evacuation?" I asked, my chest tightening as if I knew the answer, which, of course, I did. It was heartbreaking. The theory of everything had led to the destruction of his dimension and everyone had been evacuated. "No," I whispered. "The children. They left the children behind."

"And the sick," Tom said, wincing. "And the elderly."

I closed my eyes, remembering the looting, remembering stepping over dead bodies in the street.

In his dimension, physics had been God. The National Laboratory had been funded through the roof. Forget the Space Race. Why go to the Moon when you could go to another world? But a few decisions by a team of physicists had led to the release of strange matter, a substance that consumed other substances, converting non-living matter into black rock.

It had consumed half of New York in two days – buildings, sidewalks, street lights, cars, even the non-organic matter in the dirt, killing the grass and trees.

And to think in my dimension Einstein had considered his letter to President Roosevelt recommending the development of an atomic bomb his greatest mistake.

"The United Nations ordered an evacuation of Earth," Tom reminded me. "By the time the strange matter had spread up to Canada and out into the North Atlantic Ocean they had set up clinics around the world, giving out an injection they called the 'Solution.' It changed our molecular structure and allowed us to slip through the gaps from one dimension to another."

A memory passed through my mind of the protesters who had stood outside the clinics, chanting anti-evacuation slogans as we lined up for our shots in Lincoln. I could hear their voices in my mind. "No child left behind! No child left behind! No child left behind!" I grimaced. It seemed George W Bush had managed to get elected in that dimension too.

"And when they jabbed us with that needle we slid into another dimension, and the volume of sliders created a wormhole in the fabric of space and time that constantly brings us back to the date of the Evacuation," Tom explained. "We were unable to keep track of each other, which was why no one under six years old was allowed the Solution."

I remembered hearing about a woman in South Africa who had driven her car into one of the clinics, killing herself and her three year-old daughter in protest. But the thought of a three year-old sliding into a dimension on its own made the orphanages set up by the United Nations look like the lesser of two evils.

I sat up straighter as I realized the woman in the balaclava had arrived in my dreams around the time Tom had arrived in Green Grove. "My killer. Is she an evacuee?" I asked Tom.

Tom pressed down on the accelerator, as if he was running from my question. "Yes," he said through gritted teeth. "It took a few slides, but I finally heard evacuees had started killing their other selves and taking over their lives." He glanced at me, appraising the look on my face, which would have been horror with a capital "H".

"You have to understand that when we slide into a new dimension we have no identity," Tom continued, as if excusing these murderers. "It could be that we were never born or that we have a double in the dimension and have to go into hiding. The result is you have doctors working as janitors and celebrities entering lookalike competitions to make a buck."

"But how do they hide the bodies?" I asked, doing the math on billions of murders in infinite dimensions. "There would be dead doubles turning up all the time." I thought of my other selves lying in shallow graves and shivered.

Tom took a hand off the wheel and placed it on my thigh. My temperature rose at the warmth of his hand through my jeans. "There is no evidence," he said. "This is how we kill our other selves." He nodded at his hand. "When we touch them we merge with them. No muss, no fuss."

"What do you mean by 'merge'?" I asked, once he had removed his hand and I could breathe again.

"You could call it the opposite of mitosis." He paused and looked thoughtful, as if trying to think of the antonym for cell division. "The molecules in our bodies recognize each other and merge together, leaving one where there used to be two."

"Like the flames," I whispered, thinking of the two flames I had been watching in the bathtub. I thought of how many times the woman in the balaclava had reached out and touched me, spreading the cold through my body. I realized now that there had been no handgun or knives or other weapons.

"How many times?" I asked in a low voice, thinking of the number of dreams – or dimensions – where I had been killed. "How many times have I been murdered by this Evacuee Lillie?"

"I have witnessed her kill you four times. I managed to stop her in another eight dimensions." His teeth were gritted as he relived my death over and over again.

"Is that why you came to Green Grove? To Green Grove High?" I asked, my heart beginning to pound as I realized I could become number five. "To stop her from merging with me in this dimension?"

He nodded and I thought about his car trailing me as I walked home and the sensation of being watched through my bedroom window. Then I remembered his words in the clearing: "I have to stop saving you, Lillie."

"And how is that working out for you? For me?" I asked, my eyes flicking to the pastures around us, as if my other self would rise from the grasses that waved at me in the dimming daylight.

He looked at me, like it was a stupid question. After all, I was sitting in his car, safe and sound. "Fine," he said at last, giving me a small smile.

I released the breath I had been holding, but as it whooshed out of my chest, it was replaced by an emptiness as I thought about the four other Lillies she had killed. In particular, I wondered about the Lillie in the photo, which Tom had carried through multiple dimensions. "What happened to–?"

"We were married," Tom whispered. "We were living at Rose Hill. It was my seventh dimension and my first time in love with you."

A memory flashed into my mind of the greenhouse and then of the courtyard with the fountain. It was where he had proposed. A tear pricked my eye, like a bee sting. It explained my homesickness at Rose Hill. It also explained why I could see Tom on the polished dance floor of the ballroom and walking down the sweeping staircase, his hand resting on the carved banister. I had accessed her memories, the memories of the Lillie from his seventh dimension.

"Evacuee Lillie killed your Lillie," I whispered, realizing that it was the reason for his broken heart.

"And our unborn baby." For the first time his exterior was peeled back, as if the shiny paint had been stripped from a brand new car and underneath I had found a later model.

My chest heaved with my own sorrow. It was going to be a girl. We were going to name her Rose after Rose Hill. "A beautiful flower, just like her mother," Tom had said as he stroked my rounded belly.

My hand went to my stomach and I had to remind myself again that they were not my memories. Instead they were the memories of a Lillie who had lived in another dimension, who had died in another dimension. I knew she had been older than me when she had died and the number twenty-four flashed in my mind. The vein in my temple throbbed as I thought of his words, his acknowledgement that she had been his first love. My sorrow subsided and another emotion surfaced – envy.

I was jealous of this other me and for a moment I found myself wanting to live her life instead of my own. I could see myself reaching out towards her with a shaking hand and I shivered at the realization that I also had memories from the woman in the balaclava, aka Evacuee Lillie.

"How can you tell an evacuee from a non-evacuee, like me?"

Tom hesitated and then turned his head, pointing to the barcode tattoo behind his ear. "We bear this brand."

My fingers went to my own ear, brushing the hot skin behind it, knowing without looking that there was no matching tattoo. I had memories of other dimensions from my other selves, but I was from this dimension. "Jo has a tattoo," I whispered. "Is she from your dimension?"

Tom nodded and my heart squeezed, as if he had reached into my chest and closed his fist around it. "How? When?" My eyes stung with tears again as I realized that the Jo who had cut her hair and had thrown herself at Mr Bailey was an evacuee.

I turned towards the window and let the tears roll down my cheeks, as I thought about my Jo – the girl who had watched hundreds of hours of musicals with me, singing along to all of the songs in *Gentlemen Prefer Blondes* and laughing as I danced around her bedroom like Audrey Hepburn in *Funny Face*. "What if we called 911?" I asked suddenly.

Tom shook his head. "You may as well be calling the Circle," he said.

"What is the Circle?"

He gritted his teeth. "A band of vigilante evacuees. They have basically become our government."

"Then what if I went to the Circle?"

Tom let out a short bark. "The Circle is all about the secrecy of the theory of everything. They have been terrorizing evacuees into merging since the Evacuation. If we decide not to merge they call us 'Enemies of the Circle.' I was added to their hit list a couple of hundred years ago," he said, making them sound like bounty hunters. He glanced out his side window and it suddenly struck me that these vigilantes were just like his own Evacuee Lillie; a danger to his life.

"The theory of everything has a price tag and the Circle does not want us selling state secrets."

"Dimension secrets," I corrected dolefully.

I thought about the pros and cons of merging for an evacuee. The pro column read like a thesis – a ready-made family, friends and career. That being said, Tom was not exactly a janitor. How could he drive a Benz and live in a mansion without following the example of the Circle like Evacuee Lillie? "How do you make a buck?" I asked, nervously shifting my weight on the plush leather seat.

"I swindle my grandmother through Lorraine, while my other self is off at boarding school or skiing in the French Alps," he told me. His tone was light-hearted, almost cheeky, but I could hear a twinge of guilt in his voice, as if he knew he was on easy street. Of course, he was. He was living the high life while others were cleaning toilets or killing themselves, but I was relieved to know I could tick him off the list of murderers.

The sun had set by the time we pulled into my street. I caught a glimpse of my reflection in the side mirror. I was pale and drawn under the streetlights, my dark circles making my eyes look like deep holes – wormholes. I stared into my eyes as if looking for my other selves through the fabric of space and time.

As soon as the SUV came to a standstill, the front door swung open and Deb came running down the path with her hair billowing and bangles clacking, as if I had been gone a year instead of an afternoon.

"Lillie! Where on Earth have you been?" she asked as I climbed out of the Benz. Dawn was standing in the open doorway behind her and I heard the rhythmic beat of bongos that told me Blaze was elsewhere in the house. "I tried your cell. I tried Jo."

"It was my fault, Ms Hart," Tom said, climbing out of the SUV before I could remind Deb she had confiscated my cell, which was broken in any case. He gave my mother a smile that made her duck her head like a schoolgirl. Even I had to hold onto the edge of the door or be bowled over myself. That boy could have sold a drowning man a glass of water with that smile.

Tom walked around the polished hood and stuck out his hand in introduction. "Tom Windsor-Smith."

Deb suddenly dropped his hand, like it had burst into flames, and then backed up the path as if Tom was a coyote she had met on a walking trail. I suddenly remembered her reaction to his last name yesterday when she had reverse-parked the car on the sidewalk. "Come on, Lillie," she ordered, turning towards the house.

I raised my eyebrows at Tom, whose lips had formed a thin line. "She used to think of me as a son," he muttered as he watched his former mother-in-law slam the front door on his seventh dimension.

The comment made me wonder about his parents. Lorraine had mentioned them, but it had seemed from our conversation that his grandmother was his guardian – in this dimension at least.

"Lillie!"

I sighed, reminding myself to make my mother a pot of chamomile tea. "Coming, Deb!" I looked down at my feet and cleared my throat, wondering how to say goodbye after our day together, after our lifetimes together.

Tom moved towards me, lifting his hand to brush my cheek and my knees went weak under his touch. He leaned in and our lips met again. The tenderness of his kiss and the weight of his hands around my waist made me as hot as a sauna, despite the temperature being below fifty degrees.

The front door opened again. "Lillie?" It was Dawn. "Your mother wants you to come inside. Now."

I separated myself from Tom reluctantly.

"Sweet dreams," he whispered, brushing my cheek again.

I closed my eyes, soaking in his touch.

"You know," he said, as I turned towards the house. "Robert Frost was the guy who wrote that poem about the two roads. And in it, he says he wishes he could have traveled both."

He remained on the sidewalk, his arms folded against the cold, as I walked into the house, worlds apart from the girl who had walked out of it seven hours earlier.

22

I lay awake until the early hours of the morning, watching the shadows creep across my ceiling. Without Tom the questions had piled up again and I was beginning to feel like a pinprick of dust on a table, waiting for Evacuee Lillie to come along with a damp cloth.

I thought of the hundreds of empty film canisters under my bed, but it was Tom who now held the ball of twine, who told me where I had been and where I was going.

The headlights of a car passed through my bedroom for the fifth time, sweeping across my wall like a beam of light from a lighthouse. I listened to the hum of its engine, wondering if it was Tom. Maybe he was on patrol, doing laps, looking for the other Lillie.

The thought warmed me like a hot water bottle and I snuggled under the covers, mulling over what he had told me at the sandhills. There were questions I had managed to answer on my own, like piecing together the corner and edge pieces of a puzzle.

I remembered my hallucination in the darkroom last month, where he had disappeared into thin air, leaving me wondering if I was high from the chemicals. I now knew it had been a vision of another dimension where Tom had decided to pay me a visit, coming down to the darkroom where he knew we would be on our own. Maybe he had decided to clear it up from the get go, before he even gave me the lift in the rain or punched Jackson at the railroad crossing. I wondered if the Lillie from that dimension was miles ahead of me, packing overnight bags for Rose Hill.

And then there was my conversation with Tom where he had claimed his rudeness was unlike him. In the memories I had from other dimensions Tom had been a gentleman through and through.

I reached into my mind and saw myself sitting in the lounge at Rose Hill, one hand on my swollen stomach. I had been complaining about my constant cravings for peanut butter and pineapple. Ten minutes later I had a serving platter of what Tom called pineapple butter – slices of pineapple with peanut butter spread on them – which had made me laugh and Rose kick with glee, her foot stretching my skin.

I lay the palm of my hand on my flat stomach and sighed, reminding myself again that these were not my memories. They were from another Lillie from another dimension – Lillie from the Seventh Dimension. I wondered when the two of us had split and who was the original.

Neither, I thought. We were both clones of a Lillie who had long been lost in the infinite dimensions, splitting whenever two doors opened and she walked through both. I saw her as an onion being peeled layer by layer with each split and hugged myself, as if I could hold my own layers together.

My eyes were hanging out of my head when Deb woke me the next morning for a shift at Tree of Life. My dark circles made me look like I had been sucker punched twice.

I stood for twenty minutes with a customer who was tossing up between a poncho and a woolen sweater, daydreaming of the dimension where Deb had decided to let me sleep in and wondering if that Lillie was dreaming about me too.

"What do you think?" the woman asked, pulling the garments down over her short, frizzy hair one at a time.

I plastered on a smile and told her the poncho suited her body shape, like it mattered. She went with the sweater; I knew she had gone with the poncho in another dimension.

I took my lunch break early and headed for the bakery.

I scanned the tables for Tom, knowing this was where we had hung out in other dimensions. My heart sank when I saw he was a no-show. I stood in line behind a college guy who used to date Melissa and his new girlfriend, who I recognized from the Duck-In Diner.

"Hungry?" a voice asked as I scanned the menu.

I turned and saw Tom. He was looking picture-perfect as usual in a gray coat that made his pale blue eyes look wintry. He grinned down at me and I threw my arms around his neck, nuzzling into his collar until I found the warmth of his skin.

"I kind of have a craving for pineapple butter," I joked.

"You remember," he murmured, his arms squeezing me until I was breathless.

Tom ordered two salad sandwiches with chips and freshly squeezed juice.

"Pineapple?" I asked with a laugh when they delivered the tall glasses of bright yellow liquid to our table.

"With a hint of peanut butter," he responded with a wink.

I smiled at his joke as I picked up half of my sandwich. "I have a thousand questions, but only twenty minutes for my lunch break."

He looked around and grimaced. "This is kind of public, Lillie," he said, even though there was no one at the surrounding tables, except the college guy and the girl from the Duck-In Diner, who were in the middle of their own loved-up conversation.

"You are such a scaredy-cat," I teased. "A scaredy Tom-cat."

He looked at me with recognition and I knew it was a nickname he had been called by another Lillie. My mind went to the eight year-old Tom who had held her hand as they skated on the lake, going faster and faster until he called out for her to slow down.

In the memory, I closed my eyes against the icy wind. "You are such a scaredy-cat," I had taunted, in return for him calling me a chicken. "A scaredy Tom-cat." My voice had echoed across the lake and suddenly there was a crack, as the ice broke beneath my skates.

"You saved my life," I whispered and then shook my head. "You saved her life," I corrected, reaching across the table to touch his hand. I traced the deep lines on his palm, as I remembered those hands grabbing me as I fell through the ice; the coldness had been like a clamp around my chest as I hit the water.

The blade of one of my skates had clipped his chin, splashing blood across the ice, but he had held me tight and pulled me out, warming me with his body as we walked to Rose Hill. No, I corrected myself again. He had been warming Evacuee Lillie.

"I should have let her drown," he said bitterly.

A stab of pain went through my chest and I withdrew my hand.

How could he have made the decision to let her drown? How could he have known that they would both be evacuated from their dimension years later and that she would draw the short straw and slide from dimension to dimension on her own? That she would decide to merge with her other selves rather than go it alone? It would be like looking at a baby and knowing it was going to become the next Adolf Hitler or Charles Manson.

Lillie from the Seventh Dimension, on the other hand, had drawn the long straw and landed in the lap of luxury, i.e. Tom. I was surprised when another pang of jealousy went through me as I thought of her climbing under the covers and into his arms each night. His bare chest was smooth and muscular under her hands and his breath was soft in her ear as he whispered goodnight. I closed my eyes, torn between blocking out the memories and watching them like old home movies.

When I opened my eyes, Tom was poking his sandwich and shifting the chips around on his plate. A strange sensation settled in my stomach as I watched him, like–

"Déjà vu," I whispered.

He looked up and a twinkle came into his eyes, like shards of glass sparkling in his pale blue irises. "Do you know want to know what causes déjà vu?" he asked.

"They say it happens when one eye records a scene faster than the other," I said. Told you I liked trivia.

He shook his head. "It happens when you have the same experience in two dimensions," he said.

I guess I could understand how in a recently split dimension we could both be sitting at this table in another universe, like if I had ordered a ham sandwich instead of a salad sandwich. And how I could pick up my glass and take a sip of my juice at the same moment in both dimensions. I thought back to one of my last sensations of déjà vu in the quad. It seemed Sylv did flash her underwear too much if she was doing it in multiple dimensions.

"Want more trivia?" Tom asked in a low voice.

"Do I want more trivia?" I asked, as if it were a trick question. There were a thousand blank pages in my inner encyclopedia that needed to be filled.

"OK," Tom conceded with a smile. "What about ghosts?"

"What about them?"

"Do you know what they are?"

I gave him a blank look.

"Go on. Guess."

"Um." I flicked through the pages of my mind. E… F… G… Ghetto… Gherkin… Ghosts… "Cats," I announced.

He gave me an amused smile. "Cats?"

"Yep. Their eyes glow in the dark and they say when cats get up in the rafters or in the crawl space, they howl like banshees."

"Sorry, Lillie," he said with a low chuckle, "but ghosts are not cats."

I pouted.

"Ghosts," he said, leaning in as if we were telling scary stories around a campfire, "are visions of other dimensions. They can seem like hallucinations."

Like Tom in the darkroom, I thought.

He leaned back in his chair. "It can be a trip to get a glimpse of someone who lives in your house in another dimension or someone walking through a wall that exists in your dimension, but not in theirs. You can imagine too what people think when they see someone who is dead in their dimension, but alive in another."

I remembered Deb telling me how she was visited by her mother – my grandmother – a week after her death. Deb had walked into the kitchen and there was Gran, washing the dishes. I wondered if she would have been scrubbing dried vegetable lasagna from plates if she had known she had died in our dimension or if she would have been out spending the last of her social security. Of course, her only hint would have been a dream about dying or a cold shiver down her spine.

I sipped my juice thoughtfully, wondering what Jo would give to see her mom, even if it was in another dimension. I could remember her once saying she could imagine watching musicals with her mom, which told me she had survived in at least one dimension. But my Jo was gone. She is an evacuee, I reminded myself.

"Another piece of trivia," I begged Tom, as a waitress cleared my plate.

Tom thought for a moment, his eyes following the waitress until she was out of earshot. "Soulmates."

I looked at him and his eyes drew me in.

"Soulmates," he continued, "are two people who have loved each other in another dimension."

"Us," I whispered.

"Lillie."

I looked up at the sound of my name and saw Mr Green standing a couple of feet from our table, looking between the two of us with a bemused smile. He was nowhere near as thin as he had been the last time I had seen him and his cheeks had a healthy flush.

"How are you?" he asked.

"Good. And you?"

"Great," he said, his eyes returning to Tom.

"This is Tom," I explained. "Tom, this is Mr Green."

I thought he would remind me to call him Dave again, but his attention was elsewhere. "Nice to meet you, Tom," he said, sticking out his hand.

"Likewise," Tom said, standing up and greeting him.

"Have you been in town long?" Mr Green asked, holding onto the handshake.

"A while."

The older man nodded and then dropped his hand. There was an awkward silence before Mr Green said, "See you around, Lillie. Tom."

I frowned, thinking it had been years since Mr Green had called me Lillie, instead of Pipsqueak. I lowered my voice and explained to Tom how Mr Green had months, maybe weeks to live.

Tom shook his head. "That man will live a lot longer than a few months."

"But the doctors said it had spread…" I started, and then my mouth fell open as I realized Mr Green had merged, like his daughter. "How do you know?" I asked, not wanting to believe the last member of the Green family had become an evacuee.

Tom turned his head and pointed to the tattoo behind his ear. I reached out and touched the black markings. "Ouch."

"Hot?" he asked with a grimace. "It can be a pain, literally. It heats up when evacuees are around, but it can be a bit hit and miss. I think the technology is breaking down."

"Maybe those two are the evacuees," I said, nodding at the college guy and the Duck-In Diner girl, who were playing footsies under the table. I knew I was grasping at straws, but Mr Green was my last link to my Jo.

Tom shook his head. "I saw your Mr Green on the street earlier. The tattoo heated up then as well."

I slumped in my seat, wondering why the evacuees were sliding into my dimension instead of the infinite other dimensions in the universe – Evacuee Lillie, Evacuee Tom, Evacuee Jo, and Evacuee Mr Green.

"Entanglement," Tom said when I asked. He told me the story of a girl who had saved the life of a boy by stemming the flow of blood after he was hit by a school bus. Ten years later the same boy saved the same girl from choking in a restaurant. They later married and had children. "It is quantum physics," he explained.

"Spooky," I said.

He smiled. "Einstein actually called it 'spooky action at a distance.'"

I wondered whether I was also entangled with Evacuee Lillie. "Is she going to kill me? Evacuee Lillie?" I whispered, not wanting to be her fifth victim. It was like walking around with a bull's-eye on my back.

Tom put his hand on mine, his thumb stroking my skin. "No," he said with a small smile. "You are safe, Lillie. She is gone. Thank God," he added.

"Where?" I asked.

Tom looked at me with a furrowed brow.

"Another dimension," I realized. I should have been celebrating at the thought that she had left my dimension, but the thought that she could return put the cork firmly back in the champagne bottle. "For how long?" I pressed. "She could slide back in tomorrow."

Tom shook his head. "You are talking about another dimension. In this dimension she has been and gone." He elaborated when he saw my blank look. "Evacuees slide into a dimension together on the date of the Evacuation, which means we can only visit a dimension one time and one time only. If we slide out, we slide out." He made a cutting motion with his hand.

"Really?"

"Do you think I would have chased her out of eight dimensions otherwise?"

I looked at him for a long time, our eyes connecting across the table. "I think you would have chased her out of a thousand dimensions over and over again to save my life," I said.

He nodded soberly.

"How do you make her slide?" I asked, unsure if I wanted to know.

"I think your lunch break finished about ten minutes ago," Tom said quietly.

"Do you kill her?" I persisted.

He leveled his eyes at me and I thought he was going to say we had to call it a day. "You cannot kill an evacuee," he said.

I blinked. "What?"

"When we die we simply slide into another dimension."

"What if you have a heart attack?"

"I would slide."

"What if you are hit by a truck?"

"I would slide."

"Drown?"

He looked at me as if asking if really wanted him to repeat himself and then he looked at his watch again. "We can talk about this tomorrow," he said.

"But Tree of Life is closed on Sundays," I whined like a child, "which means I will be under house arrest again."

He lifted my hand and brushed his lips against my skin, sending a rush of adrenaline through my body. "I'll be at the park at noon," he murmured. "In case you get paroled."

And even though I knew we had spent hundreds of years together, I started counting the seconds until tomorrow anyway.

23

When the girls turned up for our Sunday session the next morning, Deb was like a levee at the front door. She sprung a leak though, under the weight of the reasoning from Jo and the sass from Sylv.

"One visitor," she told me.

"Sylv."

"Jo?"

"No. Sylv." Of course Deb thought I would ask for my best friend – and I would have if I could have – but that girl on the porch, stamping her feet in the cold was an evacuee, like the Lillie in my nightmares.

I pressed my hand against my bedroom window, my nose inches from the pane, as I watched Jo walk out the front gate and down the street. Her hair had been dyed brown again and the ends of her ragged bob had been trimmed. She turned, as if sensing my gaze, and I hid behind the curtain.

"Good God," Sylv said as she walked into my bedroom.

I spun around. "What?"

"Deb puts you in the hole for a couple of days and you turn into a nutcase, like that busybody Humpback Harding."

"What do you mean?" I asked indignantly, swiping at the curtain a few times, as if I were dusting the fabric, instead of using it to hide from my former best friend. "I'm like a hundred and ten percent sane," I said, pushing thoughts of parallel dimensions and evacuees out of my mind.

Sylv raised her eyebrows and ran a hand through her hair, which was now blond with bright blue and green streaks. "A hundred and ten percent? I rest my case."

I raised my own eyebrows in return. "A math lesson?" I laughed. "You think a hypotenuse is an animal in Africa."

Sylv rolled her eyes. "Hypotenuse. Hippopotamus." She perched on the edge of my desk, looking like a macaw.

"I like your hair," I lied.

Sylv grinned. "Turnip told me to get rid of it by tomorrow. Should I shave it and give him a heart attack?"

"Only if you want to get suspended like me."

"That jerk said he would expel me." She sighed dramatically and then brightened. "Jo let me dye her hair last night."

"I know," I said, with a nod to the window.

"Aha!" Sylv shouted, pointing an accusing finger. "You have totally turned into Humpback Harding."

I smiled. "OK. I might have turned into her for one second."

Sylv frowned. "Is everything OK with you and Jo?"

"Why?"

"Because you just kicked her in the guts, Lillie. She had one foot in the door before she realized Deb had said Sylv, instead of Jo."

I hesitated. Jo and I were as good as gold. It was evacuee Jo I hated. "I kind of need a hand with sneaking out," I finally said. "You know Jo. She would give me a lecture."

"A jailbreak?" Sylv asked, her eyes glimmering like gemstones. "Woohoo! And here I was thinking I was going to go deaf before the day was out." She tilted her head towards the sound of the bongos from the back room.

"I kind of have to go on my own," I said sheepishly.

Her eyebrows shot up again. "Who are you meeting?"

My flushed cheeks answered her question.

"Tom!" she gasped. "Spill. I want the dirt."

"I saw him on Friday," I said cautiously, not wanting to spill dimension secrets. "He took me to the sand hills."

"The sand hills?" She clicked her tongue stud as she considered this location. "Is there a lookout?"

I laughed. "I think you and Simon should stick to the reservoir."

"Brandon."

"Sorry. Brandon."

For a moment it looked like Sylv was blushing. "We did the deed," she announced. "After the Masquerade Ball. Down at the reservoir."

I tilted my head, wondering whether, in spite of all her talk, Sylv had been a virgin like me and Jo. "And?"

I asked, crossing my fingers she would spare me the details.

"OK. I guess." She shrugged, chewing her bottom lip with a small smile as she thought about it. "What about you and Tom? Did you–?"

"We kissed," I said quickly.

Sylv clasped her hands to her chest and sighed dreamily. I frowned. What was with the swooning? Sylv was normally a bag them and tag them kind of girl. I walked up to her without a word, turning her head and brushing back her hair.

"What the hell, Lillie?" she complained, as I checked behind her ear, but there was no tattoo.

"Sorry," I said, but I had no excuse. "I have to work out how to get around Deb," I said, changing the subject.

Sylv stared at me for a moment and then asked, "Has she put bars on your window or something?"

I breathed a sigh of relief, wondering if the dimension had split and there was a Lillie who had to explain herself to Sylv. "Not yet," I said dryly.

Sylv smiled. "Well, I guess I could cover for you. If you get the TV in here and put on a decent DVD." She put on a sugary-sweet voice. "Oh, hi Deb. Lillie just went to the kitchen to get popcorn like one second ago. You would have passed her in the hallway. No? She must be in the bathroom then." She grinned, her nose crinkling, and I laughed, reveling in her lightened mood.

"Now," Sylv said. "We have to get you glammed up for your date."

It was my first opportunity to prepare for Tom. The past two times I had run into him on the hop, but this time I pulled on my good pair of jeans and a pale yellow knit Sylv had nicked from Deb. Sylv blow-dried my hair so it had a bit of shape and clipped back my bangs with a gold-colored hair clip. She tried to pull it into a ponytail a couple of times, but I slapped at her hands until she gave up.

"I wish I had proper make-up," she said, appraising my dark circles.

"You know what they say about a poor workman blaming his tools."

"What if his tools are a broken hammer and rusted nails?" Sylv complained, and then she perked up as she had a thought. "What about Deb? She must have make-up."

"First her top and now her make-up? Do you want me to be locked up for life?"

"Oh ye of little faith," Sylv said, which I thought was ironic, coming from an atheist.

Sylv found Deb in the back room, in the middle of a bongo lesson with Blaze. I could hear Dawn singing along to the beat, a weird wailing sound. It made the pan pipe sound like Mozart. The noise stopped and I bit my lip, wondering if Sylv was going to blow my cover. I heard her say, "Me and Lillie are giving each other makeovers. Do you mind if we borrow your make-up? I think your blue eye shadow would really suit her. You know, like mother, like daughter."

A few minutes later, Sylv returned with an assortment of blush and eye shadow in a hand-woven basket.

"The colors are all wrong," I moaned, pawing through the bright greens and blues.

"You think?" Sylv asked, applying bright orange eye shadow to her eyelids and batting them at me.

I laughed.

"Is that your mom?" Sylv suddenly asked.

My eyes snapped to the doorway, but Sylv was reaching into the basket. She dug out a handful of photos, the edges of which were curled with age. I snatched them from her and held them to my chest. Photos of Deb? Really?

There were three black and white shots. The first showed a small girl holding a bunny rabbit. Even in monochrome there was no mistaking those large emerald eyes. The next was of a teenage girl, perhaps a year or two younger than me, who was dressed in a cheerleading uniform. A cheerleading uniform? I laughed out loud. Maybe that was when she had bought the ice skates. The final photo showed a more familiar Deb. She was probably my age. Her hair was long and flowing. Her smile was wide. And she was straddling a motorbike. Yep. A motorbike. And on the front was a guy in leather, his face turned from the camera. It could have been my father for all I knew.

I put the photos in my desk drawer, feeling like I had found a ball of twine that could lead me through the maze that was my mother.

I ended up sticking with my own brown mascara, but I did let Sylv put a bit of blush on my cheekbones and a dash of gold eye shadow on my lids.

"To draw attention away from those dark circles," she explained.

I slipped on my gold-colored flats. "Do I look like an Oscar?" I asked, as I studied my reflection.

"You look like a model," Sylv said, stepping back and surveying me like a proud mother.

Unlike Deb, I thought as I climbed out of the window, my legs like rigor mortis in my too tight jeans. I was letting her down left, right and center at the moment.

I snuck along the side of the house and climbed over the fence with a final wave to Sylv, who had agreed to watch a stack of Marilyn Monroe flicks after my search for non-musical DVDs turned up an instructional yoga video and a few PETA documentaries.

When I reached the park I scanned the dustbowl for Tom, my eyes skimming a handful of kids tossing a baseball in the diamond, their voices like the shriek of birds. I turned and surveyed the street, beginning to feel sick to my stomach as I wondered if he had decided to ditch our date.

It was like a shot of morphine when I saw the SUV glide down the street and perform a U-turn. I opened the door and climbed in within a second of it pulling into the curb, as if Evacuee Lillie was on my tail.

"Are you OK?" Tom asked, his blue eyes wide. Worried.

I lowered my gaze to his lips, which were slightly parted as he waited for my answer.

"Fine," I breathed, letting my eyes go to the clock on the dashboard and feeling foolish when I saw it was noon on the dot. "Except I just broke out of Alcatraz. Deb must be a prison warden in another dimension."

Tom smiled an easy smile. "You should meet my grandmother." He waited for a delivery van to pass before pulling out onto the street. "She reminds me of the Red Queen. You know, from *Alice in Wonderland*." He frowned. "Maybe she was the Red Queen in whatever dimension Lewis Carroll was channeling." But then he shook his head. "The timing would be wrong. It was published in the 1800s I think."

"1865," I confirmed, surprising myself with this literary knowledge. "And his name was Charles Dodgson. Lewis Carroll was his pen name."

Tom raised his eyebrows and then shrugged. "Well, Red Queen or no Red Queen, I could wrap my grandmother around my little finger by the time I could talk."

"What a surprise," I said sarcastically, wondering if anyone was immune to his charm.

Tom shrugged. "What can I say? You can get away with anything when you know how."

"Murder," I concurred, without thinking.

His hands tightened around the steering wheel and I knew he was thinking of his first love – Lillie from the Seventh Dimension. There was a pang in my chest as I thought about her too.

I looked out of the window and saw we were heading towards the railroad crossing; the houses were fewer and farther between here with trees filling the gaps. My spirits soared. I was looking forward to seeing Rose Hill with my new memories, wandering through rooms that had belonged to me in another place and another time.

When I saw the skid marks on the road I glanced over at Tom, recalling the look on his face as he had belted Jackson.

It suddenly made sense. Tom had chased Evacuee Lillie from this dimension, but then Jackson had come close to killing me himself. I closed my eyes, remembering my dream of being hit by the train and the coldness that had spread through my body. I shuddered, realizing that in another dimension Jackson had slammed on the brakes at the last minute and the dimension had split, leaving me alive and another Lillie dead.

I could see the funeral in my mind, my mother laying a Lily of the Valley on the wooden casket with a shaking hand. Tom was there too, standing in the background as I was lowered into the ground, his hands balled into fists at the side of his body, raging at the loss of another Lillie.

"Why were you at the railroad crossing?" I asked, remembering that he had said he had been off track.

His lips tightened and I guessed it was a question he would rather not answer. "I wanted a break," he admitted. "I thought I could be a teenager again for one dimension." He stared through the windshield, as if boring holes through the glass.

I swallowed hard. "You wanted a break?" I asked. The words rotated through my mind, each syllable stabbing at my heart. A break. A break. A break. A break from Lillie in the Thirty-Fifth Dimension. I stared at him wide-eyed, wondering why he had chased Evacuee Lillie out of my dimension if he wanted a normal life. For one dimension. My dimension.

"And being a teenager means hanging out with Melissa and the Mutts?" I asked coldly, thinking again of Lillie from the Seventh Dimension and how he would have hung out with her in an instant.

He shook his head. "It means letting go of my past. Of my Lillie." He winced and his voice dropped to a whisper. "And I did."

"You think you let her go? Your Lillie?" I asked incredulously. "Look at me, Tom. Do I remind you of someone?" I glared at him. "Do I?" I grabbed his arm, my fingers wrapping around the thick material of his jacket as I gave him a shake. "Look at me!"

He did as he was told, his irises shining like silver mirrors.

"If you could slide into your seventh dimension again you would in a heartbeat, but you said it yourself – once you slide out, you slide out." I knew I was hurting him, but I could care less. I wanted to hurt him, like he was hurting me.

Tom pulled the wheel to the right and we skidded to a stop in the dirt, pebbles pinging on the undercarriage. We sat in silence, as if at the crossroads again, and I wondered if I should bail. I guess in another dimension I did, because I thought I could see the other Lillie in the side mirror, her gold sweater shimmering in the sunlight as she walked towards town with a heavy heart.

"Lillie," Tom said, reminding me I was in the SUV, in this dimension at least. "I let go when I fell in love with you." He turned to look at me and I felt myself being sucked into his orbit, like a satellite.

"Like every other Lillie," I said. "You call that letting go? Trading in one Lillie for another?"

Tom shook his head. "The Lillie I married was my first love – my only love – until now." He closed his eyes and his words hung between us, waiting for me to pick them up. My heart swelled as I realized I was his second love. Not his twenty-fourth or thirty-first, or thirty-fifth as I had thought.

He reached across and popped open the glove compartment. It fell open and out rolled my cardigan, the one I had been wearing when he had rescued me in the rain. I must have left it in his SUV.

"You know, in this dimension they call that stalking," I said with a growing smile.

"Lillie, I thought I would never fall in love again. I–"

I leaned forward and kissed him, my hands on the back of his neck, pulling him towards me, until it seemed like we would merge.

When we drove up the avenue at Rose Hill I surveyed the grounds with nostalgia. It was like every tree, every blade of grass held a memory.

We passed an older couple as we walked into the foyer – a man wearing beige trousers and a navy sweater, and a woman dripping with jewelry. I returned their smiles, feeling at home with the swanky guests.

"Welcome back, Lillie," Lorraine said, beaming at me with red-lipsticked lips. Of course, she was referring to my last visit with Jackson, but her words resounded, warming me from the tips of my toes to the top of my head. She held a hand to her chest as we passed and I wondered whether she was thinking of the broken heart she thought I had given Tom.

Tom led me through the hotel, down the hallway and past the ballroom. The doors were open and I caught a glimpse of its chandeliers glistening as they caught the light. I paused, thinking I could see us in the crystals, dancing our bridal waltz, before Tom led me through another set of double doors and into the grounds.

"I should have brought my camera," I said. The two rolls of film I had finished on my last visit had been just a nibble of what was a multi-tiered cake. I now knew that a hundred yards to our left was a hedge maze that had been established in the early 1900s. I also knew that where the rose garden was planted there had been an old oak in the Seventh Dimension with a tire swing hanging from one of its sturdy branches.

"Next time," Tom said as we walked along a path lined with golden-rod, our feet crunching on the gravel.

When we reached the "Keep Out" sign, Tom unclipped the chain that blocked the flagstone path.

I hesitated, before taking his hand again, holding it tight as we walked along the uneven stones from my nightmares. My flats slipped on the moss and I had to cling to Tom with my other hand, like we were ice skating again.

When I saw the courtyard with its fountain, my heart went into my throat and I glanced over my shoulder, even though I knew Evacuee Lillie had been and gone from this dimension.

"I know this courtyard," I whispered.

Tom nodded. We both knew it was where I had been killed, where our – I mean, their – baby had been killed. I touched my stomach, tracing its flat lines. But my melancholy subsided when I remembered it was also where Tom had proposed.

I closed my eyes and saw him handing me a jewelry box. No – handing Lillie from the Seventh Dimension a jewelry box. She was sitting on the edge of the fountain and as she lifted the lid I heard Tom say, "Marry me, Lillie." A warmth spread through my chest as if I had heard the words with my own ears.

"It would have been at least three centuries since I last set foot in this courtyard," Tom said, moving towards the fountain and running a hand along its brickwork, his fingers finding the grooves. "In the greenhouse too."

He returned from his reverie, taking my hand again. "I had the kitchen prepare us a picnic," he said, and as we rounded the fountain I saw a tartan rug spread out on the flagstones and a wicker basket surrounded by a feast of sandwiches, sliced fruit, cheese and crackers.

The weather was cool, but the sun was shining, shimmering on the glasses of mineral water. Tom leaned against an oversized cushion propped against the damp bricks of the fountain and I was folded into his arms, popping grapes into my mouth and listening to his heartbeat under his T-shirt, as steady as a march.

"They say the human heart beats an average of fifty times per minute," I told him. "Do you want to know the average heart-rate of a mouse? Five hundred beats a minute."

"You and your trivia," he said with a chuckle. "It used to drive me up the wall."

I sat up and looked at him through narrowed eyes. "You do know I am my own person. My own Lillie."

He nodded. "I know." He considered me with those pale blue eyes and then reached up to trail his fingers through my hair, combing it from my temple to the nape of my neck.

I closed my eyes. "What was she like?" I asked. "The Lillie you married?"

I opened my eyes as he withdrew his hand.

"As serious as a heart attack," he said with a sad smile on his lips. "You had to build up a sweat to get her to loosen up. Have a laugh."

His words warmed me to the core. I had been worried we were so alike that I would continue to wonder if it was me or her that he was kissing.

His eyes grew distant, like he was seeing into another dimension. "She was as bound to her notebook as you are to your camera. She wrote poetry. She was even published in a few anthologies."

"Wow," I whispered, leaning up against him again. A published poet. My chest swelled with pride, even though in my own words I was my own Lillie. I decided

I could take a little credit, as I realized my newfound knowledge about Lewis Carroll and other literary tidbits had come from Lillie the Poet.

Tom leaned into my ear and spoke in a low voice. "I call him my love, my soulmate. This boy, now a man, and soon a father. Together a few short years–"

"–that seem like an eternity in my dreams," I finished, recalling the words as if I had written the poem myself. I sucked in a sharp breath and whirled on him. "You didn't tell her? About the theory of everything? About the Evacuation?"

He shook his head sadly, turning his head to look at the fountain, as if seeing the moment of her death. "I wanted that normal life." He scowled at himself, at Evacuee Lillie.

"If you wanted a normal life you could have merged," I pointed out.

Tom shook his head. "The first time I saw anyone merge was when Evacuee Lillie merged with my wife in my Seventh Dimension," he said. "From that moment I realized I was not going to get along with anyone associated with the Circle."

We fell silent, and I pulled a throw rug over my legs and watched the red crossbills flit in and out of the hedge until I worked up the courage to ask my next question. "Tell me about the Lillie from your dimension. You said you used to be friends."

It took him a while to answer and I glanced up at him, wondering if he had heard.

"Friends," he said slowly. "Did I say that? I guess we were friends. It was a long time ago though. Another lifetime." He stared into space for a while, his irises deepening to a cerulean blue, before he asked, "What do you want to know?"

"How did you meet?"

"My parents used to come back to Green Grove every summer in my dimension, at Christmas as well." He rubbed his forehead, as if the conversation were hurting his head. "Deb and my father were childhood friends." He paused. "In this dimension too."

"What?"

He shrugged. "I guess that was why she freaked out when she heard my name. My father grew up in Green Grove. It was my mother who came from England. From money. My father was a poor budding photographer, living in the sticks."

"A photographer?" I asked, thinking about his criticism of my photos and his hatred of photography in general.

"He got my mom hooked. They traveled around the world taking photos together. You have one of their books. The Geldings?" And then he added as an explanation. "My mother was a Windsor-Smith. My father is a Gelding."

My eyes widened as I realized he was talking about my favorite photography book – the one the girls had given me for my eleventh birthday.

"I was born in Australia," he said, which explained his accent, "but my parents sent me back to England when I was about five. I barely saw them after that, except for at Rose Hill. My grandmother would bring me out here to meet up with them. She changed my last name to hers when I was eight, given she was my legal guardian and all."

"What happened to your parents after the Evacuation?" I asked.

He tilted his head to stare up into the foliage and from this angle I could see his tattoo: W=VxT...

"They wanted to photograph the end of the world."

I could hear the bitterness in his voice and realized this was where his hatred of photography had come from. His parents had put their photography above everything, their own lives, their own son. I kicked myself for talking about my camera earlier.

"When I was around seven Deb drove me out to Rose Hill," I said, before the silence could settle again. "She asked for your father, but no one was home."

He looked down at me. "In my dimension we never missed a summer."

My mind went to Tom from my dimension and I wondered whether he was dreaming about Evacuee Tom like I was dreaming about Evacuee Lillie.

My Tom spoke again, breaking into my thoughts. "By the way, it was her that liked trivia."

"Who?"

"The Lillie from my dimension."

"Oh." I had forgotten that I had her memories too, like any other Lillie from any other dimension. I wondered which of us had been the first trivia-buff. I liked to think it was me.

"She also had a talent for making a mess." He smiled fondly at the memory. "That girl could clutter an empty room. She held onto everything, old pens, movie tickets. She even had a shoebox of rocks we had collected in the sand hills."

Well, that explained my messy streak. It also told me Evacuee Lillie had crushed on Tom like Sylv crushed on Taylor Blackwood. Movie tickets? A shoebox of rocks? I wondered if Tom realized their relationship had been unbalanced, like a seesaw with him on the ground and her in the sky.

"How about another treat?" Tom asked, propping me up and reaching for the basket.

I raised a hand in protest. "My stomach is struggling with the two sandwiches, the slice of cheesecake and the ten thousand grapes." I had steered clear of the other sliced fruit, the oranges especially. I ate oranges like a zombie ate flesh, juice dripping down my chin like blood.

"I think you will find room for this treat," Tom said, pulling a jewelry box out of the basket. I had a flash back – or a flash forward – as he opened the jewelry box and I saw the tiny key on a delicate white gold chain. I reached to my neck and fingered the patch of skin at the base of my throat, knowing I had worn this key in another dimension, the Seventh Dimension.

"The photo and key are the two things I hold onto when I slide," Tom explained.

"You sure travel light for someone with a truckload of baggage," I joked.

He smiled and lifted the necklace. Its chain glinted in the sun as it swung in a figure-eight, the symbol of eternity.

"What does it open?" I asked, as he put it around my neck, his fingers brushing my skin.

"I will let you work that out for yourself."

I frowned, searching those wisps of memories for a clue. There was another box, a wooden box. It had contained the engagement ring. I squinted, trying to bring the memory into focus, but then Tom leaned in and kissed me gently on my neck. He moved up towards my lips, and I pushed away the past and succumbed to the present.

Tom knew not to come in when he dropped me home, and watched me walk up the path from his SUV.

I pushed open the front door and waved over my shoulder.

When I turned I saw my mother rushing up the hallway, a blur of color in a psychedelic poncho. "Lillie! How dare you disobey me so deliberately?"

Dawn stood in the kitchen doorway and behind her was Blaze. Like I said, they were the sleeping-on-the-couch-for-a-month kind of visitors. "We thought you had been in another accident," Dawn said.

I glared at her and then at Deb. "Sylv would have told you where I was. I suppose you sent her home?" I said, looking around as if I needed a witness.

"Yes, I did," Deb said, folding her arms under her poncho. "And, yes, she did. She said you were out with a boy."

"You met him the other night. Remember? Tom?"

"I thought I told you not to see him again," she said coldly.

"Really? I don't think–"

"No, Lillie. You don't think. You don't think at all." She pointed down the hallway. "Go to your room."

I scowled. What was I? Five? My maturity increased ten-fold when I slammed the door behind me, the drywall shuddering with the force.

I slumped onto my bed "Ow." I pulled out a hardcover book from underneath me and as the pages fanned out I saw a slideshow of Australia. I checked the name on the front: The Geldings.

I doubted Sylv had been looking through it. Had Deb?

24

Deb dragged me to Tree of Life the next day, even though it was dead on a Monday. I joked that we could have set up shop at the cemetery and sold a thousand spirit boards instead of the one gemstone we sold to an eight year-old kid and the handmade card we sold to his mother.

I wondered if there was a gemstone for a sense of humor when Deb responded by handing me a cloth and telling me to polish the glass shelves. They were an inch deep in dust. My mother liked dusting about as much as she liked duck hunting and, let me tell you, the entire Northwest Nebraska knew about her hatred for duck hunting. Last season, she had been arrested for running around naked at a local ranch, covered in red paint.

I headed for the shelves, knowing she was watching me like a hawk. I was on around-the-clock surveillance, having to ask permission to go to the bathroom and basically sneeze.

When midday arrived I was given five minutes for lunch, which was more like a bathroom break than a lunch break.

I sprinted to the bakery like I was trying out for track, the key on my necklace hitting my chest with each footfall. The bell tinkled above my head as I barreled through the door and into a pair of strong arms.

"I have five minutes," I told Tom breathlessly, resting my head on his chest. The warmth of his sweater made me feel like I was bundled up in a quilt. "Four and a half minutes," I corrected myself.

He stroked my hair without a word, letting me catch my breath, which was easier said than done while wrapped in his arms. "Shall we order?" he finally asked. "We could have a pie-eating competition. I once ate a pie in three minutes flat." A boyish grin spread across his face and, in that moment, he was seventeen, instead of immortal.

I let him order me a sandwich and a soda, but managed about one bite and three sips before Tom tapped the face of his watch, which had been ticking like a time bomb.

"One more minute," I begged, but he shook his head. "Thirty seconds," I pressed. "Twenty? Please?"

"Less time today. More time tomorrow," he said sagely.

I stopped to read a poster in the window of the Ezy-Buy as we walked to Tree of Life, and then browsed the bargain bin at Muse, which specialized in vintage records.

Tom pulled on my hand. "Lillie," he said sternly.

"But they have a limited edition ABBA vinyl," I said, brushing the thin layer of dust from its cover and holding it up as if I was an avid collector.

I dropped it back into the bin when I saw Jackson. He was about fifty yards down the street in front of the supermarket, sinking into the backseat of a sedan. He was wearing his suit from the Masquerade Ball and black sunglasses. His short wavy hair was slicked back and parted as if it were photo day back at Green Grove Elementary.

"Dammit." I slapped my forehead as the penny dropped. "Jackson had his court date today. Do you mind?"

"Yes."

"It was a rhetorical question," I said, walking towards the sedan.

Mrs Murphy was standing on the sidewalk talking to a man with a briefcase who looked like a lawyer while Jackson sat in the sedan, staring out at the road. When I tapped on the window he spun around, startled.

"I forgot about your court date," I said apologetically as he lowered the window. "What was the verdict?"

He hesitated, biting his lip before he spoke. "They gave me community service and suspended my license until next summer."

"Sorry."

Jackson ran a finger along the seam of his seat nervously. "They told me the train was going sixty miles an hour. It was carrying more than two thousand tons of grain." He looked up and I could see myself reflected in his lenses. "I could have killed you, Lillie."

I could have told him that in another dimension he had killed us both, but Mrs Murphy had finished her conversation and was walking around the hood of the sedan. I stepped backwards onto the sidewalk, as Jackson pushed a button and raised the window.

An arm wrapped around my waist and I leaned against Tom. In our reflection in the car window I could see he was staring daggers at the boy in the backseat.

I gave him a nudge. "What is up with you and Jackson? Do you have a history with him in another dimension or something?"

"No," Tom said, as he watched the sedan drive down the street. "But you do."

"Oh." I blushed. "Really?" My mind went to Jackson and how his smile made me feel like I was standing in the sun. How he made me laugh, made me forgive and forget his flaws. If I closed my eyes and searched the deepest, darkest corner of my mind I could imagine myself in his arms, instead of here with Tom.

Being late to Tree of Life cost me my break the next day. I shook my head at Tom as he passed by the front window twice, my hand pressed up against the glass.

Deb handed me a cloth. "Fingerprints," she said, clucking her tongue.

I spent the afternoon trying to get a glimpse behind her left ear for a tattoo, but when she restacked a shelf of massage oil I saw that she was tattoo-free. Maybe this was her latest hobby – being a mother.

That night a set of headlights lit up my room, flashing like Morse code. Dash. Dot. Dash.

I dressed with the speed of a shopaholic in a dressing room, pulling on a red sweater and a pair of jeans and snow boots. The tips of my boots scraped on the weatherboard as I climbed out of my window, making noise enough to wake the dead.

I crouched beside the house, the cold dirt beneath my hands as I waited for one of its occupants to switch on a light. I imagined a window sliding open on its rotting tracks and my mother poking her head out into the night, but I knew that was happening in another dimension.

In this dimension, I scaled the fence and slid down the other side to meet Tom.

We could have stood there for hours, two lovers canoodling on the sidewalk, but Tom folded me into his coat and we walked down the street towards his SUV. Our breath fogged on the frigid air, reminding me of our walk home from ice skating in his first dimension.

I was thankful for the heated seats as I climbed into the Benz. The clock on the dashboard flashed a few minutes past midnight. Green Grove was asleep, but we were wide awake.

I looked over at Tom as he pulled out onto the road, wondering how I could sleep if we shared a bed night after night. I smiled fondly as I thought of baby Rose. I guess sleeping had been an issue for Lillie from the Seventh Dimension too. I held a hand to my chest as the jealousy stabbed at me again, twisting like a knife in my heart.

A lone pick-up truck idled at an intersection, its headlights sweeping across us as we passed. A moment later, it pulled into our lane, filling the interior of the SUV with light.

Tom checked his rearview mirror as we turned another corner and his jaw clenched. "Shit."

"What?" I turned and looked through the back window, but was blinded by the headlights.

"We have company."

"Do you think Deb hired a private eye?" I asked with a laugh.

He glanced in his rearview mirror again. "You buckled up?" he asked and, without waiting for a response, he pulled into a side street with a sharp turn that had me hanging onto the edge of my seat.

"Tom!"

"Sorry." His eyes went to the rearview mirror again, but I could have told him the truck was behind us, its headlights bouncing off my side mirror as it took the corner with the same speed as we had, its tires shrieking as they skidded slightly.

My skin prickled. "Who is it?" I asked and then yelped as Tom took another fast corner onto Wyoming Crescent. He flicked off the headlights and the road in front of us sank into darkness, broken up by pools of light from the streetlights.

A heartbeat later the truck swung onto the same street, its headlights like a searchlight.

"Lillie," Tom said, as he pressed down on the accelerator. "When I pull up around the next corner I want you to get out and run home."

"What?" I looked out of my window and saw we had performed a lap of east Green Grove. My house was on the next street. "No." I turned to him, pleadingly. "Let me stay. Let me help."

"Lillie," Tom said through gritted teeth. "Let me handle them."

"Who are they?" I asked.

"The Circle," Tom said.

The panic bubbled up like a fountain. "What do they want?"

Tom grimaced. "They want me to merge." He thumped his hand on the steering wheel. "Dammit! I should have known when I saw him at the café…" his voice trailed off as he pulled the SUV over, the tires scraping the curb. "Get out, Lillie," Tom said, sounding like Jackson at the railroad crossing.

"No."

"Lillie," Tom said with desperation. "Please!" He leaned over and unclipped my seatbelt. "Go!"

There was a roar as the truck overtook us and skidded to a stop, blocking our path. "Oh my God," I whispered, as I recognized the vehicle and then its occupants.

Tom threw the SUV into reverse, spinning the tires as he backed up the curb and did a 180-degree turn. We screeched up the street, the acrid smell of burning rubber blowing through the vents.

"Put on your seatbelt," Tom ordered, as I was thrown around like a doll, in too much shock to hold onto anything. "Lillie! Put it on!"

"It was Mr Green," I said dully. "Mr Green is part of the Circle?" I thought about his face, staring out at me with an expression that was nothing like the man who had dressed up as Santa Claus each Christmas until we were thirteen. Yes, thirteen. And with him, in the passenger seat, had been the girl from the Duck-In Diner. I was in a goddamn town of Evacuees.

I managed to pull myself together and clicked in my seatbelt as Tom launched the SUV across the railroad crossing, giving the suspension a workout.

We were heading into the Open Valley where Tom knew the roads like the back of his hand. Thank God, because we were driving in the dark, the light from the crescent moon glinting on the markers in the middle of the road.

A set of bright headlights illuminated the interior again as Mr Green and the girl from the Duck-In Diner played catch-up. I watched the speedometer climb to seventy as we slid around another tight bend.

I was tossed from side to side. Left. Right. Left. This. Is. It, I thought, as we lost the headlights one second and found them the next. "Tom! Slow down!" While he was a cat with a billion lives, I knew I had one life to live and one death to die.

He eased off the gas, looking in his rearview mirror again as the headlights vanished for one second, two seconds, three seconds... I looked back at the black strip of road bordered by the shadows of the trees. "We won!" I shouted and then laughed like a maniac.

"Maybe they turned off their lights," Tom said, checking over both shoulders, as if the truck would come crashing through the woods. He pressed down on the accelerator again. "I need to get them off my scent," he said. "The chauffer at Rose Hill will take you home."

"What do you mean 'get them off your scent'?" I asked. My throat closed up and I choked out my last words. "Are you leaving Green Grove?"

I leaned forward, pressing a hand against the glove compartment for support, as I began to hyperventilate. No. I had to hold it together. I straightened up, sucking in a deep breath. "What can the Circle do to you?" I asked. "What can they do that would make you leave Green Grove?" I stopped short of saying "leave me."

"They have an antidote," Tom said. "For our condition. It stops us from sliding." He looked at me, his eyes glinting in the soft glow from the dashboard. "They can kill me, Lillie."

I frowned. He had told me they were immortal. "Like *kill* kill?"

He nodded. "Yes. And I would be like *dead* dead."

I blinked as I remembered having seen a syringe filled with the antidote. I waded through the memories, diving for the memory like a diver for pearls, but it sank like a stone.

"I would have taken it time and time again and ended this limbo," Tom said, his hands gripping the steering wheel as we turned another corner, "but I had to keep you safe from Evacuee Lillie."

"But I am safe. You said so yourself."

He looked at me with a softened expression. "I have another reason to live now."

A set of headlights suddenly came over the crest ahead, turning our world white.

"Tom!" I shouted, as the truck came at us head on.

Tom pushed down on the accelerator. "Brace yourself, Lillie."

I put my hands up in front of my face, thinking of how in another dimension I had probably decided to stay at home in bed instead of sneaking out with Tom, but I knew deep down it had not been an option. The dimension had not split. I was here in the car with Tom and that was that. I snuck one last look at him though my fingers, knowing I had no regrets.

We were both about to lose the game of chicken when Tom flicked his lights back on high beam, blinding our opponents. He then turned the wheel sharply until the SUV lurched sideways and we slid past the truck on two wheels, low hanging branches scratching the roof.

I was thankful I had buckled my seatbelt, as I hung sideways, suspended somewhere between my seat and Tom.

I hit my head on the ceiling as the tires reconnected with the road. "Ow."

"Are you OK?" Tom asked, glancing between me and the road.

I nodded, holding a hand to my head and turning in my seat to watch as the truck lost control. It spun wildly, its taillights like lightning bugs and its headlights swinging through the forest until we heard a loud crash. The air seemed to vibrate with the collision, like rolling thunder.

"I think the question is, will Mr Green be OK?" I whispered.

Tom pressed down on the accelerator again and shrugged.

The lights were on at Rose Hill, lampposts lighting up the drive and floodlights illuminating the gardens.

"I thought you said you were OK," Tom muttered as I climbed down from the SUV. He brushed his fingers across a graze on my forehead.

"I am." I tilted my head until his lips were inches from mine. "As long as you stick around."

He smiled and leaned down to kiss me. I kissed him back desperately, holding onto him as if we were a couple of kids standing on the edge of a high dive.

We were pushed into the deep end when we entered the foyer.

"Are you the boy claiming to be my grandson?" a voice asked.

The Red Queen, I thought as I took in an older woman wearing an expensive looking red pant-suit. A cream-colored silk scarf was knotted around her neck and in her lobes were drop earrings; pearls, of course.

I glanced at Tom. His face was waxen as he stared at Mrs Windsor-Smith.

His grandmother regarded me with an arched eyebrow, like I was running around her estate in my underwear. "I think the girl should go home."

Tom blinked, as if a spell had been broken. "Come on, Lillie," he said, putting a protective arm around my shoulder.

"Wait," she said. "Lorraine!"

Lorraine poked her head out from an office behind the reception desk like a gopher from its hole. She looked at Tom and then at me, chewing her red lips nervously.

"Call the chauffer. For the girl."

"For Lillie," Tom corrected.

His grandmother waved his words away. "Lorraine," she barked again and Lorraine let out a squeak and picked up the phone to call the chauffer.

Tom drew himself up, but I squeezed his arm and shook my head. He was going to have to charm the pant-suit off this woman and that was not going to happen with me at his side.

I patted his arm as it slid from my shoulders and nodded a farewell to his grandmother, before walking out of the door and down the front steps of Rose Hill. It was like leaving home for the first and last time.

There was no conversation from the chauffer during the car trip, except to ask my address. I told him a couple of doors down and then snuck back into my bedroom via the window.

I sat on the edge of my bed, moonlight from the window falling across me like a crisp white sheet. Who can say when I fell asleep? Three? Four? But when I woke up, fully dressed on my duvet, the light was tinged with gray.

I kicked off my shoes and crawled under the covers, dozing until the light turned yellow. Then I rolled out of bed and went to the landline, creeping through the house, which was full of the sounds of sleep. I could hear

Blaze snoring loudly in the back room and a softer snore from Dawn. I knew Deb would be doing much the same in her bedroom.

I flipped through the phonebook and dialed the number for Rose Hill, listening to it ring out over and over again. The sound was shrill, as if the line was screaming his name in my ear. Tom! Tom! Tom!

I went to work again, spending the morning doing inventory. It took me an hour and a half to count the gemstones. I counted them one by one, as if counting the seconds until my lunch break. Today I was going to the bakery, whether Deb liked it or not.

At midday I slipped out while she was with a customer and half-walked, half-ran to the café. I pushed through the door, coming close to knocking over a mother with her kid.

I apologized breathlessly, my eyes scanning the room as I walked between the tables, knocking into two chairs and bumping into a waiter. But I knew before I reached the back of the café that Tom was a no-show.

I sat there for fifteen minutes and then walked slowly back to the store, looking for his SUV in the row of parked cars. I was sick to my stomach wondering how he was going with his doppelganger grandmother.

I phoned Rose Hill again when I got home, but it rang out again. I considered calling Jo and asking her for a lift to the Open Valley, but given my run-in with Mr Green I thought it would be a dangerous decision.

I was going to have to wait until I went back to school the next day, if Tom was still here. My stomach somersaulted at the thought that he may have slid.

25

Tom was nowhere to be seen at school on Thursday. I wandered through the corridors and around the quad like a lost dog looking for its owner. I eyed his locker with a hollow in the pit of my stomach as I thought of Mr Green and the Windsor-Smith Matriarch.

"So did you and Tom do it on Sunday?" Sylv wanted to know.

"Sylv!"

Sylv rolled her eyes. "Sorry. I meant did you and Tom make love on Sunday?"

I was saved by a group of senior girls who walked past whispering insults like "slut" and "ho." I thought they were talking about Sylv, but then the group changed course and one jostled Jo, making her drop her bag. She scooped it up and shuffled towards me with her head down. I eyed her warily.

I hated myself for hating Evacuee Jo. She looked like my Jo. She acted like my Jo. She was my Jo, except for the tattoo. The black mark that had given me Tom had also taken my best friend.

"Watch it," Sylv snapped at the girls, but the taunts continued all morning.

When Jo got a good mark off our biology teacher, there was a snide comment. "Who do you have to sleep with around here to get a good mark?" The answer came back, "Ask Jo."

It was when she was pushed from behind in the bathroom while walking into a cubicle and cracked her shin on the toilet that my heart of ice began to thaw.

"You should see the school nurse," I suggested, as she rolled up her pant leg at lunch and applied a cold drink to the lump.

She shrugged. "Another day. Another bruise," she said fatalistically.

Before I could respond, Sylv arrived wielding a magazine like some kind of medieval weapon. "What the fuck is this?" she asked, throwing it in front of Jo. It hit her bowl of pumpkin soup, splashing orange droplets onto her gray sweater.

Jo looked at the magazine like a grenade had landed on her lunch tray.

I tilted my head and saw an image of a rock chick holding a guitar and making the devil sign. The image slid from view as Sylv snatched it up and shook the magazine until its spine broke, repeating the question louder and louder until we had the attention of the entire cafeteria.

Jo flinched like a puppy being kicked as Sylv flung the magazine at her for a second time. She grabbed it with both hands, holding it against her stained sweater like a shield.

"What the hell are you talking about?" I asked Sylv.

"Page twelve!" Sylv shouted. "Show her page twelve!"

Jo shook her head, her short black hair whipping around her cheeks. Fantastic. World War III was about to begin in Green Grove.

"Show me page twelve," I snapped, grabbing the magazine and flipping the pages frantically. My mouth fell open, as I saw the double page spread advertising a label called Dead Kitty. It was Jo, reclining on a red velvet chaise, dressed in a short black dress and black and white striped tights.

I looked from the glossy magazine to Jo, gob smacked. "Is this you? In a magazine? Modeling?"

Sylv made a "hrmph" sound.

Jo looked like she needed to go to the bathroom. She jiggled in her seat, her face screwed up as she begged us to hush. "I made friends with the girl at Grunge Ghetto and Dead Kitty is her new line. She needed models," she explained. Jo had been shopping at Grunge Ghetto? That explained why she had been looking like Morticia Addams.

"Let me get this straight," Sylv said, half-addressing Jo and half-addressing her audience of about fifty students. "When you get approached for a photo shoot you end up in a double spread, but when I get approached it's for a titty magazine?"

Jo blushed and stared into her bowl, like she wanted to dive into the orange mush.

Blake and Ethan start up a chant of "Fight! Fight! Fight!" from across the cafeteria.

Jo lifted her head and drew in a deep breath. "You should be thanking me," she said with either complete bravery or utter stupidity. "I warned you about that dirtball and I was right."

I grimaced at the implied "and you were wrong."

"Thanks for the tip," Sylv spat, "but I think I'll pass on taking advice from the competition." She gave the table a shove before turning and striding towards the double doors. My strawberry milk toppled onto its side, gushing across the table towards Jo, who ironically burst into tears.

Jo pushed back her chair, its legs shuddering on the vinyl, and ran to the bathroom, the sound of the spilt milk dripping off the table mimicking the sound of her shoes slapping on the floor.

That afternoon, Jo ditched track to walk home with Yours Truly.

I knew not to talk about the double spread. If Evacuee Jo wanted to be a model in this dimension that was between her and Sylv. As we walked, I unwrapped my scarf, letting the cold air circulate around my neck.

"I like your necklace."

My hand went to the key. "Thanks. It was a present from Tom." My eyes suddenly misted and I busied myself with my scarf again, looping it around my neck until it was a bitch to breathe.

"You want to talk about it?"

"About what?" I asked with a sniff.

Jo shrugged and we continued on without speaking until the end of the street.

We paused at the pedestrian crossing, the toes of our sneakers hanging over the edge of the curb.

Jo held out her cell. "Call Rose Hill."

"I have," I said, a whine in my voice. "Like a thousand times."

"Then make it a thousand and one."

I took her cell. I knew the number by heart. The tone of each key had become my theme song over the past twenty-four hours or so.

"Good afternoon, Rose Hill. This is Lorraine."

It took me a second to speak.

"Lillie. Hi," she answered warmly. Was it warmly? It sounded like it was warmly. "Let me see if Tom can take the call."

I tried to read between the lines as I listened to the hold music. Did she mean let me see if Tom wants to take the call? Or if his grandmother will let him take the call?

Lorraine came back on the line. "Sorry, Lillie."

I hung up, my thumb pushing on the button until the skin around my nail turned white.

Jo frowned. "Bastard."

I shrugged, like I could care less. As if.

"You want to come in?" I asked when we reached my front gate.

Jo looked embarrassed. "I have a date."

My eyes widened. "A date?"

"With Jackson." She winced, as if I was going to dissolve into tears again. Ironic, considering she had been mood-swing central since she had became Evacuee

Jo. "Are you mad at me, Lillie? Please say no. Please say no. Please say no." As if *she* needed the rule of repetition.

"No!"

"Are you sure?" She raised her eyes to the heavens. "Phew. I was worried. I mean I know you have... had Tom." Her eyes widened as she realized what a kick in the guts her correction from present to past tense had been.

"Jackson is a friend. Period," I said quickly. At least in this dimension, I thought.

Jo did a tap dance on the sidewalk. Yes. You heard me. Jo. A tap dance. If I had not already known about evacuees I would have guessed then and there that she was not my Jo. "He said he's liked me since Elementary. Can you believe it?"

I was still having a hard time believing the tap dance, but I nodded as I suddenly recalled his drawing of Wal-Mart and Jo. And how he had remembered that Jo and I had gone to the Rainbow Retreat. God. How stupid had I been to think he liked me? Very.

And maybe Jo had liked him all along too, I thought, as I recalled her words, "Maybe you could spare a few for the rest of us".

That night I lay awake in bed, holding the key around my neck like a good-luck charm and watching for the headlights of the Benz. Whenever a car went past, I propped myself up on my elbows, waiting for the driver to flash a message to me. A love letter in Morse code.

By the early hours of the morning I had fallen into a rare dreamless sleep. It seemed Tom had also abandoned me in my dreams.

26

I phoned Rose Hill again on my lunch break from Tree of Life.

"He literally drove out of the gates two minutes ago," Lorraine told me.

Uh-huh. And you can call me Lillie Windsor-Smith.

I walked down to the bakery. It was blowing a gale, the icy wind making a noose of my hair.

I ordered a pineapple juice at the counter before taking a seat at my usual table in the back corner. I was onto my second juice when the door opened and in walked Tom.

His eyes found me in an instant, like he knew I would be there waiting. Of course he did. I was always waiting for him. In every dimension, I thought miserably.

"I think we should go for a drive," he said. This time, there was no hesitation.

The luxurious interior of his SUV seemed to shrink as we headed towards the Open Valley, the silence between us filling its nooks and crannies until it was like a third person in the vehicle.

Tom seemed nervous, tapping his finger on the steering wheel and chewing his bottom lip, like a schoolboy waiting for the principal.

He stopped to check for traffic at the corner, careful to look past me instead of at me. I leaned forward, trying to catch his eye with a small smile on my lips, but I may as well have been the breeze from the air vents.

"Um..." I started, and then stopped. I had a billion and one questions to ask about his grandmother – what had she said? What was she going to do? What was he going to do? When? Where? Why? How? – but I was worried about the answers, given his uneasiness and the manner in which he changed gears rapidly, like I might grab his hand if he came too close.

"Um..." I paused again and then followed up with a burst of inappropriate laughter that belied my nerves. I looked out the window at the grasses that waved in the wind, like a rolling ocean beneath the snow-filled clouds.

As we drove through the railroad crossing, the tires hit the tracks with a thud-thud that sounded like gunshots. It seemed to rouse Tom from his reverie and he spoke suddenly, the words rushing out of his mouth like he was ripping off a Band-Aid.

"My grandmother is an evacuee," he said. "A merged evacuee."

I waited for him to go on, but he had returned to chewing his bottom lip.

"You found your family," I said hesitantly. My mind was racing through the scenarios. Maybe his grandmother knew what had happened to his parents,

I thought, deciding on a positive outlook. Maybe Tom had been wrong and they were here as well. A family reunion.

"The two of us have crossed paths before," Tom said, like he was reading my mind. "In my seventh dimension."

The Seventh Dimension. I scratched my jeans with my fingernail, like a nervous twitch.

"She let us…" Tom paused, casting his eyes to me for a moment. "I mean she let Lillie and I live at Rose Hill."

My fingernails dug into the denim. Dig. Dig. Dig. Lillie. And. I.

"I had no double in my seventh dimension," Tom explained. "My father had been killed in a motorbike accident as a teen, which meant I was never born. My grandmother pulled a few strings and created an identity for me so I could have a life."

"And so you could get married," I said, as I imagined Lillie walking through the formal gardens in a flowing white dress. No. Not imagined, remembered. I could see Tom waiting next to a gazebo, dressed in a black tuxedo. His smile was broad and his eyes sparkled like cut diamonds as I walked towards him with Sylv at my side. There was no Jo.

"She wants me to go with her to England," Tom suddenly said, bringing me back to the present.

A family reunion in London. My heart ached at the thought of losing him for a day, let alone a week, but did he mean… "Forever?"

Tom glanced at me. "Lillie, she wants me to merge with her grandson. The Tom from this dimension."

I hissed, the sound like the seal being broken on a soda can.

"My grandmother is part of the Circle," he explained.

"Like Mr Green?"

Tom nodded. "How do you think she knew I was here? He let her know as soon he saw me in the café. He was out looking for me the night she arrived. The night I was with you." He squeezed the steering wheel, his knuckles turning white before he released his grip, giving up. "My grandmother has me booked on a flight to London on Monday."

"Is that what you want?" I asked, realizing this was not one of those dimensions where Tom had his grandmother wrapped around his little finger.

"Of course not." He turned to me, his eyes flashing like lightning. "I am not a murderer."

I looked at him, wide-eyed, knowing this was another fork in the road, but neither direction led to a destination we wanted.

His nostrils flared as he stared straight ahead at the road. "I have to slide."

He may as well have driven the car into a brick wall, splattering my heart against my ribcage. "Stop."

"What?"

"Stop the car!" I fumbled with the door handle, gasping for breath. It was like the oxygen had been sucked out of my lungs. I took off my seat belt and opened the door, letting in a rush of wind and sparking a warning signal from the dashboard.

"No, Lillie. Wait!" Tom slammed on the brakes and the dusty road that rushed like a raging torrent beside me became a steady stream.

I jumped out and ran along the narrow strip between the trees and the road. My feet swished through the uncut grass, which slithered around my ankles like snakes hissing the word "slide".

"Lillie!" Tom shouted.

"Go away!" I choked against the wind, my throat thick with emotion. I could taste the tears coursing down my face. He was breaking my heart again, because he was breaking his promise again. I groped through my memories, looking for a promise that I knew had been both made and broken.

"Listen to me." Tom grabbed my shoulder. The contact was like a knife in my back. I fell to my knees and he crouched beside me whispering my name in time with my ragged breathing.

"I want you to come with me, Lillie."

I looked at him sideways, as if waiting for a blow to the head.

"I want you to slide too," he begged. His voice was strained and I realized was scared. Scaredy Tom-Cat.

"I can do that?" I asked, my hair flying around my head like Medusa. "I can slide?"

"Did you really think I would leave you, Lillie? I would rather merge than slide into another dimension without you." I watched his chest rise and fall under his sweater as he took a deep breath. "I have to tell you something," he said and then shook his head. "No. Let me show you." He stood up and offered me his hand.

I let him help me to my feet, leaning on him like a crutch as we walked back to his SUV.

The Benz was parked lopsided, half off the road with both front doors open, shuddering with each gust of wind. It looked like a prop from post-apocalyptic film and its warning signal grew louder we approached, sounding through the valley like a homing beacon. Beep. Beep. Beep. This. Is. It. I knew we were about to reach another twist in the book and, like last time, I wanted to skip ahead to the last page.

"Look," Tom instructed, guiding me towards the SUV and pointing at the side mirror.

I leaned in to look at the pale-faced girl in its reflection. Meanwhile, Tom reached in through the door and pulled the mirror from the visor. He lifted this second mirror behind my head and carefully drew back my hair from my face as if it were a curtain made of antique lace.

I closed my eyes as his fingertips brushed my ear, blushing to think he would see their pointiness. But then I realized he would have seen them countless times in other dimensions. I wondered if Lillie from the Seventh Dimension wore her hair in a ponytail, not needing a shield like me.

I opened my eyes. "No," I whispered when I saw my reflection again.

"Yes," Tom said.

"No!" I straightened up, my back as rigid as a washboard.

"Lillie," Tom said, catching my arm before I could run. "I told you I had saved you in eight dimensions, but had been too late in four." His eyes begged for forgiveness, his pale blue irises like shimmering lakes. I wanted to submerge myself in them, sink to their sandy bottoms and drown. "This was the fourth dimension, Lillie."

I wanted the wind to whisk away his words, but it had died down, leaving us in the eye of its storm.

"She killed me?" I asked, but it was more a statement than a question. I had seen the black tattoo myself, the mix of numbers and letters behind my ear, which marked me as an evacuee. I lifted the veil of hair that had hidden the truth and touched my tattoo. My fingers ran over the smooth skin, feeling the heat that made my cheeks burn like I was blushing. I looked in the mirror again and saw that my cheeks remained ashen, despite my rising temperature.

My mind went back to that night six months ago when Evacuee Lillie had leaned over my bed. I had thought it a dream and then a memory from another dimension, but it had been neither. "She killed me," I said again, thinking of my nosebleed and my muddled memories over the past six months. And then there was my constant blushing that I had put down to having a crush. My voice became accusatory. "You said she was gone. You said I was safe."

"She is gone, Lillie," Tom said. "For the first time it was Evacuee Lillie who was killed in the merge. You lived." He offered the smallest of smiles. "You won."

I shook my head, holding my hands over my ears, like I could block it out. "No," I whispered.

"Yes. How else could you remember our ice skating accident as if it was your own memory? Before you merged it would have been like looking through the peephole. You would have only had part of the picture. Lillie, the merge has opened the door to other dimensions.

"And what about your memory of us getting married?" he continued. "It will be another five years before that happens in the other dimension." He clenched his jaw and I knew he had been reliving the date of her death over and over again in the three hundred-odd years since his seventh dimension.

My tongue touched my chipped tooth, which I now realized had been inherited during a merge with the me of another dimension.

Tom went on to explain how he had followed me around after the merge – not to protect me, but to spy on me.

I understood his demeanor now in those first few weeks. The brick wall he had built between us had hidden a love-hate relationship between him and the other Lillies. He hated Evacuee Lillie, but loved Lillie from the Seventh Dimension. And here we were like the Father, Son and Holy Ghost. The Unholy Trinity.

"I wanted to be sure she was gone. I enrolled in school to be certain," he explained. "I soon realized from your jokes that you were not Evacuee Lillie – or any of the other Lillies." He managed another small smile and I remembered the look on his face when I had joked about the tampons and then there was his question in the car – "You like to laugh, don't you?"

But then I thought about the dreams of murdering or being murdered and realized Tom was wrong about Evacuee Lillie. She was alive as long as her memories were alive. I held onto the doorframe as she spoke to me through her memories, reminding me of the last time Tom had left her behind.

Tom and I had been standing in line for the Solution in Lincoln. It had taken us several hours to reach the start of the line and in that time we had speculated what we would find in other dimensions.

"Each other," Tom had decided, pulling me into a hug.

I had leaned my head against his chest, listening to the beat of his heart beneath his T-shirt, letting the rhythm drown out the sound of the protesters, who stood behind barricades on either side.

"But will we be able to find each other?" I had asked hesitantly. "They say we can be split up, even though we are entangled." I pulled away from him to retrieve the information booklet from my back pocket, flipping through the pages for information on the Solution.

Tom had pulled me close again. "I will find you Lillie," he said into my hair. "I promise."

But when we slid I had landed in a new dimension on my own. This was where the memories became dim, as if Evacuee Lillie had slammed the door shut on them, leaving a string of scenes that were like mismatched garments. I shuddered as I came across a memory of dying. And another. And another. It seemed she – I – had been killed over and over again by creatures that did not exist in this dimension. I scrunched up my eyes against the memory of my flesh being torn and the sound of my own screams, like the wail of a fire engine in my mind.

And then she found Tom. Years after landing in his seventh dimension, her eighteenth, she had spotted him in Lincoln and followed him back to Rose Hill.

"She had been looking for you for more than a hundred years," I whispered, as we stood in the valley, "but you had broken your promise. You had given up." The jealousy of Evacuee Lillie welled up in me again, as I thought of Lillie from the Seventh Dimension.

I shook my head, backing away from Tom.

"Lillie. Please," he said. "I had searched for her in every dimension, but then I fell in love."

"With another Lillie," I spat, letting the hundreds of years of heartache for Evacuee Lillie wash over me in waves of bitterness. "A replacement. How could you?" I reached up to my neck, my fingers finding the cold metal of my necklace. "And you said Lillie from the Seventh Dimension was your first love." I pulled down and the back of my neck burned as the chain slid across the skin and then snapped. I felt the weight of the key in my hand for a moment before I threw it at him. It hit his chest and bounced, landing at his feet. "I was your first love."

We stared at each other as we realized I had said "I was," not "she was." I was talking about Evacuee Lillie in the first person. Tom hesitated for a moment before taking a step forward. It was a moment too late though, because by the time his wristwatch ticked over I had thrown myself into his SUV and pulled the door shut behind me.

"Lillie!" he shouted, but I slammed down the lock and turned the key. My foot pumped the gas as I threw the stick into first and lurched forward. The passenger door on the other side swung shut and I heard it lock automatically as I revved the engine again and eased off the clutch.

I had only ever driven twice illegally with Jo and one of those times had been a stick shift. Who fucking drives stick shift? I wondered, as I crunched the gears. I could guarantee this SUV had been custom-made. "Europeans," I muttered.

Tom was pulling at the handle and yelling at me through the glass. He pulled his sweater over his head in a fluid movement and wrapped it around his hand, readying himself to smash the back window, but I lurched forward again, hearing the tires churn the loose gravel.

I forced the vehicle into second, the gears crunching, and then third as I sped up along the road. I could see Tom in my rearview mirror, growing smaller and smaller with each surge of the engine. This was when the levee broke and the tears poured down my cheeks, blurring my vision and making him look like a mirage in the middle of the road.

Suddenly a white dust filled the rearview mirror and I realized it had started snowing. A freak October snowstorm. The word "freak" resounded in my mind as the swirling flurries coated the windscreen, melting on contact with the heated glass. I flicked on the blinkers twice until I found the wipers, which cleaned the windscreen with the precision of a cut-throat razor – back and forth. Freak. Show. Freak. Show. Freak. Show. The insult from Melissa made me laugh hysterically now. If she had only known the half of it.

I slammed on the brakes as I came upon an intersection, spinning the wheel in the direction of Green Grove. The SUV slid out a few feet until the traction system kicked-in. A small delivery van passed, beeping its horn and flashing its lights angrily.

I reached up with one hand and pulled on my seat belt and then laughed at myself again. I could slam head-on into a tree at eighty miles per hour and not die. First, I would be cushioned by the multiple air bags and state-of-the-art crumple zones. Second, I was an evacuee and I was going to live forever and ever, Amen.

The heated steering wheel made my palms sweat, but I tightened my grip and pushed down on the accelerator. The van driver was probably an evacuee like me, I decided, shrugging off the near collision. If I had killed him he would have slid for eternity too.

I saw flashes of myself pulling a black balaclava over my head. I saw my hand reaching out and touching Lillie after Lillie after Lillie. I banged my hand on the steering wheel. What the fuck? Evacuee Lillie had merged with more than four Lillies, I realized as her memories emerged from the corners of my mind.

One. Two. Three. Four. Five. Six. Seven. Eight. Nine. Ten. Eleven. Twelve. Thirteen. Fourteen… "Twenty-six," I breathed, the tears continuing to roll down my cheeks, dripping from my chin. "I was the twenty-sixth." And that was not counting the times my own dimension had split and she had merged with me in the kitchen or darkroom, instead of in my bedroom.

I gasped as I remembered where I had seen the antidote. Tom had used it to chase me out of dimension after dimension. He had tried to kill me. Correction: he had tried to kill Evacuee Lillie. I guessed he had not told me about the antidote initially in case I remembered him holding the syringe to my neck until I slid into another dimension and then another and another, as if caught in my own rule of repetition. The realization left a taste in my mouth like tea laced with arsenic, but it was Evacuee Lillie who made me ill.

"Twenty-six," I whispered. "Twenty-six."

The railroad crossing loomed ahead and I saw the familiar "Look For Trains" sign between the snowflakes. I pushed down on the gas and the speedometer rose from seventy to ninety. Suddenly the thin layer of snow coating the tracks ahead lit up like the Fourth of July, as a train rounded the bend at breakneck speed.

I slowed for a heartbeat, before gritting my teeth and pushing down on the accelerator. "One. Two. Three. Four. Five..." I whispered, counting down the Lillies with each passing second.

I knew I would reach the railroad crossing before I got to twenty-six, and so would the train. It was like an icy hand had gripped my heart. I made the last-minute decision to slam on the brakes, pushing my foot to the floor. Too little. Too late.

I was sliding towards the train, which had already gone through the crossing, blaring its horn. Its thunderous cars followed, whizzing by my windscreen, waiting for me to crash into their side. I pulled on the wheel and the SUV careened off the road and rolled.

I woke up upside down. It took me a moment to work out where I was and a funny story came to mind about Deb being in a serious car accident when she was my age. She had been wearing hair rollers and had removed them while hanging upside down in the car, not wanting the paramedics to see her in that state. I reached up – or was it down? – and touched my hair, which rested on the crumpled roof. Warm sticky blood covered my hand. I suddenly felt sick. I wanted to get out, but my hands seemed too weak to get the belt off.

I must have blacked out a few times before I heard a window being smashed and the car alarm ringing out, interrupted by Tom, shouting, "Lillie, stay here. Don't go. Don't slide."

I blacked out again.

27

There was a beeping in my ears when I woke and for a moment I thought I was still in the SUV, hanging upside down with the blood rushing to my head. My eyes flew open and I stared up at the ceiling as if raised from the dead.

I was lying in a bed, tucked into the starched white sheets like a letter in an envelope. I rolled my head to the left and saw a machine monitoring my heart rate with a high-pitched beep. I also saw a bag of clear fluid that hung on a stand, connected by a tube to an IV drip that pinched the back of my hand.

"Lillie? Lillie!"

It was Deb. She was leaning over the metal rail on the side of the bed. Her long hair was knotted into a loose bun that highlighted the dark circles under her eyes. Panda eyes.

I moaned.

"Stay still," she begged. Her hands hovered a foot above me, as if holding me down. "Hush, hush, hush," she chanted, but five hundred hushes could not have convinced me to stay still. I pushed myself up in the bed. My arms were like lead, as if they had been dormant for days or weeks. The right seemed heavier than the left and I realized it was in a cast.

"What day...?" My voice was a rasping whisper. I swallowed. "When?"

"Monday," Deb said. "The car accident was last Saturday. They had to sedate you. We thought..." Her voice choked off.

"Tom," I groaned, struggling to sit up as if I could go to him, but he was in his thirty-sixth dimension. I remembered his words as they had loaded me into the ambulance, his warm breath in my ear and his cheek wet with tears.

"I will find you," he had said, squeezing my hand. "I promise."

I laughed now, a short husky bark that came from deep in my chest. Of course he would find me. In his thirty-six, thirty-seventh, thirty-eighth dimension and beyond. But it would be another Lillie, who he would marry and have children with and live happily ever after.

My ever after was like a black hole by comparison, an unknown, full of darkness. I had a thousand memories that belonged to other Lillies, but none that told me how to slide without killing myself. I lifted my arm with the cast slowly and touched the drip in my other hand.

"Lillie," Deb said, putting a hand on my arm. "Leave it."

I followed the tube until my fingers found a piece of plastic. I wanted to slide. I wanted to hold Tom to the promise he had made hundreds of years ago, to the renewed vow he had given me two days ago. We would find each other in a new dimension.

"Lillie," Deb warned and then she shouted, "Nurse! Nurse!"

I was pumping the syringe, trying to OD on whatever was in the bag.

"Stop!" Deb clamped a hand around my cast. "Lillie!"

"Good morning," a cheerful voice interrupted and my cast was released. "You sure slept like a log these past couple of days." The nurse approached the side of my bed, tilting her head, as she surveyed the scene. "You thirsty, dear?" she asked, attending to the IV drip. "This here is for hydration. A saline solution," she explained and I collapsed into the pillow with a sob.

The nurse tapped a plastic box that was hidden under the blanket and I looked down to see a second drip in my hand. "This is the morphine." She winked at me like we shared a secret – what a laugh – and then pulled out a set of keys that jangled jarringly as she unlocked the box and studied a glass vial before locking it again.

I closed my eyes, tears rolling down my cheeks as I thought about the Lillie who had died in the car accident in the Open Valley. Tom had told me that when you died you slid. I imagined him holding her hand as she drew her last breath and the cold spread through her body.

I knew I had drawn the short straw with this split dimension. If I slid on my own, I would be on my own for a number of lifetimes, perhaps for an eternity, not knowing how to find Tom and not knowing if he would find me.

"The doctor will check on her this afternoon," I heard the nurse tell my mother as my eyelids grew heavy and I drifted into a sleep filled with dreams about Tom.

I woke for a few minutes when the doctor came in. I overheard him talking about a broken wrist and stitches. He touched my head and the skin on my forehead crawled like it was covered in cockroaches.

I heard the word "lucky" followed by "improved" and laughter welled up in my throat, dying before it reached my mouth.

I let myself slide into sleep again, where I could relive my other lives with Tom over and over, again and again.

It could have been an hour or a week later that I was woken by the hydraulics of the bed and found myself being folded up until I was in a sitting position.

"Sweetheart," Deb said softly. "The food is here. Do you want to eat?"

I kept my eyes closed, leaning back into the pillows as if I could hide in their cushioned comfort. The thought of food made me want to heave, even though my stomach was as empty as my chest. It was like my insides had been scooped out, leaving a gaping hole that nothing could fill, not even the chicken casserole that I could smell on the tray in front of me.

It seemed that Deb had given up on my vegetarianism. I wondered if that meant she had also given up on me.

••••

They started reducing my morphine somewhere between my seventh trip to the bathroom and the arrival of my fourth tray of food. I knew this because the pain began to increase each hour, from a nine, to a ten, to an eleven and then to a five hundred.

My sanctuary was to sleep, perchance to dream.

The girls came to visit me in hospital.

First came Jo. I could feel the tattoo behind my ear heat up as she settled in the seat beside me, making my face feel flushed.

"Lillie," she whispered. "Can you hear me?" She fell silent for a moment. "The PSATs are next week," she said. "I spoke to the guidance counselor and he said I had to let him know by Tuesday if you…"

She trailed off and the room sank into silence again, except for the beeping and the muffled voices in the corridor.

"You know," Jo whispered, starting another one-sided conversation. "My dad is completely cured. The doctors are calling it a miracle."

She thought she was giving me good news, but the news was as good as it was new. My skin began to burn beyond the heat of my tattoo. I had to tell her about her dad. I had to tell her about herself. I wondered whether she even knew she had a tattoo behind her ear, let alone that she was an evacuee.

"Hi," a voice said from the doorway. Sylv.

I opened my eyes ever-so-slightly and watched through my lashes as Jo made room for Sylv. They had made up. I guess a car accident trumps a catfight in any dimension.

"Lillie." It was Jo. She had seen my eyes open and was leaning over me, like I was a baby in a bassinet. I closed my eyes, unable to return her smile.

"How you doing, Lillie?" Sylv asked and the bed shuddered as she leaned against its rail. "Guess what? I dropped out of school." I could hear the glee in her voice. "I start my hairdressing apprenticeship next week," she continued, undeterred by my lack of response. "I went in for an interview yesterday and they hired me on the spot. You should see the hot college guys they have as customers."

"What happened to Brandon?" Jo asked.

"Brandon who? I have a date tonight with Taylor Blackwood." She gave herself a cheer. "It turns out he has a policy on not dating high school girls."

"Does he also have a policy on not washing his hair?" Jo asked. I would have laughed a week ago, but now my face remained as slack as a corpse.

When they said their goodbyes, Jo squeezed my hand.

"Jackson says, 'Hi,'" she said and then sighed. "I know this sounds stupid, but I think we might be soulmates." She laughed at her own sappiness, before letting go of my hand and following Sylv towards the door.

My eyes opened. "Jo?"

She rushed back to my bedside. "Lillie!"

"Jo, I have to tell you–"

A throat cleared in the doorway and we looked up to see Mr Green. His lips stretched into a smile without sentiment.

"Look at you, Lillie," he said, walking into the room. "You banged yourself up a treat." Like Sylv, he leaned against the bed and it slid under his weight. "Yep," he said, looking at the top of my head. "We thought you were a goner." His eyes met mine and I knew by "goner" he meant he thought I was going to slide.

Jo frowned. "Dad."

Mr Green looked at Jo, as if seeing her there for the first time. "Honey, the nurse asked me to tell you visiting hours are over. We gotta go home." He grimaced, like he was sorry, but I could see through him like cellophane.

"Lillie, what were you–?"

"Go," I croaked, cutting Jo off. I closed my eyes, wanting to go back to sleep, wanting to see Tom in my dreams.

She hovered for a moment, her shadow passing across my eyelids. "I'll be back tomorrow," she promised.

"You go ahead, honey," I heard Mr Green say. "I have a message to give Lillie."

My eyes flew open. A message? From Tom? Who else? If I had the muscle mass I would have sat up and grabbed Mr Green by the collar until he told me every word.

He was watching the door, waiting until it closed with an audible click of its latch. He looked at me out of the corner of his eye like a vulture and then turned his head, his body following until his round stomach rested on the metal rail, as evidence of his transformation from call-me-Dave into evacuee Mr Green.

"What do you remember, Lillie?" he asked, tapping his index finger on the rail. Tap. Tap. Tap. "What do you remember about…?" He hesitated.

I looked at him, realizing that there was no message, unless he was typing it in Morse code. Fuck. Fuck. Fuck. They say not to shoot the messenger, but I could have used a machine gun in that moment.

"I remember you chasing us last week," I said through gritted teeth. "I remember the tattoo behind my ear. The Evacuation." I lifted my chin in defiance.

Mr Green nodded thoughtfully and then his hand shot out as fast as a rattlesnake and caught me around the neck. "Then you must remember the Circle," he growled.

His fingers formed a vise, which tightened until the veins in my neck bulged and I thought my eyes would pop out of my head.

"Loose lips sink ships, Lillie," he warned, as I gasped for breath. "You keep your mouth shut and this here will be smooth sailing." He gave me a shake, my head bouncing like a bobble-head doll, and raised his eyebrows, as if waiting for a response.

I blinked a couple of times and he released his grip, letting me suck in a lungful of oxygen. I rubbed my throat with my good hand and then pointed to the space behind my ear. "I think these tattoos are going to rock your boat," I said, my voice scratchy. "Jo will see hers – everyone will – and there goes your dimension secrets. They say a picture tells a thousand words..." My voice dropped off, as I remembered Tom saying this to me a week ago, a lifetime ago.

I closed my eyes, as if I could make myself slide back in time, and when I reopened them I saw Mr Green was smiling, his fat lips stretching until they were paper-thin.

"I would like to think that after four hundred and ninety-eight years we have ironed out a few flaws." He leaned in close, his breath smelling of stale coffee. "You see, the Circle has a knack for fixing problems. We make them disappear. Like that." He snapped his fingers and I flinched.

"I have to say though," he said straightening up, "I did consider sliding out of this hellhole the second I tracked down my double." He shook his head. "A truck driver?" He laughed and then his eyes returned to me, burning like coals. "But then I saw what a balls-up dimension this was, with the tattoos and the unmerged evacuees. I decided it was worth the extra couple of weeks it would take to merge because of the cancer." I remembered Jo saying last month that he had started forgetting things like that she had her license. I scowled as he patted his stomach, as if congratulating himself for curing his cancer.

He trailed off as I reached across to my tray table, fumbling until my hand closed around the butter knife. I rolled over with a small moan and looked at my reflection in the shiny metal of the bed rail. A set of bleary emerald eyes stared back at me and when their irises moved upwards I saw a white bandage that covered the circumference of my head. Hair stuck out at odd angles between the gauze, lank and in want of a wash.

I brought the knife up behind my ear, turning it this way and that until it revealed the space behind the cartilage. The blade showed a clear patch of pale skin with no markings. I touched the skin and realized it was stove-hot, tattoo or no tattoo.

"What did you do? How did you–"

Mr Green shook his finger and clucked deep in his throat. "Unlike your friend Tom, I toe the line on… What did you call them? Dimension secrets?" He chuckled, repeating the words under his breath as if adding them to his vocabulary.

My friend Tom. "Where is he?" I asked in a whisper. "Has he gone?"

Mr Green nodded with a smirk and I fell back into the pillows, wrapping my hand around my neck to hold in the sound of my sobbing. A single tear slid from the corner of my eye. Yes, Tom had shared dimension secrets. But it had been on a need-to-know basis, leaving so much – too much – unknown.

I removed my hand, propping myself up on an elbow. "Jo deserves to know," I said. "They all do. What happens when they slide? What will Jo think when she turns up in–?"

"Because everyone else knows so much about the afterlife," Mr Green said, cutting me off. But then he sighed and suddenly he looked tired, worn out, like the old Mr Green. "Jo will remember when she slides. Everyone will. Think of it as pressing a reset button."

"A reset button?"

Mr Green raised an eyebrow. "Did you think you would live forever?" he asked, but it was without malice. "You should be thankful that eternal life is reserved for evacuees."

I frowned, thinking of Evacuee Lillie and how her memories filled my mind. I had her habits – her untidiness, her love of trivia. "I thought I was an evacuee." But of course, Tom would not have loved me if I was Evacuee Lillie.

Mr Green shook his head. "You won, Lillie."

I won. Tom had used the same word. They made it sound like a war.

"And the winner takes it all," he continued. "You came out of the merge a winner, but with a truckload of memories not of your making." He shrugged. "Think of it as a bonus."

"A bonus?" I blinked back the last of my tears, wondering what was the point of winning if I lost myself when I slid? According to Mr Green and his reset button analogy, I could slide as Lillie from the Thirty-Fifth Dimension and arrive in a new dimension as Evacuee Lillie.

Why then would Tom ask me to slide? I narrowed my eyes at Mr Green. I had no reason to trust him and every reason to trust Tom.

"Evacuees are the losers Lillie," Mr Green continued. "I worked that out in my first hundred years, which was when I joined the Circle." His eyes clouded for a moment. "In those days we were just a group of likeminded Evacuees," he said.

I snorted as I remembered Tom telling me they were a band of vigilantes who had become their government.

"We wanted to spread the word that merging allows us to live normal lives," he said. "It makes us one with the dimension."

"It also makes you murderers," I pointed out.

"I thought we had established that you are not an evacuee," Mr Green said with a raised eyebrow.

"Merging either kills non-evacuees or evacuees," I said.

Mr Green scowled. "Evacuees are like cockroaches. We will be here after Armageddon."

"What about the antidote?"

His scowl twisted into a snarl as he realized I knew another dimension secret. "All you need to know is that I am determined to keep the theory of everything a secret at all costs," he said. It was a threat and it made me wonder if they would be chasing Tom through his thirty-sixth dimension and beyond. It sounded like he knew too much.

"For the good of science," I said sarcastically.

"For the good of humankind," he corrected. "Do you think this is a life we want to pass on to anyone else? Stuck in this God-forsaken time warp, this abomination? Do you really think you would be helping them? Do you think it helped you?" He spread his hands out above the bed, indicating my injuries. "Tell me that Lillie."

His mask had slipped for a moment, and underneath I had seen a sad and sorry man. The moment passed and his face hardened. "If I catch you sharing dimension secrets I will give you more than a sore neck," he warned.

28

How do I describe the next eight months? That length of time between November and June that was like a knot in my ball of twine, with me on one side and summer on the other? It seemed like eight years for starters, with each second ticking by at the speed of an hour. And while they say time heals all wounds, I knew I was looking at an eternity with a hole in my heart.

The snow became my cocoon. It was falling thick and fast by mid-November and the town went into hibernation, except for the rumble of snowplows and salt trucks. The occasional car followed, creeping like a sleepwalker in the dim daylight.

Tomorrow, and tomorrow, and tomorrow, creeps in this petty pace from day to day, I would recite to myself, as I lay in bed until late or slumped over my desk at school. Shakespeare. A throw back from Literary Lillie from the Seventh Dimension.

There were a few times when I woke from my slumber for a few minutes or even a few hours. But it was late December before I smiled and February before I laughed again. The girls staged two interventions – one at the Duck-In Diner and another where Sylv threatened to dye my hair pink and purple – but by Christmas they had given up shooting for the stars and settled for the Moon instead.

I was talking after all, as in stringing more than two words together. The casts had come off my arm and leg. I had also started brushing my hair, which was growing back from the accident. I found that if I pulled it into a ponytail it covered the scar and surrounding shaved patch, letting me look into a mirror without thinking of Tom.

Of course, I thought about Tom a lot. My dreams had become less like a Band-Aid and more like rubbing salt in the wound. I became an insomniac, drinking coffee and staying up until the early hours to avoid seeing him in other dimensions. I averaged five hours of sleep a night, but those five hours were filled with a lifetime of memories with him.

I would lie in bed after waking up, wondering if I had seen into his thirty-sixth dimension. It made me think about sliding for the millionth time. I would have done it in a heartbeat, would have run the risk of becoming one hundred percent Evacuee Lillie if I could remember how to A: track him down; and B: slide without killing myself.

I had given the latter a shot and had a scar the size of Alaska as a result.

I confronted Mr Green about sliding at Thanksgiving, when he came over for our annual tofu turkey. I sat across from him during the appetizer, main and dessert, eyeballing his fat face, which seemed to have swelled to twice the size since he had started putting on the pounds again.

When he excused himself to go to the bathroom, I cornered him in the hallway.

"You have to tell me how to slide," I said, my voice low in case we were overheard.

He raised a caterpillar-esque eyebrow. "I have to tell you how to slide?" he asked and then laughed, a deep bubbling sound.

"And how to find Tom," I added with a firm nod, even though my knees were trembling. I had kept my mouth shut in lieu of his rough-up, but I needed answers to my questions and that was worth risking my neck. Hell, it was worth risking my spine.

His laughter suddenly stopped and he slammed his forearm into my chest, pushing me up against the wall. "I have to tell you shit," he spat, his round nose inches from my face. "You want to slide? Go ahead and kill yourself. The slide will kill you anyway." He gave me one last shove and I felt the drywall behind me bend, coming close to breaking.

Mr Green was lying about the reset button. I would bet my eternal life on it. Like he said, he toed the line on dimension secrets. He was not going to share the ins and outs of sliding with a non-evacuee.

I started going to the public library with Jo in December, checking out tomes on physics and reading them cover-to-cover for a clue on how to slide. It was during this time that I educated myself on Einstein.

I learned why the sky was blue, explained by Einstein with a formula for the scattering of light. I read about the fabric of space-time, which had four dimensions – height, width, depth and time, and how gravity was the weight of the universe on our shoulders, pushing us, not pulling us, towards Earth. But for me, it was the weight of universes.

I read of his search for a unified theory, dubbed the theory of everything. His contemporaries believed Einstein had wasted the last thirty-odd years of his life on this theory. And I guess in my dimension he had.

While I schooled myself in physics, Jo tutored me in a range of subjects from English to Biology, thinking I wanted to study for the SATs.

I let her teach me about sentence structure and integers, knowing she would leave me alone if she thought I had a purpose, even if it was to put one foot in front of the other until the end of our junior year.

April arrived with the speed of a snail crossing the Southwest and I submitted my major work for Art Studies. We were allowed to submit our major works individually. Like I said the class was made up of social outcasts and two restraining orders later the school board decided teamwork was not worth the lawsuits. I got an A, which gave me a bit of a buzz, if that was the word for a spark lighting in my chest and then blowing out within the same second.

A few weeks later an exhibition of our major work was held in the gymnasium. Jackson roped me into the exhibition committee, which meant I gave up an afternoon of sipping coffee and staring out of my window at the veggie patch to set up partitions and hang the works.

Mr Hastings was giving directions like it was an exhibition at the Met. I knew he had merged, the skin behind my ear heated up whenever he came close. And he had a new lease on life, like Mr Green with his cured cancer. He had handed in his resignation at Green Grove High and was moving back to New York at the end of the school year to relaunch his career. He already had a show booked.

"OK. Explain," Jackson said, after he had hung my work. He squinted like it was an optical illusion.

"I would if I could," I said truthfully.

The image had been exposed multiple times and showed me standing in the center against a white background. At my feet was another Lillie, curled into a ball. Leaning against the white wall behind me was a third Lillie. My foot could also be seen in the bottom corner as a fourth walked out of the frame. There were twenty-six Lillies in total and it had taken me at least seventeen overexposed negatives before I got the shot. I called it "The rule of repetition."

I continued to hang the works one after another, canvases of dead insects, and sketches of semi-naked women and fairies. I paused when I picked up a drawing of a girl with unbrushed hair and traced my fingers across the freckles that dotted her nose. It was Jo. She was laughing, her mouth open and head tilted towards the sky. The signature in the bottom corner read "Jackson Murphy".

I envied Jo. As they say, ignorance is bliss, and thanks to Mr Green she was completely and utterly ignorant that she had merged with evacuee Jo, leaving her like me, somewhere in between yourself and someone else.

29

I took the SATs in June, the week after school wrapped up. It was kind of like going to another world where I had three and a half hours without Tom, as I identified sentence errors and solved all kinds of problems that started and ended on a piece of paper.

Jo skipped town the next day, starting out on a two-month road trip with Jackson.

"To celebrate the state giving back his license," she explained, as we watched him pack the trunk.

"And my parents giving me back my baby," Jackson added, patting the rusted roof of his repaired hatchback.

It was about eight in the morning, but it was as hot as midday. Jo was wearing a sleeveless top and shorts, showing off her toned arms and thighs. I looked ready for a blizzard by comparison, wearing jeans and a shirt with three-quarter length sleeves. It was as if my bones had frozen during winter and I was now like a leg of lamb thawing on the counter. But it would take more than a day to defrost me.

I shivered and stepped out of the shade of the cottonwood.

"Did someone walk over your grave?" Jo asked.

I laughed without humor. "You said it, sister." I crossed my arms for warmth and tilted my face towards the sun. "Where will you go?"

"Arizona."

"We want to check out Phoenix," Jackson called out, heaving a second suitcase into the tiny trunk. "And take a look at that big hole in the ground."

I guessed the destination had been his decision. Jo would fry like a hash brown in Arizona, but then she told me how she had been looking forward to the road trip for months.

"Arizona," she breathed, looking into the distance as if she could see the sign. "When I think about that state I have a funny feeling, like homesickness."

I remembered that Jo had not been at my wedding in the Seventh Dimension. I could now guess where she had been – Arizona. In another dimension Mr Green was probably the head of Area 51.

As we were saying goodbye, Jo asked for the hundredth time for me to be their third wheel.

"We saved you a seat," Jackson added, tilting his head towards the back, where there was a foot-by-foot of saggy car seat cover with luggage piled on either side.

"You just want me for my map-reading skills," I joked.

Jo rolled her eyes and explained to Jackson, "When I first got my license, Lillie got us lost in the National Park. I spent three and a half hours driving in circles. Sylv was ready to drink her own urine."

"Those trails were unmarked," I protested with a laugh and then stood up from her open window. "Go. Have fun."

The engine of the hatchback whined as Jackson reversed down the drive. I wondered if they would make it to Arizona without breaking down and hoped they had packed a few bottles of water, otherwise they would have to pull a Sylv.

I raised my hand in farewell as they drove up the road. Jo pressed her hand against the window and mouthed a goodbye, and Jackson leaned on the horn until they turned the corner.

I suddenly felt like my life was a play and I had stayed long after the curtains had closed and the actors had exited stage left.

Sylv stayed for the encore too. And for the after-party.

She was stuck in Green Grove for the summer because of work, not that you would catch her complaining. She loved working at the hair salon, even though they had her sweeping the floor and washing hair for minimum wage.

I think it was the gossip she loved.

"Humpback Harding comes in every month for a blue rinse and a perm," she told me conspiratorially, as we hung out in front of the shop. "And Melissa came in the other day for an appointment. It turns out those long locks are hair extensions."

I had to admit it was good gossip.

"Her hair ends at her shoulders," Sylv continued with a laugh. "And guess what? Kimmy said she will teach me to mix colors tomorrow. She thinks I could be their next colorist."

I eyed her purple streaks. "Is she blind?"

Sylv laughed and leaned against the hot brick wall, closing her eyes and soaking up the sunlight.

I watched a couple of kids zoom by on their scooters.

"I forgive you, Lillie," Sylv suddenly said.

My eyes widened. "Forgive me? For what?" I ran through a list in my mind, scanning the years. Was she talking about when I had pushed her off the swing when we were seven? Hang on. It had been Sylv who had pushed me off the swing. I remember I had stubbed my toe and it had bled through my sandal. Hmmm. Maybe it was when I told her mom she had skipped school in fifth grade. Wait. Had I told on her for skipping school or for smoking at the reservoir?

I shook my head. My memories were mixed in with those of other Lillies. Who knew where one dimension ended and another started? I had hundreds of memories of my father, for example. Like the one from my first day of school. I could see him bending down to tie up my shoelace at the front gate, but as he stood he turned into Deb. She kissed me and wiped away a tear from my cheek. "Have a good day, sweetheart. I'll be here waiting at lunch." I knew the latter was my own memory and the former was a memory from a dimension where my father was actually listed on my birth certificate. It was kind of like having the opposite of amnesia.

"I forgive you," Sylv continued, "for losing your shit this past year. You know, you were kind of the lynchpin that held us together." She sighed, opening her eyes and rolling her head on the bricks to look at me. "We had sixteen good years though, right?" She was clearly not counting the last twelve months. I think there were some candles and a cake when I had turned seventeen in March. "You and me and Jo."

I was the lynchpin? I resisted the urge to laugh. I could barely hold myself together. Jo was the lynchpin. Or at least she had been my lynchpin, until she became Evacuee Jo. I stared at Sylv, suddenly realizing that I was to her as Jo was to me. A guide. A ball of twine.

"Sorry," I said, placing a hand on my chest until I located my heartbeat. It had become a habit, checking my heart for a beat like others checked their voicemail for messages.

Sylv shrugged and made a "meh" sound. "What are you going to do?" she asked rhetorically. "If we could choose our path I would be wearing Versace on a catwalk in Milan."

And I would be in another dimension with Tom, I thought.

Sylv stood up from the wall and smoothed the back of her skirt. "I have to love you and leave you. My dustpan and broom are calling." She paused, tilting her head on the side and surveying my hair in its ponytail.

"What?"

"Come with me," she said, taking my hand. I allowed myself to be led like a child by its mother.

••••

Who knew hair could be so heavy? Like a fur coat draped over your head, I thought as I stepped out of the salon an hour later.

My freshly washed and styled hair had been cut to my shoulders with sweeping bangs that tickled my eyelashes. I ran a hand through the strands, light and feathery between my fingers.

A few hundred feet up the street I stopped outside the Duck-In Diner and stared at my reflection. The cut flattered my face, widening my narrow features and making my eyes look larger than life. It also completely concealed the shorter section of hair from the accident. "A brand new Lillie," Sylv had said as Kimmy finished my blow-dry. I laughed dryly and my reflection laughed as well. Like I needed another Lillie.

I looked beyond brand new Lillie at the booths, as if looking for a familiar face, or rather two familiar faces. They would see me and wave me in, and we would laugh at the duck bill visors and squabble over the last waffle fry like the old days.

A spoonful of grits hit the window in front of my face, sliding down the pane. A young boy was giggling at a nearby booth. His mother scolded him while shooting me apologetic looks. I nodded an acknowledgement, before turning and heading home.

And then I saw him. In the street. Like I would see anyone else. Like I would see Humpback Harding or Mr Green, or one of the girls. He was walking out of the Ezy-Buy with a newspaper under his arm and a set of keys in his hand. Tom.

It was like I had been hit by the train again and I thought I would wake up either in hospital or not at all. I dropped my camera and heard it clatter on the sidewalk, its lens shattering. But the sound was distant, as if it had fallen down a deep well or down a rabbit hole, like in *Alice in Wonderland*. The blare of music through the open doors of the record store became muted, as did the roar of cars up Main Street, full of college guys doing laps during their summer break. All I could hear was the rush of blood in my ears, like static from a TV.

Tom shielded his eyes against the sun as he stepped off the sidewalk. I managed to move forward too, putting one foot in front of the other like a sleepwalker, but I was wide awake.

I stopped dead, my shoe scuffing the concrete as I saw him walking towards a red sports car. The shiny paintwork stood out like a sore thumb against a backdrop of rusted station wagons and beat up SUVs.

"Tom!" a voice called out and I whipped my head around to see Melissa with her hair extensions in a dripping wet braid and her leopard print bikini visible through her white tank top. Becca was trotting behind her, looking like a poodle with her head of damp curls.

Tom turned and when he saw Melissa he leaned against his car, a slow smile spreading across his flawless features. But it was a smile of amusement, not of recognition and it picked up what the sports car had put down. This was not my Tom. This was the Tom from this dimension, who had been at a boarding school in Kent. I wondered what he was doing in Green Grove when he could be spending his summer on the beaches of Spain. Maybe he wanted to take a look at Rose Hill. It was going to be his inheritance after all.

As Melissa passed I had a sudden urge to push her under one of the lapping cars, but I bent down and scooped up my camera instead. Tom from the Thirty-Fifth Dimension would have no memory of Melissa – and, while I would have paid for front row tickets to this show, the thought that he had no memory of me either made me head for the nosebleed section.

It was like the volume had suddenly been turned up full-blast as I half-walked, half-ran down the alley between the bakery and the Ezy-Buy. My feet thudded in my ears as they hit the sidewalk with a Slap! Slap! Slap! and my mind shouted, Tom! Tom! Tom! until I reached my house.

"You had a haircut," Deb said, as I rushed through the kitchen. She was sitting at the table, beading: a hobby she seemed to have settled on. Her healing necklaces and peace bracelets were in high demand at Tree of Life – there was even a waiting list. Yep. She had found her niche.

"It looks lovely," she called after me.

I grunted a response.

In my bedroom, I yanked open my drawers and dug through my clothes, looking for my favorite pair of jeans. I teamed them with a light pink billowy top with short sleeves and a dark pink ribbon threaded around the neckline. At the last minute I grabbed a jacket, despite the heat of the day. It was hard to know what to wear on the last day of your life.

Between Main Street and home, I had made up my mind. I was going to slide. OK, I might have to do myself in. And, there was a chance the reset button might be pushed. But there was no way, no how I could stay in this town, in this dimension with a Tom look-a-like haunting me, like the ghosts of Tom past, present and future. I wondered whether this was what I had been to Tom when he came to Green Grove, a recurring nightmare. A constant reminder that the world was round and there was no way to make it flat again.

I went into the kitchen again.

"You hungry?" Deb asked, as I pulled apple chips and muesli bars out of the pantry, dumping them into my bag.

"Picnic," I mumbled.

"Maybe I could come with you?"

I looked up from buckling the strap of the bag and let out a laugh.

Deb blinked at me and then set her lips into a thin line, before picking up her needle and threading a couple of clear beads onto the fishing line.

I hovered for a moment before dumping my bag and pulling out a chair, its back legs squealing on the linoleum. What were a couple of minutes when I was going to be gone for an eternity?

Deb paused in her beading when I sat down, like I was a prairie dog that would be startled by sudden movements. I picked up a strand of fishing line and started threading Rose Quartz onto its needle.

"I should have let you love him," Deb suddenly said and I knew she was talking about Tom.

I picked up another crystal and watched it slide down the fishing line.

"Were you in love with his father?" I asked. "William?"

I heard a sharp intake of air and thought she was going to clam up, but instead she said, "Yes."

I let the word hang in the air and she breathed it in like incense, a fond smile on her lips as she exhaled. "We were best friends growing up," she explained. "He was there when I lost my first tooth and learnt to ice skate, and I was there when he rode his first motorbike, sitting on the back with my arms tight around his waist."

Deb looked alarmed when I pushed back my chair and went to my bedroom, but I returned a moment later with the three black and white photos of Deb.

She bit her lip as she looked at them, pausing on the photo of the motorbike. "I thought we would be together forever," she said.

I nodded, thinking of Evacuee Lillie.

"And then along came Annabelle Windsor-Smith."

Like Lillie from the Seventh Dimension, I thought, resuming my beading.

"We had been friends, but they were soulmates."

And now they were traveling the world taking photos together. No wonder Deb hated photography.

Deb shook her head, as if clearing out the last of her skeletons and looked down at my beading. "What a beautiful bracelet."

I let her take it from me and tie silver clasps onto each end.

"Hold out your wrist," she said.

I obeyed and she looped it around twice, before securing the clasp. She spun one of the crystals with her finger and I thought she was going to remind me that it was the crystal of love, but then she released a ragged sigh. "I would have gone to the ends of the Earth for William. And I should have."

It was like she was giving me permission. "I love you, Mom," I said, the words tumbling out of my mouth and surprising both of us.

"I love you too, sweetheart," she said and then I was in her arms and she was rocking me like a baby.

I could have cried on her shoulder for a thousand lives.

The walk to Rose Hill was both too long and too short.

As I cut through the vineyards, heading in the direction of the mansion, I dug into the depths of my mind, looking for the solution to sliding. The Solution. A light bulb illuminated the word in my mind. It had been the name for the injection, but it was also the name for the series of equations of the theory of everything. The letters and numbers of my tattoo came to mind, as well as their meaning.

"Distance equals Speed multiplied by Time…" I whispered, climbing through a wire fence that separated two vineyards. And then the remainder of the equations followed, one-by-one, as I called them like long-lost friends, knowing their sound waves would cause a chemical reaction that would allow me to slide. "Energy equals Mass…" I continued on and on until I found myself in the formal gardens at Rose Hill. I had one last equation, but I wanted to be in the courtyard when I slid. If Mr Green had been telling the truth and I was lost in the slide I wanted it to be my final resting place, so to speak.

I thought my heart would be pounding as I walked up the flagstone path, but it was as slow as a funeral march. I stood in the courtyard, listening to its steady thud beneath the bubbling of the fountain and the trill of birds in the canopy. The dappled sunlight moved across my upturned face, tickling me with cool shadows. I held on tight to the straps of my bag and closed my eyes.

This. Is. It, I thought.

"Hello?"

My eyes flew open at the sound of his voice, both rough and smooth. For a moment I thought I had slid and found Tom in my second dimension, but when I turned I saw it was London Tom. I flushed, like a child caught with my hand in the cookie jar.

He studied me with those piercing blue eyes. His hair was half an inch longer than my Tom, curling around his ears. He was wearing a bright red T-shirt that clung to his form and I resisted the urge to throw myself at him, tuck myself into his arms and lay my head on his chest.

He frowned, an expression that seemed as foreign to him as smiling was to my Tom. "Do I know you?" he asked.

I blinked back the tears, wondering whether to tell him we were soulmates. "No," I whispered. A few dreams of other dimensions did not mean he knew me at all. He was looking at me through a peephole. It was like crossing paths with someone who had taught you in fifth grade in another dimension and spending five minutes wondering where you had met. Unless you were merged, none of this made sense. And even then... I thought of Jo.

"Lillie?" His tongue rolled across the double Ls with familiarity and my eyes widened.

Tom shook his head and laughed at himself. "Sorry. I know I sound like a stalker, but for the past – God, eight months? – I have been dreaming about you every night." He winced, as if I was going to start screaming for help. "I know. I know. I need my head read. I mean, what was I thinking flying halfway around the world to meet the girl of my dreams?" He grinned apologetically. "Sorry. That sounded cheesy."

I suddenly realized the space behind my ear was as hot as the sun. "Did you die?" I asked sharply. "In your dreams?" My heart was squeezing, squeezing, squeezing. No. No. No, I thought, clutching my chest as I remembered Tom saying he would rather merge than leave me.

He nodded, regarding me like I was clairvoyant. "In the first dream I was killed by..." he hesitated, giving a nervous laugh "...myself."

My hand moved to my throat, as a small sob came out of my mouth. Tom had pipped me at the post. I was about to risk my life and limb to be with him, but it turned out he was ten steps – or eight months – ahead.

He had merged, risking killing either himself or the other Tom in a game of Russian Roulette. The prize was keeping his promise. "I will find you," he had told me, and here he was in the flesh, but not in spirit. The chamber had spun and the gun had gone off, leaving me with a Tom who thought the world was flat.

This was what Mr Green had meant when he said Tom was gone. The weight of his loss was like a thousand dimensions on my shoulders and I sunk to my knees, releasing my throat and allowing my sobs to echo through the courtyard.

"Are you OK?" the merged Tom asked nervously. He held up his hands, as if showing me he was unarmed and began talking rapidly. "I have this as well. I thought you might— I mean, I know it sounds silly, but…" He nodded towards his pocket, before reaching down as slow as you like and retrieving a necklace. My sobbing subsided as I watched the key spin on its broken chain, catching the sunlight like a mirror ball. "Do you know what this is? Is it yours? Because…"

I put out my hand and he lowered it into my palm without another word, the chain curling like a tiny snake. I climbed to my feet and turned towards the fountain. The mossy bricks were damp under my hand as I walked around its edge. I stopped when I reached the opposite side and bent down, scratching at the earth that clung to the clay until I could see an etching of a key, like a brick stamp.

I used my fingernails to prise the brick from its lodgings. It was two inches wide and in the gap behind was a wooden box. I used the key to unlock its lid. In the Seventh Dimension this box had contained an engagement ring. In the Thirty-Fifth Dimension it contained…

I opened the lid and saw a crumpled photo. It was the photo of us from the Seventh Dimension.

Tom leaned over my shoulder, making my skin tingle with his proximity. "Is that... us?" he asked, his smooth features crinkling as he searched his memory. There was a pause. I was holding my breath.

"Wait," he said and his pale blue eyes seemed to shimmer in the afternoon light. "I think I remember..."

I exhaled.

ACKNOWLEDGMENTS

I would like to thank first and foremost my wonderful agent Meredith Kaffel. You have been the mentor in my monomyth. Thank you for leading me to the ultimate boon and ensuring *When the World Was Flat (and we were in love)* did not end up as just another file on my computer

A heartfelt thank you also to my amazing editor Amanda Rutter for loving this novel as much as Meredith and I. I am pinching myself even now that you wanted to share my story with the world. Thank you too for the honor of being able to call myself a Strange Chemist.

An enormous thank you to all those who read the multiple drafts of *When the World Was Flat (And We Were In Love)*, including friends, family and fellow authors. Special thanks to my friend and writing buddy Jennie Cowley, who was the first to read – and thankfully to love – this novel. You have been the fuel in my tank on this road to publication.

Thank you to my family for their constant love and support, even when I am buried under a pile of books or in the middle of a manuscript. In particular, thank you to my mom Pauline Jonach and late stepfather Ron Revitt. You introduced me to the arts and encouraged me to follow my dream of being an author. A shout out also to my sister Kara Jonach, who was on hand whenever I needed a hand translating from Australian to American. And much love to my long-suffering husband Craig Barnard for understanding my long nights and weekends spent writing *When the World Was Flat (And We Were In Love)*.

Lastly, thank you to all of those who will read this novel. I hope you enjoy reading it as much as I enjoyed writing it.

ABOUT THE AUTHOR

Ingrid Jonach was raised in Australia by two artists and spent much of her childhood hiding under tables at art exhibitions, where she would nibble the complimentary cheese over a well-worn copy of *The Magic Faraway Tree* by Enid Blyton.

Her love of reading led to a love of writing. By the time she graduated from high school, Ingrid had decided she wanted to spend her days sitting around in her pyjamas, writing stories.

She graduated from university a few years later with a Bachelor of Arts in Professional Writing with Honours. She then worked at the local newspaper, where she was able to live out her dream of writing stories for a living, but they never let her wear her pyjamas to work.

Ingrid currently lives in Canberra, Australia, but you can find her on her website or on Twitter.

www.ingridjonach.com
twitter.com/IngridJonach

EXPERIMENTING WITH YOUR IMAGINATION

"Exciting, funny, clever, scary, captivating,
and – most importantly – really, really
awesome."
James Smythe, author of The Testimony

EXPERIMENTING WITH YOUR IMAGINATION

Five years ago… the gods of ancient mythology
awoke around the world.
This morning… Kyra Locke is late for school.

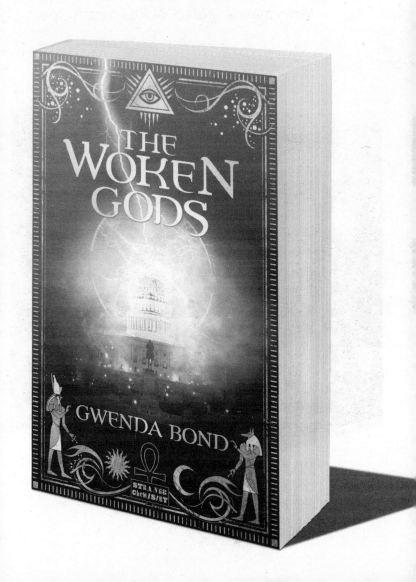

EXPERIMENTING WITH YOUR IMAGINATION

Whoever said being a teenage witch
would be easy?

EXPERIMENTING WITH YOUR IMAGINATION

"An enjoying, compelling read with a strong and competent narrator … a highly satisfying adventure."
SFX Magazine

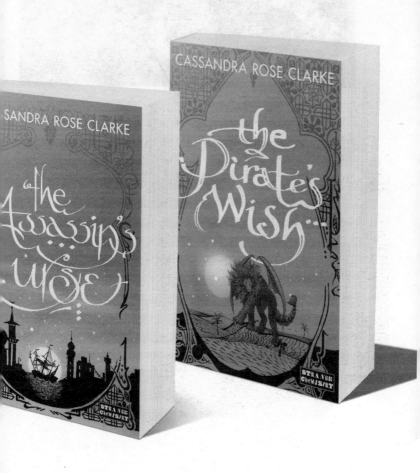

BUY STUFF, LOOK COOL, BE HAPPY

Never miss an Angry Robot or Strange Chemistry title again. Simply go to our website, and sign up for an **Ebook Subscription**. Every month we'll beam our latest books directly into your cerebral cortex* for you to enjoy. Hell, yeah!

READER'S VOICE: *Gee, that sure is swell. I wish other publishers were that cool.*

SHADOWY ANGRY ROBOT SPOKESTHING: *So do we, my friend, so do we.*

Go here: | **robottradingcompany.com** |

...our Inbox, if that is more convenient for your puny human needs.